I. O. U.

Books by Nancy Pickard

I.O.U.
Bum Steer
Dead Crazy
Marriage Is Murder
No Body
Say No to Murder
Generous Death

Published by POCKET BOOKS

I.
O.
U.

Nancy Pickard

POCKET BOOKS
New York   London   Toronto   Sydney   Tokyo   Singapore

POCKET BOOKS, a division of Simon & Schuster
1230 Avenue of the Americas, New York, NY 10020

1

IN NEW ENGLAND, WE GET FOG THAT WOULD HAVE GIVEN
Daphne du Maurier the creeps. I don't mean poetic mists that slink in
on little cat's feet, or those delicate white clouds that hover halfway
down Fujiyama on those Japanese prints. I'm talking fog that descends
like a blanket—whoomp—and stakes itself down like a tent. Waking to
one of those fogs, you want to lift the flap and peer out into the morning, but you can't because, to paraphrase Gertrude Stein, there's no
"out" out there. There's only fog, white and impenetrable as bone,
hiding your left foot from your right if you dare to leave your home,
swirling around your ankles until your feet disappear, hiding child from
mother, husband from wife, curb from sidewalk, car from post, earth
from sky.

I think we had one of those fogs the day we buried my mother.

I say "think," because although it was foggy that morning, I may be
exaggerating the extent of it. Maybe it was my brain that was thick as
clam chowder and my eyes that were cloudy with tears, or maybe I've
confused it with the fog of pneumonia that filled my mother's lungs and
killed her, but I think it was the weather.

I could ask somebody, I *should* ask somebody if I want to be accurate
about this account, but I think I'd rather let that day remain foggy in
my memory. Let the clouds swirl eerily around the casket, let the mist
settle like grief on the shoulders of the mourners, let the merciful fog
hide us each from the other, and let it drop like a curtain between me
and the sight of my mother's grave.

* * *

"—by the blood of the eternal covenant—"

The rented, nondenominational preacher bowed his head and closed his eyes, signaling the beginning of the end of the graveside service.

Instead of praying, I watched him.

He was a man of indeterminate age, thickly built, with a face that could have been carved onto one of those painted "olde fisherman" statues they sell down at the harbor; he looked like a lobsterman who'd found God. He was dressed conservatively in a brown suit, too tight across the shoulders, with a cheap tan shirt and a skinny yellow and brown tie. He stood, short legs akimbo, as if riding the waves on the deck of a boat, with his shoulders squared and his large, roughened hands folded over his crotch as he prayed. His words seemed to be addressed to the dead grass at my feet.

I hooked the toes of my shoes over the chair rung.

Those words, landing at the toes of my good black funeral pumps, made me feel uneasy. The blood of my mother surely did run through me, there was no denying that. And now with her death I felt a queasy sense of failure, as if there were, indeed, some eternal covenant I had failed to keep with her.

I shifted my weight on the hard, brown metal folding chair on which I sat in front of my mother's coffin, under a green canvas canopy. It was March, on a rather mild but foggy morning, at the Harbor Lights Memorial Park, on a cliff above the ocean, in Port Frederick, Mass. I had lived in "Poor Fred" all of my thirty-some years. For the last decade or so, I had been employed in town as the director of the Port Frederick Civic Foundation, which dispensed charitable funds to worthy causes. For good or bad, in sickness and in health, for richer or poorer, and probably 'til death us did part, it was my town.

The moist air was thick with the smell of turned earth and that oniony scent of new-mown grass. How the caretakers had managed to find grass to mow in March, I didn't know. Maybe they had sprayed the smell around, to go with the plastic flowers scattered about on other graves. My sister's perfume, and my stepmother's, mixed uneasily and hung in the air, too, along with hints of my husband's aftershave, and my father's, as if all of those conflicting fragrances had been captured and bottled within the invisible molecules of humidity that were softening my skin, loosening the wrinkles in my skirt, and straightening the curls that I had heated into my hair that morning at home.

I kept taking sharp breaths, trying to be unobtrusive about it, trying

2

to suck some oxygen in, but managing only to make myself feel as if I were filling my lungs with fragrant water. Could a person drown in fog? I wondered, feeling claustrophobic and a little desperate.

I sneaked a look at my sister, Sherry Guthrie. I guess I wanted her to trade secret glances with me, to acknowledge our mutual pain and loss. But she had her head bowed and her eyes closed. Of course. When did she ever do anything that wasn't entirely conventional? She looked so much like Mom—tall and blond, just like me—but she was so much tougher than our mother had been. I thought: *Why couldn't you have split the difference between you? If you were softer, nicer, maybe I'd like you better, Sherry. And if Mom had been held together by tougher sinews, like you, maybe she'd be alive . . .*

If, if, if.

My head wouldn't bow, my eyes wouldn't close.

"—and that the hour of our death is known only to you—"

Yes, I thought, striving for detachment. I wouldn't think about breathing, I would think about the preacher's benediction: *The hour of our death is known only to you.* Okay, so when did Mom really die? Was it three days previously when her heart and brain stopped? Or was it when she originally entered the psychiatric hospital so many years ago, leaving "real life" behind her? Maybe I'd ask the preacher what he thought about it. It was a decent philosophical question to ask a theologian. Or maybe I didn't want to hear anything else he had to say, considering how he was already making me squirm. Maybe I particularly didn't want him quoting Bible verses at me. Those old guys in both Testaments were great ones for making vows they'd rather die than break. But I'd never made a vow to my mother. And what promise had I ever made to her that I hadn't kept?

None. I sucked in another little breath. None. *None.*

My brother-in-law coughed. Somebody standing behind us echoed him. My stepmother, Miranda, known appropriately as Randy, sniffed a couple of times. I resented each delicate, sensitive little sniff. She and my dad had bowed their heads and closed their eyes on cue, but I suspected that Randy was praying for my mother's diamond drop necklace to drop her way. My dad was probably praying the fog would lift so he could get in at least nine holes of golf that afternoon. They had flown in for the funeral from Palm Springs, where they had fled in 1971 after Dad ruined his own reputation by bankrupting our family business. He had then destroyed what was left of our family life by deserting

3

his desperately ill wife to marry Randy. She'd been twenty-two years old at the time, making her a geriatric forty-one now. My dad was sixty-three, and he still wasn't old enough to know better.

"—God of boundless compassion, our only sure comfort in distress—"

This preacher wasn't filling me with solace, but rather with an awful, itchy, restless sense of dissatisfied finality. Like eating dinner without dessert. Like having sex without the orgasm. But it *was* final. Mom *was* dead. And it *was* a blessing, yes it was, just as so many people had repeated to me, over and over, until I could have hit the next one of them who said it. It was over. Over. Over. After all these years.

I had behaved very strangely the night she died.

I did odd things, starting with the fact that I didn't tell anybody—not even my husband—when the Hampshire Psychiatric Hospital called me.

I seemed, even to myself, to take the news calmly.

"Did she?" I said, in a voice that felt as cool and clear as New England town ponds used to be. My heart, however, was beating fast and my arms felt as hot as if I were standing over a stove. "Was she? . . . Yes, the Harbor Lights Funeral Home . . . Thank you . . . Thank you . . . Thank you."

I hung up the telephone, grabbed my keys and purse, slipped into a down jacket and walked out of the house. My husband, who was somewhere upstairs, didn't even cross my mind. When he tapped on our bedroom window, drawing my attention to his face behind the glass, I waved and called up, "I'll be back." There wasn't any way that he could have heard me; I could only assume that he thought I was making a late-night run to the nearest convenience store. And since we lived off the beaten track, about thirty miles off of it, he'd figure it would take me a while to drive there and back.

It was another thirty miles or so, along a winding two-lane black-top highway, to the hospital. I rolled back the sunroof—it was a heart-breakingly clear night—so that I could glance up and see the stars. "First star I see tonight, I wish I may, I wish I might, have the wish I wish tonight . . ."

I didn't wish her alive again; I wished her on her way.

I opened the window on my side, admitting the wind, which was bracingly cold. I could feel the planes of my face when the wind stroked it, as if the weather had thrown me into bas-relief against the night. As I drove, it seemed to me as if my car and I were the only things that moved, as if we were driving off the frieze like a sculpture come to life. I felt so alive on that journey.

It was strange, I think I knew that.

But it got stranger, or at least it seems so to me now, looking back on it.

I drove to the hospital and went to her cubicle in the intensive care unit in the medical wing. They'd already dismantled the tubes and oxygen tent and they'd even thoughtfully gathered her belongings for me and packed them in the suitcase I kept in her closet. They had that case—with its pitifully few belongings—out at the nurse's station where they tried to hand it over to me when I walked past.

"We're sorry," they said. So kind, so understanding. They were knowing enough not to say, "We're sorry she died." Who could be, after all? Wasn't it a mercy? They were sorry, that was all, and that was sufficient.

They had meant to be tactful and helpful by clearing out her room. New sheets, even. Empty hangers. Bare walls where photos and bright pictures from magazines had once hung. I flipped on the overhead light and then quickly flipped it off again. I drew the white curtains that shut the nurses off from any view of me. And then I did the strangest thing of all: I lay down on her bed.

I wasn't so flipped out that I pulled back the covers and got in, but I did lie back on top of them with my hands crossed over my chest and my feet together and my eyes closed.

Dead. My mother was dead. I curled into a fetal position similar to the one in which she had spent the last days of her life. Like a baby.

Baby. Mother. Daughter.

What had she felt, lying here? From that position on my side, I could, if I rolled my eyes a bit, see almost all of the room and a rectangle of the corridor. I could smell the soap the hospital used to wash the sheets, and the disinfectant they used to clean the bathroom. I heard a beeping from a monitor in the room next door. It was soothing and sad; somebody was still alive.

I closed my eyes.

My mother had lain here. I tried to feel her body, to melt into my memory of it, but there was still only me alone in the bed. I hadn't cried yet. Well, that was true if you counted the minutes since she died. Before that, plenty of tears.

Was I all cried out? Dried up?

I didn't feel dry, I felt moist and tender inside, as if somebody had turned me inside out and beaten me lightly.

When I heard footsteps approaching, I had the sense to jump down, to smooth my trousers, and to straighten my blouse.

A nurse stood in the doorway, shining white.

"Ms. Cain, is there anything we can do for you?"

"No, thank you."

"Do let us know if there is anything—"

"I will, thank you."

Let them know if there was anything they could do to help? Is that what she was going to say? What irony. Such irony. Considering that I had always blamed the American medical establishment. It was their fault, because they didn't create a miracle, and because they weren't even smart enough to tell me—finally, absolutely, and without a doubt —what ailed her. Paranoid/schizophrenia, said one doctor. A chemical imbalance that mimicked alcoholism, said another. Blood clots. Strokes. Epilepsy. Even, toward the end, Alzheimer's. Purely physiological. No, no, strictly emotional. No, no, no, hormonal. Hormones! I remember looking at my mother, after I heard that one, and thinking: If this is menopause, I'm not having any.

I followed the nurse back to the central nursing station where I accepted hugs and grave handshakes. Then I hoisted Mom's suitcase and walked for the last time down the corridor to the elevator. Sometime I would return, and ride up to the fifth floor to say goodbye to the nurses who had served her for so many years before her final illness caused her to be transferred to ICU. Some other time, not this night.

I drove home to tell Geof and to start calling people. And once again, the stars appeared preternaturally bright and the wind blew against my face like *pneuma*, the mystical breath of life. On the way back, I wondered, did I sleepwalk through my mother's illness? Was my mother's death awakening me?

"—and let perpetual light shine upon her. Amen."

I certainly wasn't acting very wide awake at her funeral.

"Jenny?" My police lieutenant husband, Geof Bushfield, leaned toward me. "You okay?"

6

I stared at him. Okay, compared to what? I wondered. Compared to somebody whose mother is not inside that box? Not trusting myself to speak, I nodded at him. For him. When he turned away, I wasn't quite sure I recognized him. He certainly was handsome, whoever he was, with that big man's physique and that strong face and that thick brown hair just starting to turn gray.

The rented preacher, his duty almost done, moved down the line of brown folding chairs, patting the women and children with his rough touch and shaking hands with the men. He was a stranger, recruited at the last minute because the Catholic priest of my mother's childhood told me he couldn't bury her in a Protestant plot. I was still fuming over that one. As if he knew that excuse fell on deeply offended ears, Father Francis Gower had added, in a complaining tone that brought to my mind the Yiddish word *kvetch,* "My old bones couldn't stand the weather, anyway. Makes me ache."

And moan, I had added silently, furiously.

So, since my sister's Episcopal priest wasn't available, either, we had accepted this stranger brought in by the funeral home.

"The Lord be with you," he murmured to me, in a hoarse voice that sounded as if it might once have called across the sea from one boat to another. I wondered if, in another life, he had, indeed, been a fisherman, and whether he might even have worked for our old family business, Cain Clams.

I didn't ask. God knows, if that were true, he probably had turned to religion to save him from poverty, after we went bankrupt, pulling many fishermen and their boats down with us.

Go away, I thought, feeling a familiar guilt as I looked up into his eyes, which looked as if they had stared at the sun and never blinked. No *offense.*

He sidestepped down the line to my sister, Sherry.

Poof, I thought as he disappeared from my view, *I can do magic.*

I stood up then, and was instantly surrounded by all of those well-meaning people who say all of those awful things that people say at the funeral of somebody who's been sick a long time.

"God works in mysterious ways, Jenny."

She certainly does, I thought.

"At least your mother's at peace now, darling."

Right, I thought, peace was just what she needed after all those years of being a vegetable. My mother, the potato, I had thought when I was

younger, and when bitter irreverence was my only defense against trag-
edy. And: *Mom, Mom, you've got it all wrong, the princess isn't supposed
to turn* into *the pea.*

"Sweetie, maybe it's better this way."

Some choice, I thought.

"God finally took her home, Jenny."

She already had a home, goddammit!

I turned resentfully away, trying to regain my composure, half afraid
that I'd said it out loud and offended the nice preacher. Buffeted by the
loving, well-meaning crowd, I was unprepared for a painful tug at my
elbow, an urgent whisper at my ear.

"Forgive me!" a voice said.

"What?" I responded. Caught off guard, both physically and emotionally, I tried to turn toward the voice, but I was frustrated by somebody pushing heavily against me. I stumbled, and frantically tried to
regain my balance. I thought I heard somebody say, in that same, fierce
whisper, *"It was an accident. Forgive me."*

Anonymous hands kept me from crashing headfirst into my mother's
coffin. They dusted me off, and helped me to regain my equilibrium.
"Jenny, are you all right?" somebody said. "You okay, honey?" "Maybe
you'd better sit down, dear." Nobody seemed to be aware of how close I
had come to braining myself against the brass handle on Mom's casket.
Nobody appeared to realize that I'd been pushed. At least, that's how it
had felt to me, like a deliberate shove. And the whisper: It hadn't
sounded as if it were imploring me to "forgive," but rather, demanding,
even threatening. I whirled around to try to glimpse who it might have
been, but I was stymied by reaching, grasping, comforting hands and by
kindly faces pushed lovingly, infuriatingly into mine. I began to doubt
my own perception of the incident. I had been pushed, hadn't I? That
was a shove, wasn't it? Well, maybe not, I decided. Maybe somebody
had been accidentally pushed against me by another person, and maybe
I'd stumbled because I was so fatigued I was nearly falling asleep on my
feet. That must have been it. Nobody would push me. That was crazy.
The day was so strange, the fog was so otherworldly, that I was willing
to believe that it hadn't happened at all. Maybe I'd daydreamed it, or
hallucinated it.

But there was one thing I knew for sure.

I had to get out of there. Right then. Now.

Before they started to lower Mom's coffin into the ground, and I had to watch.

I pushed tactlessly through the crowd, leaving my family to cope. I felt as if I couldn't breathe, as if they were all sucking the air out of me. I stumbled out from under the canopy, past the graves of some of my family, and I kept walking until I found a tree by the side of the cliff, a tree that looked old enough, thick enough, and strong enough to support my sorrow.

I leaned against it, facing the ocean.

But there was nothing to see except a frightening white eternity of fog into which a person might step off and never be seen again. In three hundred years, there had been three thousand shipwrecks off the coast of Cape Cod alone, and days like this were the reason why. Ship captain fathers went down with their sailor sons, entire families drowned en route from Europe, without ever setting foot on the New World of their dreams. My family, the Cains, was a sea family, too. Not mariners, in the sense of being the hardworking ones who hauled the nets, but lucky merchants of the sea. And we'd gone down, all right, our golden days ended, as sure as if somebody had pulled a plug on our little boat of a business, and let the sea come rushing in.

I turned back, and stared at the grave site.

They were all there, gliding slowly about in the fog like characters in a surrealistic movie. My husband, Geof. My sister, Sherry, her husband, Lars, and their children, Heather and Ian. My father, Jimmy Cain, and his second wife, Randy. My employees at the foundation, and my employers, too. My mother's doctors, and their nurses. My father's ex-employees. My mother's friends, my friends, and quite a few people I didn't recognize at all. Why had they bothered, any of these people, to come out on this miserable day for this miserable family that—

"Jenny, dear?"

I looked up to find that my mother's most loyal friend, Francine Daniel, had followed me. Long after everyone else had sidled away from my mother's bedside, Francie had continued to visit her, holding her limp hands, gossiping with her as if she heard, as if she understood, and might even reply. Now, Francie's kind, round, auntly face looked pale and pinched, her gray hair looked as limp as mine felt, and she held her coat bunched against her chest to ward off the chill. Her brown eyes held an expression of such deep concern and love that something inside of me almost cracked. But I didn't let it. I couldn't allow that.

"I'm all right, Francie."

"Good, honey."

"Francie? Tell me something. What was she like, as a friend to you?"

"She was a wonderful friend."

"Was she fun to be with?"

"Oh, yes."

"When Sherry and I were little, what kind of mother was she?"

"As sweet as you can imagine."

"That's how I remember her. Why'd she get so sick, Francie?"

"Oh, Jenny." She sighed. "These things happen."

"But you were here, and I was at college—"

"I can't tell you anything—" She sighed again. "—that you don't already know. Honey, you don't want to dwell in the past. We all loved your mother, and she loved you girls, and that's all that's important now. I know it's hard, but you have to let her go."

"But Francie—"

She put her arm around my stiff, resisting shoulders and gently led me back toward the green canopy where the gravediggers were lowering my mother's coffin into the ground, the very sight I had most wanted to avoid. Geof came walking toward us, and when I saw the worried expression on his face, I had to stoop suddenly to pretend to read the inscription on the gravestone of one of my father's sisters. Her grave lay just outside the green mat of artificial grass the cemetery had put down around the freshly dug grave, and a corner of the green mat had rolled up. Under that corner, I glimpsed a flat bronze marker. I reached out to uncover it fully, in order to see which of my other aunts or long-dead cousins was buried there.

But Francie grasped my elbows and pulled me to my feet.

With her own foot, she kicked the green mat back into place, covering the flat, bronze marker.

"I'll take her," Geof said to Francie.

She turned me over to my husband. I was so tired, so confused, and so sad, that I didn't even mind being treated like a small child being passed from one adult to another.

"It's almost over," Geof said, hugging me to him. "Only a little while longer, and we'll be home again. I'm proud of you. You've been wonderful, Jenny, through this whole thing. Just hold on for a little while longer, and then we'll be home and you can get some rest." He brushed my hair with his cheek. "I love you very much."

I.O.U.

"Did you see me nearly fall into the grave?"

"No, what happened?"

"It felt as if somebody pushed me."

"You mean on purpose?"

I backed down again from the sheer unlikelihood of it. "I guess not. I mean, surely not. They said, 'forgive me.' I mean, they sort of hissed it, in this kind of angry whisper. And then they said it again, and they also said, 'it was an accident.' " I shrugged. "So I guess it was an accident."

He hugged me tighter, and led me to the waiting limousine.

I knew Geof was right: I desperately needed some bone-deep, narcotically forgetful, sleep. But I thought he would probably rather not know that my mom's kind of "rest" sounded pretty attractive to me at that moment. I was so tired, from so many years of . . . so much. I wondered if those stories of afterlife experiences were true. Did my mother fly into a long tunnel of light, and then into the waiting, cradling arms of a being of love? I hoped so. No, on second thought, that wasn't what I hoped for her at all. I wanted her, after all those years of immobility, to run and leap and scramble into heaven, shouting and singing and carrying on like a wild woman. It was only for me, at that moment, that the idea of being cradled and comforted forever sounded wonderful.

I didn't lean on Geof; I took his hand and matched his long stride.

I held myself—and my pride—erect all the way to the limousine, where a liveried driver waited beside an open door.

2

From the Harbor Lights Memorial Park, we traveled in the black limousine back to my sister's house, through the white mist that hangs like a soft curtain in my memory. There were nine of us in the car, counting the driver: Geof and I, my sister, Sherry, and her husband, Lars, their two children, and Dad and Randy. I sat up front by the driver. Geof had deposited me there because, I suspected, he sensed correctly that I wouldn't want to be squeezed into the back seats with the rest of my family.

I could see only the lines in the road, the lights of oncoming vehicles, the brakelights of those in front of us and, now and then, sketchy outlines of the peaky gables on private homes, and the flat roofs of office buildings. The limo driver leaned forward at a 45-degree angle toward the steering wheel, and his brow furrowed with the effort of seeing well enough to keep us on the road. We all drew in our breaths and the children shrieked at one point when headlights came at us suddenly as we crested a hill. *This is frightening,* I thought, *I should feel afraid.* But I liked the feeling of being cocooned in cotton, of moving forward blindly into white nothingness.

"Well," my stepmother said in her Betty Boop voice, "I thought it was a lovely service."

Nobody responded.

There were cars following us back to Sherry's for an open house and buffet. Slowly and carefully leading the way, our driver took a short cut, slicing through the harbor industrial district rather than winding through town. Unfortunately, the route he chose took us past the former home of Cain Clams, which had been our family business for three generations—until Dad sunk it, and it ended up being sold to Port Frederick Fisheries.

Inside the car, the silence lengthened and grew awkward as we approached the plant. Its roofline appeared through the fog—which I hoped would swallow it up whole, as diners had once gulped our clams. But there was no such act of divine mercy. Or even luck. Instead, we rounded a bend in the road and *voilà!* hit a patch of clear weather that allowed us to view the canning plant in painful detail. Beyond the plant, we saw the wharf and dozens of little boats, their masts looking like toothpicks poking out of the fog.

"Let there be light," Geof murmured.

Lars Guthrie, my brother-in-law, laughed softly.

The two sons-in-law didn't have to worry about hurting their father-in-law's feelings; Dad never listened to anybody.

"Remember how it smelled?" my sister asked.

"Pee-u," her son said. Ian was a tall, skinny ten-year-old, whose wrists and ankles always seemed to immediately outgrow his mother's every attempt to cover them. I glanced back at him, and smiled at the sight of at least four inches of bare arms and a couple of inches of bare legs above his good black dress socks. Like his twelve-year-old sister, Heather, Ian wasn't even born yet when the plant folded, but he'd heard the rest of us discuss it, usually in sepulchral tones, all of his brief life. He held his nose, sounding comically nasal. "Yuck. Fishy."

"Stinko," Heather agreed.

I smiled at my pretty, coltish niece.

With our windows rolled up, we couldn't tell if Port Frederick Fisheries smelled as bad as Cain Clams used to smell, particularly on humid days. I remembered it as the scent of failure. Sherry seemed to regard it as the smell of humiliation. All those years later, we still couldn't eat clams without gagging.

"When I first met Jimmy," our stepmother said brightly, "I thought he always smelled like clam dip."

There followed another silence, an appalled one.

Somehow we each resisted the temptation to say, "When you first met Dad, Randy, you were his new receptionist and he was a married man."

A handsome fellow, even when unshaven, uncombed, and fresh out of bed, James Damon Cain III looked particularly elegant on this morning of the funeral of the woman to whom he had been married for twenty years. It was strange to think he had now been wed to Randy for almost that long. Their years together surely had been easier than the twenty he spent with my mother, I mused, paved as they were with lots of money (from trust funds the bankruptcy hadn't touched) and with virtually no responsibilities.

Dad hadn't said a word yet.

I wondered what he was thinking as we drew abreast of the old plant site, where, in the fog which had gathered again, the metal buildings appeared like spaceships floating on a sea of their own steam.

Port Frederick Fisheries, which now owned the lands and buildings, had long since replaced our 100-year-old wooden plant with these structures that looked as if they could last a lot longer than a mere single century. PFF had taken the architectural drawings that Dad had commissioned for the additions he had planned—the ones that threw us into bankruptcy—and then they had simply redesigned them to fit their own purposes. The first thing they'd done, though, was to remove the old wooden sign that my great-grandfather had erected and which his son and then my father had repainted through the years, the sign that said, "CAIN CLAMS, Purveyors of Fine Seafood Products Since 1869." The new sign was a block of capital letters painted onto the front of the foremost steel building: "PFF."

"Like graffiti."

My stepmother turned her head toward me. "What, Jenny?"

"Their sign. It looks spray painted. Like graffiti."

"It doesn't look at all like graffiti," my sister said.

"PFF," I pronounced. "Pretty Fine Fish."

On the jump seat, Ian giggled.

"Pretty Fat Fish," he said.

"Ian," his father warned him.

I smiled back at my nephew. "Paltry Fish Fry."

Heather, on the other jump seat, said, "Pasty Fish Fingers."

"Yuck," Ian said, and giggled again.

"Stop that," their mother admonished, not to them, but to me.

"Oh, Put your Face in a Fan," I told her, and her children flew into paroxysms of laughter. To them, I said, "Pack a Fresh Flounder. Pickled Fish Fillets. Pat a Fat Fisherman."

"Pat a Farty Fisherman!" Ian squealed, and then laughed so hard that he slid off the jump seat onto his grandfather's shoes. "Part a Fatty Pisherfan!"

"Ian, get up from there," Sherry demanded, while his father picked him up by his shirt collar and hauled him back onto the jump seat. The children tried valiantly to get themselves back under control, but it was impossible. Every time they looked at each other—or at me—they burst into giggles again.

The person responsible for this unseemly outburst also had a hard time getting herself under control. I laughed and laughed along with my niece and nephew, and it wasn't until I heard the silence that I realized they were all staring at the back of my head. My hysterical tears of laughter had turned into plain old tears.

My stepmother practically climbed over the seat, trying to reach for one of my hands to hold.

I jerked away from her, and fumbled for tissues in my purse.

"Sorry," I mumbled.

So many losses.

"Jenny?" Geof said.

How had it all happened?

"I'm *fine*," I snapped.

And why to us?

"Particularly Fine Fish," Ian whispered.

I turned my head and tried to smile at him.

"Shh!" His sister reached across the car to swat his arm, and then she glanced back at me, looking frightened.

At the Guthries' house, which had been designed in a determinedly anti-New England style by a disciple of Frank Lloyd Wright, the pillars of Port Frederick society moved through the buffet line sedately, as befits pillars, scooping up salmon and tuna, roast beef and chicken wings.

With determinedly dry eyes and with fresh makeup borrowed from Sherry's dressing room, I sat in her bay window, trying to be invisible. I didn't want to be comforted. I didn't want to talk to anybody. I didn't want to stumble, or offend, or lose control, or run away, or make a fool of myself. But despite my best efforts to hide behind Sherry's draperies, people kept making the mistake of approaching me with Chinette plates full of food and with sympathetic faces full of good intentions. They kept trying to say the right things, which were invariably the wrong things. I kept taking offense—and, as the afternoon wore on, trying less and less hard to disguise it—thus making awkward situations all the worse by piling my own rudeness upon their innocent tactlessness.

One of the people I unintentionally insulted that day was Calvin Farrell, my mother's obstetrician, who had delivered Sherry and me. The white-haired old man strolled over to the bay window to say hello, accompanied by his longtime nurse, Marjorie Earnshaw. Some people thought, because Doc had never married and because Marjorie was divorced and because they'd been working together so long, that she'd probably been his mistress for many years. Personally, I doubted it. I had a feeling that Doc Farrell viewed Marj as neuter, like his office furniture, and that she viewed him as a necessary means to a desired end—retirement security.

"Doc," I greeted him. "Marjorie."

"Jennifer—" was all he managed to get out before I interrupted him.

"You doctors certainly make me appreciate broken legs," I told him, stepping right up onto one of my pet soapboxes. "You look at a broken leg, and you say, look! It's broken! *Because* he fell off the roof, *because* the ladder slipped, *because* he propped it backwards against the house, *because* he was nervous *because* his wife was watching him and she got exasperated when he screwed up little jobs, *and so* he really wanted to do this one thing right—get the cat off the roof—*and so* he was thinking about his wife and heights and how he was afraid the cat would scratch him *and so* he screwed up again and fell off the roof and broke his leg and killed the cat by landing on it. *Because. And so.* Magical words." I snorted. "That's all I ever wanted you doctors to say. *Because. And so.* I wanted you to say, Jenny, your mother lies vegetating in a mental ward because . . . and . . . Fill in the blanks. All I ever wanted any of you to do was to fill in the blanks."

"I'm sorry," the good doctor said, and let it go at that.

Marjorie protested, "Jenny, that isn't fair—" But she got no further, because he openly nudged her in the ribs and then grasped her elbow to move her away from the threat of me. Even I realized that for Calvin Farrell, considering his usual gruff persona, it was a moment of supreme tact and restraint, particularly in reining in Marj, who'd never been shy about expressing her opinion to anybody at any time.

They backed away, a smart move on their parts.

I, however, was not getting any wiser as the day progressed.

The next person I insulted was Samuel Hayes, the young owner, editor, and publisher of *The Port Frederick Times.* Sam's father had run the town's only newspaper before him, and his father before that. Ours was a town of family businesses, all right, many of them into their fourth and fifth generations, most of them inextricably intertwined, with cousins sitting on corporate boards with their uncles who married their mothers' sisters whose fathers owned . . .

"Listen, Sam, I have a bone to pick with that paper you run," I said, when he made the mistake of walking up to me. Sam was only thirty-one, but he was a hardwood chip off the old-fashioned block of his father, even to the point of dressing like the old man, complete with rimless glasses, suspenders, and a red bow tie. I fished a clipping out of the pocket of my skirt—I'd been carrying it around with me for two days, waiting for just such an opportunity as this—and waved it at him. "This is my mother's obituary. Now listen to this . . . 'Mrs. Margaret Mary Cain, aged 60—'"

"Jenny, I know what it says," he objected.

"You listen," I commanded. " '—died yesterday of a long illness. Mrs. Cain, formerly married to James Damon Cain III, former owner and president of Cain Clams, was the daughter of Frederick S. Thorne, who was a prominent local merchant in the first half of the century. Her maternal grandfather, Soren Threlkeld, immigrated to this country from Sweden with his parents in 1865, and became well known later in life as a prominent local farmer and politician.' The next three paragraphs, Samuel, give more family history, even including a synopsis of the collapse of Cain Clams. Now listen to this, here's how it ends—"

"I am already familiar with it, Jenny!"

"I know, Sam, but listen. 'Mrs. Cain is survived by two daughters, Jennifer Lynn Cain, who is the executive director of the prominent Port Frederick Civic Foundation and whose husband is Police Lt. Geoffrey Bushfield, who is the eldest son of the Bush, Inc. plumbing and hardware supply family, and Sherry Cain Guthrie, whose husband, Lars Guthrie, owns and operates Lars Brand Labels, and two grandchildren, Heather Guthrie, 12, and Ian Guthrie, 10.' "

"So what's wrong with that?" Sam asked, testily.

"Where's my mother in all of that?" I heard my voice rising, and knew people were staring, but I'd been storing up this fury for two days, and now I was rolling with it. "Where is all of the other information I gave the paper? About the grade school and high school she attended, and . . . and . . . how dare you define her by her former husband, for God's sake. And her father and her grandfathers! And her daugh-

17

ters' husbands! Christ, Sam! Who cares about all of these other people? Where is my *mother?* Who was *she?* What about *her* life? I told your reporter she had a wonderful imagination and she made up terrific stories to tell us at bedtime, and she made the best potato soup you ever tasted. Isn't that important in life? What's wrong with an obituary like that? Who was she when she wasn't my father's wife? Or my mother? Or Geof's mother-in-law? Where is my mother in this . . . this . . . travesty?"

The young publisher stood rigidly, staring down at me.

"Well, Samuel?" I challenged. "What do you have to say?"

"You're being naive, Jenny," was what he had to say, and then he added stiffly, "I'm sorry you're so disappointed in our work. I thought we were being respectful of your family by not dwelling on the negative impact that the failure of Cain Clams had upon this community. We could have said so much more that you wouldn't have liked at all. Frankly, I thought I did you a favor. Perhaps, with time, you'll come to see it that way, too."

Sam Hayes turned on his heel and walked away from me.

"Perhaps with time, you'll come to be less of a pompous ass than your father was," I muttered, "but I doubt it."

Over at the buffet table, my sister was flashing admonitory looks at me, but I ignored her. It had never been one of my aims in life to keep from embarrassing my little sister. In front of the chicken wings, Geof raised an eyebrow at me, as if to inquire: *Are you sure you know what you're doing?* When I shrugged, he smiled slightly, and turned back to his conversation with two of his fellow police officers. I thought I'd found a pretty effective way to discourage companionship, but brave friends continued to venture to my bay window that noontime, and all the while I talked and talked and talked, and they smiled nervously and eventually found tactful ways to edge away from me.

Finally, I was happily, deservedly, isolated.

Until my stepmother plunked herself down at my side.

"Jenny, dear," she said brightly, as was her habit, both to call me "dear," as if she were my senior, when in fact she was only a few years older than I, and to act unrelievedly "bright," as in sunshine, not I.Q. I was usually a little nicer to her—God knows, I was grateful to her for taking Dad off our hands—but this day of my mother's funeral brought back old, bitter memories of Randy's adultery with my father. I thought I'd forgotten—even possibly forgiven—all that, but today it felt as fresh as it had when I was seventeen years old. As she sighed down onto the cushion beside me, I looked at her with disfavor. Randy had gained a little weight in the last few years, but it only served to make her look more voluptuous, which is not precisely the quality one seeks in a stepmother. Her dark hair curled sleekly around her pretty little heart-shaped face, and her navy silk dress fit her snugly in all of the places where my slim mother's figure had failed her. For my mother's sake, I resented Randy's boobs most of all. She'd been at her infuriating worst all day, and now she chirped, "Isn't this nice?"

I leveled my hardest gaze at her, the one that imparts the silent message: *Bug off.* It had never worked with Randy before; actually, it had never worked with anybody, but I enjoyed using her for target practice now and then. Unfortunately, it didn't work this time, either. She just frowned prettily, and inquired, "Do you have a headache, dear?"

"Yes."

"Tell me who everybody is again, Jenny. I can never remember anybody's names, since we don't get back here very often."

Although I heaved a martyred sigh, I quickly found myself feeling a warm, sentimental, teary glow at the pleasure of naming for her so many really distinguished people from my little old hometown. Randy may not have been impressed—she didn't look it—but I discovered that I was impressed, both by the accomplishments of these nice people and by the fact that they cared enough about us to show up. Over there was the mayor and her preacher husband. There was the curator of Oriental art at the museum, talking to the manager of the repertory theater. There was the director of a home for battered women, and a couple of social worker friends of mine. And there, standing in a semicircle as if posed for a photograph for our next annual report, were all of my trustees at the Port Frederick Civic Foundation . . .

". . . left, that's Edwin Ottilini, who's an attorney, then Lucille Grant, a retired teacher. Next to her, there's Roy Leland, runs United Grocers, Jack Fenton, chairman of First City Bank, and the one on the right's my chairman, who's also the chairman of Port Frederick Fisheries . . ."

"Pete Falwell," Randy interrupted. "I haven't forgotten him."

"Yes, that's Pete," I said. The contrast between Pete and the old man standing next to him was painful for me to see. The other man was Jack Fenton, my dear friend and advisor, who was nearly eighty now, and looking so stooped with age, and unwell. Pete, ten years his junior, still carried his height vigorously; like my dad, he was perpetually tanned, always managing to look as if he had just stepped off a tennis court, even in March, in New England.

"Old family friends," I murmured, feeling a swell of affection for all of them.

"Some friend," Randy said, "taking Jimmy's business."

"Pete didn't exactly steal it, Randy. Dad practically gave it away through mismanagement."

"I'll never believe that."

I gritted my teeth. This was an old argument. She brooked no disparagement of "her Jimmy." I tolerated no criticism of my trustees, particularly those four old men who had been on the board at the time I was hired. I owed them so much: They had employed me back when the Cain family name carried no weight, only controversy.

"Jimmy says—"

I wasn't interested in what "Jimmy" said about Pete Falwell or Port Frederick Fisheries.

"Where *is* Dad?"

Randy looked miffed at having been interrupted. I wasn't always as polite to my elders as I could be. "Where is he?"

"Yes, Randy, where is Jimmy?"

A tiny frown appeared between her brows. She usually kept better tabs on him than this, and God knows, she needed to. It wasn't just that he hadn't lost his eye for a pretty figure when he married her, but also that if you didn't nail my father down, he'd drift away into some sort of trouble that somebody else would have to get him out of. Miranda earned her keep, I'd give her that; any woman did who lived with him.

Like my mother . . .

"Ahem," my father said.

Randy and I looked up.

He was on the top step of the landing, gazing benignly down upon the rest of us who were gathered in Sherry's vast living room. With his beautiful white hair, worn roguishly long, and with his impeccable Palm Springs tailoring (black suit of the coolest, finest wool, baby pink shirt with French cuffs and mother-of-pearl links, pink and cream and black tie, black tasseled dress loafers), he looked like visiting royalty from a minor principality, probably one with gambling casinos and a southern lattitude. His tanned, beautifully manicured hands were hid-

1

den in his trouser pockets. His weight was on his left leg and his right foot was thrust forward slightly, so that he appeared absolutely relaxed and confident, as if he were modeling for *Gentleman's Quarterly.* Dad smiled in a benevolent way—the prince bestowing the grace of his presence upon what he supposed to be his adoring populace. Some of the female pulses in the crowd probably did beat faster. Mine did, too, but for an entirely different reason: fear. What in the world was he up to now?

"I would like," he said, "to take this opportunity to say a few words—"

"Oh, shit!" I hissed, and peered frantically around the room for my sister. I caught a glimpse of her just as she fled into her kitchen, dragging Lars with her, in characteristic retreat. Coward! I glanced at Geof, who rolled his eyes up. Beside me, Randy stood up so fast she spilled her drink down the front of her dress. "Uh, Jimmy dear, don't you think that perhaps—"

But he waved her down. "You'll enjoy this, too, Miranda." Dad spread his arms expansively. "I want to thank you for coming out to pay your respects to my family today."

It was true that the Old Boy Network of Port Frederick was out in force, but what my father was incapable of grasping was that they were not here for him. It must have amused some of them—like Jack Fenton —and infuriated others—possibly Pete Falwell—to realize that my dad had never understood he was no longer one of them. When Cain Clams went under, he went out. Not only that, but I suspected that they'd always blamed him for my mother's problems. Only he didn't know it. He thought he was still one of The Boys.

"—and I thought I'd just take a few moments to say a few words about the woman we all knew and loved, my dear first wife, Margaret Mary—"

Randy made a choking sound.

So this was why my father had been so quiet during the ride over: He'd been gathering his thoughts for this one supreme opportunity to make an utter fool of himself. I had always stepped in and protected him whenever I could. So did Randy, I'd give her that, too. Could we do it now?

I looked at her.

She stared beseechingly at me.

I stood up and yelled: *"Oh, my God! The kitchen's on fire!"*

21

From within that same kitchen, my sister heard me and began bleating, *"Help! Help! Oh, help!"*

The next thing that happened was that Sherry's husband, Lars, came rushing out of the kitchen carrying a portable fire extinguisher bless his heart. He yelled *"Everybody out! Follow Mr. Cain! Everybody out!"*

And that's how my father came to feel like a hero, leading his family and his old friends to safety, on the day we buried my mother. Never let it be said that this family can't act as one—and quickly—in a true emergency.

Later, when the firemen arrived and discovered it was a false alarm, my craven sister denied all complicity. "I heard Jenny yell," she told them, "and so I started screaming, and Lars grabbed the extinguisher and told everybody to get out of the house. I thought it was for real, I didn't know!"

Lars, of course, could hardly refute his wife's story.

So that left me hanging out there alone, feebly claiming, "Well, I thought I saw smoke."

The firemen accepted my story, but the few remaining guests looked at me even more strangely than they had earlier when I had bawled out *The Port Frederick Times* in the person of its publisher. If I wasn't careful, I thought, I was going to develop a reputation.

3

AFTER EVERYBODY LEFT, RANDY TALKED DAD INTO DRIVING HER out to the country club for lunch, since she hadn't imbibed anything more solid than vodka and orange juice since breakfast.

I drew him aside in the hall to say, "Dad, will you tell me what you were going to say about Mom?"

He gazed at a point somewhere north of my left shoulder. "I've been meaning to speak to you about something important, Jennifer. I do wish you'd try to be better friends with your stepmother."

"Okay." It was always better to agree immediately with whatever diversion he raised, and then try to get him right back on the track of the original conversation. "Dad, there were so many theories about what may have been wrong with Mom, and I've always wondered, what did you think?"

"Miranda does her best to be pleasant to you girls."

"Yes. But how did you know Mom was sick, at first?"

He patted me lightly on my upper arm, let his glance touch mine for an instant, and smiled with blue-eyed sincerity. "I want you to try a little harder, Jennifer, for your old Dad."

I surrendered. "I will. Have a nice lunch."

He was one wiggly fish, my dad.

After he and Randy left for the club, Geof rounded up the kids to help him clean the kitchen. Nobody else in the family could have produced such cheerful acquiescence, but Ian idolized his cop uncle and Heather had a crush on Geof, so they practically whistled as they worked for him. It freed Sherry and Lars to go up to their bedroom to recover from their extraordinary funeral buffet.

Before she disappeared, I tried to get my sister involved in talking about Mom, but I had even less luck with her than I'd had with Dad.

"I don't want to have this conversation, Jenny."

She stood on the steps to the second floor, frowning down at me. Lars had already gone up.

"But Sherry, don't you ever wonder—"

"No, it makes me unhappy to think about it, and I just really don't want to talk about it. Anyway, there's something I want to tell you. Dad and Randy are driving me crazy. Can't you and Geof take them into your house for the rest of their stay?"

"We don't have the guest room fixed up yet."

"Well, when will you?"

I smiled at her, "Over Randy's dead body?"

She laughed, and said, "That's an idea. And I'll help you decorate the room."

I took advantage of her sudden good humor to chide her about deserting me. "Sherry, come on, you knew there wasn't really a fire, didn't you? I mean, you were standing in the kitchen! So why'd you tell the firemen you didn't know, and leave me hanging out there by myself, looking foolish?"

But she shut down on me again, even managing to look offended. "Of course I didn't know."

I grinned encouragingly up at her, thinking: *Please, have this moment with me.* "Right." Teasingly, I said, "But you're grateful, aren't you? What you 'didn't know' sure didn't hurt you."

"It certainly did, Jenny. Imagine what people are thinking."

So much for the moment. I sighed, and let it go the way of all of the rest of them in our lives.

"Sherry, can't we just talk about—"

"No, we can't. Take a nap instead, Jenny. That's what I'm going to do."

She continued on upstairs, leaving me frustrated, as usual.

A nap! As if that was an answer to anything. She was a great one for taking naps every day, my sister was, while I could never fall asleep unless a full day of work hit me over the head and knocked me out at night. I was certainly too tired and too restless to sleep on this crazy afternoon. I offered to help with the dishes, but Geof shooed me away, echoing Sherry. "Take a nap, read a book, do something to take your mind off things." I felt like a child who's underfoot. The only way to escape the three of them as they picked up, swept up, and washed up was to wander down the hall to the family room, which also happened to be where Sherry had been sorting through a lot of Mother's old things.

Surrounded by boxes, I rifled through them, searching for memories. And, possibly, a few long-sought answers. I found the memories in photographs, some in albums and others lying loose. They reminded me that my mother was a beautiful woman. Not as tall as Sherry, but as slim as either one of us, and even blonder. And once, she was younger than we were now . . .

"Oh—"

I sank to the carpet, a photo in my hand.

There she was, a child, all dressed up for Sunday Mass in ruffles and bows. It must have taken some strength of will, I mused, for three generations of women in her family to remain Catholic while all the men about them were Lutherans. But was it really their own will, or merely a religion-inspired fear of eternal damnation? My mother hadn't ever displayed much of the former—certainly she hadn't bucked the Cain tradition by raising Sherry and me in her church—so I suspected it was probably the latter.

I dropped that one, and picked up another photo.

Here she was as a teenager, sandwiched between my father—who looked dapper even then—and a gorgeous convertible, my father's teen dream machine, his famous 1937 Duesenberg. "Last year they ever made them," he had said often enough to cement the words into my memory. I wondered, was he more proud of the girl or the car? Silly question. Of course, it was the car.

And here were pictures of her with Sherry, Dad, and me.

Here was a professionally taken, color, eight-by-ten photograph of us when I was sixteen and Sherry was fourteen, the year before everything fell apart. Yes, there was a date scrawled on the back in my own childish handwriting. Sherry and I looked like thin blond twins; despite the two-year difference in our ages she was already the same height as I. Dad was black-haired and handsome as a matinee idol, and he sported just that kind of insipid smile, too. But my mother, otherwise pretty in her sleeveless blouse and full, belted skirt, appeared intense and worried; there was a crease between her eyes that made her appear to be trying by the sheer act of concentrating to help the photographer get us into focus. That would have been a trick all right: getting the Calamity Cains into focus. And how like my father, I thought, to hire somebody else to attempt it and how like my mother to take the burden of the effort—somebody else's effort, at that—upon herself. And how like Sherry to pose like a beauty queen contestant, one hand on a hip, her shoulders back, her (then) flat chest stuck out, and a blinding smile revealing her breathtaking teenaged confidence along with her braces. And how like me to look so pleasant, so conventionally adolescent, so goddamned cooperative. *Nice Jenny; stand, Jenny; smile, Jenny.*

Suddenly, looking at that photograph that I hadn't seen in years, I realized that the funny thing was, I was aware of it all—of my father's meaningless insouciance, my sister's pose, my mother's tension, my own bland acceptance—even then, at the moment of that picture being snapped. I could even kind of remember thinking under my smile: We're so weird!

Typical teenaged angst? If it wasn't that, then what did I know then, or suspect, or sense? That my dad was such a lousy businessman that he was bound to fail? That he was playing around with other women? That my mother was hurt and sad and sick? Did I know that? Was it true?

I put the photos and albums away without looking at the rest of them, and turned to a box of Mom's old clothes and shoes, but there wasn't much . . . a dressy black chiffon . . . a strapless black taffeta . . . a black suit . . . a brown wool dress . . . a pair of black slacks with a black turtleneck sweater. I was struck by the fact that they were all dark: Did my mother always wear dark colors, or were these depressing tones some kind of symptom we should have noticed? Funny, I mostly remembered her in sunny yellow, in pinks and golds and whites and silvers. But maybe my memory had put her behind a romantic gauze curtain and painted her in happy pastels she never really favored? Funny, too, that Sherry and I, who could have fit easily into our mother's old clothes, had chosen to pack them away in Sherry's basement rather than wear any of them. Did we think it was catching? I asked myself bitterly. Were we afraid we'd catch her madness by wearing her sweaters? No, I decided, that wasn't fair to us, or even true: We'd hidden them away in the secret hope that she would come home to wear them herself one day.

I got up and closed the door.

Then I slipped out of my funeral dress, my slip, and heels and pulled on my mother's black wool slacks and her black turtleneck sweater.

They were classic styles that would never go out of fashion and, what's more, they fit me perfectly, although my throat felt a little tight under the turtleneck.

I knelt on the carpet again.

I'd brought her suitcase from the hospital here to Sherry's house, since she was the family pack rat. Now I opened it. Brush. Comb. Kleenex. Toothbrush. More photographs, the ones I had taped to the wall in front of her bed. Jergens body lotion, her favorite.

I held the familiar yellow plastic bottle in my hands for a moment, feeling its curves, and then I pumped a dollop of Jergens into my palm. I put the bottle down and lifted my hand to my nose, and then I rubbed the lotion into my hands, working it up to my wrists, then touching it to my cheeks. Oh, I loved this rich, warm, feminine scent that reminded me so much of my mother, and that made my chest swell with sorrow and joy in equal, unbearable measure. Jergens. Nothing fancy. Practical. Off the shelf at the grocery store. But so creamy and soothing and sensual. And what did any of that say about my mother? That she was frugal? That she was vain, but not overly so, about her lovely skin? It was the only brand of lotion I remembered seeing around our house, and what did that fact imply? That she was consistent? Unimaginative? Secure? Insecure? Or maybe she only bought it because it was her mother's favorite, too, but that—

"Shut up," I said to the Jergens bottle. "You make me feel too much, and you tell me nothing at all." I put it behind me so I couldn't see it, and then I felt really sorry that I had spread it on my skin, because now I was stuck with the haunting, painful smell of it.

There was not much else in the suitcase.

I snapped it shut, then hid it behind other boxes we wouldn't have to open for another thirty years.

"What's left?" I asked myself.

Ah, everything from the funeral.

On the desk, I found a copy of Sherry's order for two boxes of engraved "Thank You" notes. And the little white cards that had been attached to the flowers. And our copy of the contract with Harbor Lights for Mom's funeral and burial. And the white, leather-bound visitor's book that our friends and family and business associates and acquaintances had signed at the Visitation last night and at the funeral this morning.

I sat down in Lars's favorite chair, and stroked the book's binding.

GUESTS, it said.

I thumbed through the white, lined pages, touching the signatures, recognizing most of them, trying to decipher the others. Amazing, how very many people had shown up. How nice of them to say this, how very kind of them to say that.

And then I found it, the thing my subconscious had been looking for all along, ever since the graveside service.

My skin turned clammy and I felt sick when I saw it.

I don't want to see this, I thought.

But I have to see this; it's been waiting for me.

It was only a few words that were scribbled, nearly illegible, and so hard to read that probably no one else who had been waiting in line to sign the visitor's book at the funeral home would have even tried to figure out what it said. But I had the time now, and no one was waiting impatiently behind me to sign this book. And so I was able—after considerable effort—to decipher the two words that were scribbled on the lines between the names of an old friend, Lucille Grant, and somebody whose name, Cecil Greenstreet, looked familiar, but which I couldn't place.

"Forgive me," the anonymous message said.

And suddenly I recalled the shove, and the two sentences whispered into my ear at graveside, fiercely, as if from some great emotion:

"It was an accident. Forgive me!"

A woman's voice? Maybe. Did I recognize it at the time? No. Did I know her? Or him? Who could know? Who was she, who *was* she!

"It was an accident."

What was?

"Forgive me!"

For what? For bumping into me, was that the accident she meant? But she had sounded so urgent about it, so demanding, surely a stumble wouldn't produce that kind of whispered passion. But was it a stumble? Was it an accident that she shoved me? It had felt purposeful, that hand grasping my elbow, and then that body pressed against my back.

Forgive you for what?

I said it out loud: "What accident? Forgive you for what?"

"Some nut," Geof declared, after I trailed into the kitchen with the guest book and a repetition of my story of what I had begun to call The Incident at the Graveyard. He listened to me, but then all he said was,

"You look nice; is that a new outfit?" He put his arms around his crew and all three of them beamed at me, and Geof said, "Did we do a great job, or what?"

"Superb," I said, finally coming awake to the point he was trying to make to me, which was that there were children present. "You guys are a sodden mess, but everything else gleams. Thank you." I bowed to them. "On behalf of the entire Cain/Guthrie/Bushfield clan, I thank you most sincerely."

Ian and Heather broke away, and ran out of the room so quickly that I felt guilty.

"I'm sorry, I wasn't thinking how that might be a story that would frighten them." I plucked at the waist of my black sweater. "These were Mom's. What do you think?"

"I think her daughter's a knockout." He finished drying his hands on a towel. "I also think that if Sherry catches you wearing them, she'll make you cut them in half, right up the middle, so she gets her 'fair share.' " He flapped the towel toward the kitchen table. "Let's sit down. You can show me the book. Don't worry about the kids; kids love being spooked."

Geof sat across from me with the white book between his hands. He read the message and then tapped it with the middle finger of his right hand. "It's one of those funeral freaks who show up at every service. Or it could be an apology from somebody who feels bad for not sending flowers, or for not visiting your mother in the hospital, or some damn thing."

"Yes, it could be," I agreed.

He looked at me with suspicion. "You're easy to convince today."

"I want you to convince me. I want to think it's as you say, because I don't know what to do if it's anything else."

"What else could it be, Jenny?"

I shrugged helplessly.

"Why does it bother you so much?"

"You're right, it bothers me a lot. Because, because—"

"It was kind of nasty, the shove."

"Yes, it was, Geof. Startling. I almost fell onto Mom's casket. And the person's voice—"

"Angry, you called it, and demanding. And there's maybe a meanness about this 'forgive me' business, too."

"You think so, too?"

29

"I think that's how it feels to you. Because why would a person write a mysterious thing like that in a guest book at a funeral? It seems screwy on the face of it, and self-centered, almost like a practical joke, but what's the joke? On the whole, though, I think it's more screwy than mean. It doesn't make any sense. It's out of the blue. There's a lack of connection here that speaks to me of a person who's not quite right in the head. And that would fit a funeral freak."

I nodded.

He smiled. "I thought I sounded quite convincing."

"Oh, you were."

"But you're not convinced?"

"I want to be."

"And there's nothing to do about it if you're not."

"There's nothing to do about it."

"Maybe there is." He slapped his palms on the kitchen table and shoved his chair back. "Where do Sherry and Lars keep their phone book? Oh, I see it. Under the phone, where else?"

"What are you doing?"

He brought the phone and the Port Frederick telephone book back with him to the table and began to thumb through the Yellow Pages.

"Geof, who are you calling?"

"Harbor Lights Funeral Home."

"555-3636."

He shot me a questioning glance, his finger in the book.

"I've had one or two reasons to call them this week, you know."

He dialed the number I gave him and asked to speak to Stan Pittman, Jr., who was the son of the owner and an old high-school friend of mine.

"Stan," he said into the phone. "Geof Bushfield. Got a minute for a question? No—" He grinned at me. "We haven't had any complaints about any missing bodies. Listen, Stan, do you get any of those people who regularly attend the funerals of people they don't even know? Yes? Well, tell me this, what sorts of things do they sign in the guest books?" Geof looked disappointed in the answer. "Really, no strange messages? Sure, I understand that you don't examine everybody's guest book, but maybe you'd do me a favor. It's for Jenny, really." Geof winked at me and nodded, to indicate that Stan had promptly agreed to do it. "Some nut wrote the words 'forgive me' in the guest book at her mother's funeral. There's nothing to it, I'm sure, but would you take a glance through the guest books for the next few funerals? Especially if you see one of your 'regulars' coming in? And let me know if anything out of the ordinary shows up, all right? Thanks, Stan. I'm sure Jenny has already said this, but thank you for doing such a nice job with Mrs. Cain's funeral."

Across the table, I nodded my approval.

"Appreciate it, Stan," he said, and hung up.

"Appreciate it," I said to my husband.

He sniffed. "Well, hell, what's the good of marrying a cop if he can't solve a little something for you? And in the meantime, we won't either of us jump to any conclusions, will we?"

"Not I," I said demurely.

He cleared his throat.

"Oh, dear," I said. "This is the part where you're going to give me some advice."

"Jenny, do you think maybe you're trying too hard to find the meaning of life in every little thing?"

"No."

"Well, then maybe I'm trying too hard to make you feel better, but I don't think this book or The Incident at the Graveyard means anything, not one damn thing." He reached across the table to touch me. "Now here comes the advice. Take it easy for a while. Be good to yourself. These have been hard years, and you deserve a chance to slow down . . . about everything. Will you?"

I thought about that for a moment, and then said, "I'll try." I stood up. "See me rise slowly from this chair. See me walk sedately around the table. See me bend down at all deliberate speed to slowly, slowly, slowly . . ." I kissed him.

Cheers, whistles and applause broke out from the doorway, where Ian and Heather had been eavesdropping.

The next day, Sunday, I moped around the house trying to take Geof's advice. I slept a lot, I wrote thank-you notes. A number of condolence letters had already arrived, and I'd carried away from my sister's house the little pile of white florist cards. Most people would be sending contributions to the mental health society, as we had requested in the obituary (at least they'd gotten that right!). But there were some who either hadn't seen the notice in time, or who just plain liked to send flowers anyway, no matter what. My old-fashioned trustees were among that group, and there was a card, crowded with their names: Lucille Grant, Edwin Ottilini, Pete Falwell, Roy Leland, Jack Fenton. There was one from an old boyfriend, another from the woman who does my hair. And one from . . . *Cecil Greenstreet?* There was that name again, as it had been signed in the guest book below the anonymous inscription, but who was he? I thought I ought to recall, but I couldn't. Maybe I was thinking of that old actor, Sydney Greenstreet. Or was I thinking of Mr. Green Jeans from the "Captain Kangaroo" show? Whoever. It would come to me. It was late in the afternoon by the time I started writing the thank-you notes.

The ninth one down in the pile made me call out: *"Geof!"*

"What?" he called up from the basement, where he was getting a head start on cutting stakes for tomato plants. When I didn't answer, he bounded up the stairs and came into the living room where I sat, still in my bathrobe and slippers. "What?"

I held out the little white card by the tips of my fingers, as if it were something nasty. Which it was, to me.

"It's another one," I told him, and my voice shook.

"Another one what?" He came nearer.

"Another one of those stupid mysterious messages."

He bent down, peered at it, and read aloud: "April 10, 1971." What the hell's that supposed to mean?"

"I don't know, but I think Dad put Mom in the hospital around then."

Geof straightened and then stared at the card for a moment. He switched his gaze to me, and then back to the card. "Don't move," he said, and walked out of the room. When he returned, he had a plastic food storage bag in his hand. He opened it and held it under the card, and I let the damn thing drop in. Then he sealed the bag.

"I'm not sure why I'm doing this," he said.

"It probably doesn't mean anything," I said.

We gazed at each other.

"And if we pick up any prints, they'll be the florist's," he added.

"I know."

We remained like that for a moment, me on the couch, him standing with the bag in his hand. Then he said, "Well, hell, at least we can call the florist."

"On Sunday?"

32

He smiled a little. "What's the good of being married to a cop if you can't—"

I finished his sentence and tried to smile back at him. "—bother people on Sundays?"

But Jack Chart, the proprietor of Chart's Flowers, said the order—which he recalled because of the odd message and the even odder way in which it was delivered—came under the door of his shop in an envelope with cash in it and instructions to spend the twenty-five dollars on an arrangement of pink rosebuds, baby's breath, and white carnations, and to send it to the service for Margaret Cain at Harbor Lights Funeral Home.

"I don't know who ordered it, Lieutenant," he told Geof. "Please tell your wife that I felt awful that it was such a chintzy arrangement, but you can't buy many roses for that kind of money. I hope she wasn't offended?"

There wasn't any way Geof could answer that question, so he said, "I'm sure it was very nice, Mr. Chart, and Jenny is grateful. Thanks for your help. If you get any other orders like that, let me know immediately, okay?"

"Oh, I hope I don't!" the florist said. "I just hate for people to think we do cheap things. I mean, well, you know what I mean?"

Geof knew what he meant.

I completed the rest of the thank-you notes, and he went back to sawing stakes for tomatoes. But the day was ruined. And so was my sleep that night.

4

A LIGHT SNOW FELL THAT NIGHT, BUT IT HAD ALREADY MELTED by the time we woke up, leaving Monday morning looking wet and shiny, as if the world had cried all night. I had not, although I hadn't slept much. Still, by that morning, which was the fifth day after my mother's death, I thought I was "fine."

Geof asked me over coffee, "How are you?"

"Fine," I said.

I returned to work at the Port Frederick Civic Foundation.

My assistant, Faye Basil, greeted me with, "Jenny, how are you?"

"I'm fine," I said.

I walked into my office, sat down at my desk, and stared at the papers on it. A few of them, I knew, were decidedly unfriendly. They were letters from residents of Port Frederick who objected to some of the projects we were funding. Planned Parenthood, for instance. An AIDS hospice. A wonderful little gallery of modern art. We were getting more daring in our funding lately—and consequently more controversial—because I was finally growing into the strength of my convictions about the functions of foundations. Or, at least, of any foundation that I ran. And that was—to my mind—to help those with the most acute needs or those who had the hardest time getting funds from conventional sources. In other words, the sickest, the neediest, the experimentors and the inventors, the geniuses who looked at first like fools, that's who I wanted to help, the people who took risks.

Which meant the foundation took some risks, too.

The men on my board didn't much like this new direction in which I was tugging them, although they had grudgingly agreed to fund a handful of "Jenny's weird projects." But not all of them, by any means. "Jennifer, have you lost your mind?" was how Pete Falwell, the current president, had put it to me once or twice when I'd made especially outrageous recommendations for funding. My husband had laughingly put it another way: "Are you trying to get yourself fired?" So the bulk of our funds still went to conservative and socially acceptable causes. Fine causes, for the most part, good causes, but comparatively rich causes. They didn't generate the hate mail or the nasty phone calls that some of "Jenny's weird projects" did. If I kept this up, my trustees were complaining, we might soon have actual picket lines at our front door. While they shuddered at that idea, and I didn't exactly look forward to it, it didn't scare me, either. There were things I had seen in the last few years, things I had done and felt and experienced, that had raised my fear threshold considerably.

On this morning, there was an anonymous letter. "Great," I muttered, after I opened it, "just what I need, another mysterious pen pal." But this one was considerably different in tone from the ones related to my mother's death. It excoriated us for giving money to "those dykes with those filthy paintings they have the nerve to call *art.*"

"So what should they call them?" I said aloud. "Fred?"

The writer was, I gathered, referring to an artists' coalition that couldn't exist without our funding. Their current show was a satirical one that featured paintings of nude men posed in the style of famous paintings of nude women through the ages. I thought it was hysterically funny to see chubby men painted in the manner of Botticelli, or a reclining nude man surrounded by fully dressed female picnickers, modeled on Manet's famous *Luncheon on the Grass.* The exception that proved the rule of the show, however, was the one nude female—limpid-eyed, extending her limp forefinger to a powerful, robed, female God. It was God granting life to Eve in a distaff Sistine Chapel, and it was brilliant.

This letter, this morning, would seem to indicate that not everyone in Port Frederick was equally impressed. Or amused. Apparently, not everyone's consciousness was raised, either, nor did they think it needed to be. I stared at the damned thing, reading it over and over, until the meaning of it began to seep into me. Ah, they were threatening us with something dire . . . but what? I had to keep staring until it registered: "burn in hell."

"Oh," I murmured, "is that all."

Burn. Dire. Dire Fire.

That's where authors of anonymous messages ought to go, I thought . . .

It was an accident. Forgive me. April 10, 1971.

My thoughts wandered far away from my office . . .

On April 10, 1971, I was in college, living in a dorm in another state 450 miles away from Port Frederick, Massachusetts. Sherry was still in high school, living at home. When I left for college that fall, my mother had seemed brittle to me. Beautiful and golden as an autumn leaf, but just as brittle. I hadn't known why. When I came home for Christmas, she'd been sweet but withdrawn, sleeping almost all of the time, so that we rarely saw her downstairs in anything but her house robe. I knew that she and my dad whispered behind closed doors that summer before school, and I'd heard the sound of raised voices frequently enough to make my stomach churn at the tension between them, but the furious whispered arguments seemed to have come to an end by Christmas when my father was away from the house most of the time and my mother spent her days alone in their bedroom. The truth was, I probably didn't notice or even care as much as I should have, because I was young and self-absorbed and resentful of their apparent lack of attention to me. My parents, I thought, could take care of themselves. Nobody told us girls that Dad's business was failing. There wasn't any hint in the newspapers that summer or Christmas, and no rumors reached our ears at the swimming pools or holiday parties. And of course, we didn't know about Dad's girlfriend, about Randy, that is. We didn't talk much, Sherry and I, because I wasn't very interested in the high-school affairs of my little sister. And I didn't want to hear—didn't even want to believe her—when she tried to complain about how "mortifying" it was to bring her friends home after school only to find Mom wandering around the house in her nightgown, stumbling on the stairs in her slippers, mumbling to herself about things that nobody else could hear . . . .

"Jenny?"

I jumped in my office chair, startled by the sound of a real voice.

My assistant, Faye, always so motherly and kind to the young delinquents in her life, walked in carrying legal documents pertaining to a recent bequest to the foundation. She placed them in front of me, and pointed. "I'm sorry, but you checked the wrong boxes. According to this, you've advised them to place the money in a personal checking

account in the name of the deceased." She smiled. "Maybe you think he
wants to take it with him."

"Faye, I'm sorry, help me fix it."

This time, she carefully pointed out to me which boxes to check,
which lines to sign.

"Jenny, have you read that letter from the Morality in Our Arts
Committee? MOAC?" Faye smiled, and took back the signed papers I
handed her. "The one that says we're all going to burn in hell for
portraying God as a woman?"

"MOAC," I said, "MOAC, MOAC. Sounds like a sick parrot." Faye
laughed, but I hardly heard her. The word *parrot* had triggered a memory. "My mother had a canary for a few years, Faye. It was definitely
hers, too, not ours. It wouldn't sing for anybody but her, or perch on
anybody else's finger without biting us. I hated that damned bird. It
looked like her, too—thin and pretty and pale yellow, like her hair, and
it hopped around its cage with these quick, little, nervous movements."
I made my fingers dance in the air. "Just like Mom used to dash around
when she was excited or upset about something."

She had darted about, like that canary, on the day I left for college,
pecking me with little nervous kisses, annoying me with silly, last-min-
ute worries so that I'd felt relieved to get out of the house and to be on
my way to school at last.

"Jenny?"

I looked up. "I'm sorry, Faye, my mind was wandering."

She gnawed on her lower lip for a moment, and then spoke in the
gentle tones of a recovery room nurse. "I can take care of the office,
Jenny. There's no good reason for you to be here, so soon after . . ."
Faye paused. "I'm sure you have many things to take care of at home,
maybe you'd be better off there . . ." She trailed off. Although she
stood right in front of me, I had the impression Faye was speaking to
me from across a vast chasm, standing on the other side, so very far
away from me.

"No," I said.

She waited.

When I realized she was still there, I repeated, "No, no."

When she was gone, I transferred my gaze from the pile of papers on
my desk to the view outside my window: bare tree branches, empty sky,
pale sun. The poet was wrong. April was not the cruelest month, March
was; at least some of the green promise of April would be kept, but

March offered no hope at all. In March, it looked as if the world had truly died and might never be reborn, the trees would never bud again, or the leaves grow, the animals would remain in their hibernation forever, snakes would drift deeper and deeper into their cold sluggishness, and birds would never nest, old bones would never warm by sun but only by fire, and even the darkest skin would pale to the color of ice, even the warmest heart would freeze, splinter like ice, and split.

The phone was ringing.

I laid my head on my arms, on my desk.

There was one thing I held on to: My mom had called me the week before they put her into the hospital. Just to say hello, she told me. Sherry was fine. Dad was fine. She wasn't feeling too well, herself, but she'd be fine. How was I? I'm fine, Mom, but I'm in a hurry, got to get to class. I love you, Jenny. I love you, too, Mom. Goodbye, honey. 'Bye, Mom.

"Jenny?" Faye started to come in, stopped. *"Jenny?"*

The next thing I knew, I was cradled in her arms, weeping into her soft shoulder pads. Although I insisted I could get myself home, it turned out she had to drive me because I'd lost my keys someplace between the parking lot and the office.

"I know this phenomenon," Faye assured me. Her father had died the previous year. "I call it the Alzheimer's of grief. You'll forget things and misplace things, until you'll think you're losing your mind. But it's just grief, Jenny. That's all your mind can hold right now, that's what's important, you shouldn't expect it to hold on to little, unimportant things . . . like your name, or your phone number, or your car keys!"

Unfortunately, Faye was still speaking to me from across a great divide, and so her wise words registered only dimly, and they were the very next things I lost. When she guided me up the walk to our cottage, she said, "Call Geof the minute you get inside." She fished for the hide-a-keys behind the front door light, and opened the door for me. "If you don't, I will. Then take some aspirin and go to bed."

"I'm fine now, Faye."

"You're sure you'll be all right until Geof gets home?"

I had no intention of interrupting him at work, not when he'd already had to take so much time off for my family affairs.

"Sure."

"Okay," she said, sounding skeptical. "What's your name?"

"Jenny," I said, sheepishly, and grinned at her.

"Hold on to that," Faye said, and kissed my cheek.

I thanked her, waved vigorously as she drove off, and then shut myself in the house. I didn't realize, until I was alone, how very much I didn't want to be. Come back, Faye! But I couldn't even chase her down in my car—I'd lost my keys and didn't have a car. Feeling desperate for company—why *didn't* we have at least a cat!—and embarrassed about it, I phoned my sister's house, but my stepmother answered. "Jenny, dear," Randy said. "There's nobody here but little ole me. Your father has gone to the club, Lars is at work, Sherry has a church meeting, and the children are at school. Is there anything I can do for you, dear?" *Dear*. My skin crawled at the sound of it. You'd think the woman was thirty years older than I, instead of very nearly my own age.

"No, Randy, dear," I said. " 'Bye."

Bitch, I said to the telephone.

Who? it inquired. *You or her?*

My friends all worked; I couldn't just call and dump on them in the middle of their jobs. Of course my best friend was a psychiatrist, so she was used to it, but something in me shied away from calling Marsha. I thought of others I might call, like my favorite trustee, Lucille Grant, or my mother's friend, Francie Daniel, but it suddenly seemed such an effort, too much effort, really. And besides, if they really cared about me, wouldn't they be calling to make sure I was all right?

I dragged myself up the stairs to our bedroom.

The pretty yellow room, with its fireplace, bay window, and cozy four-poster bed, felt bleak and cold and lonely.

I stripped, leaving my clothes where they fell.

I crawled naked into the middle of the bed, and pulled the covers over my head.

The phone rang, but I let the answering machine get it.

It rang again, immediately afterward, and I ignored it.

And again, a few minutes later.

Keys turned in the front-door locks.

Faye, not trusting me to call my husband, had phoned him herself. The lieutenant called my name from downstairs and, receiving no response, took the stairs in a few bounds. Soon, I felt the mattress sink under his weight. Through the covers, I smelled his Old Spice. Then I felt his hands rubbing my back through the blankets. He stroked and stroked . . . my back . . . down my arms . . . over my hips . . .

down my legs to my feet . . . up to my back . . . even my hidden skull. And then he lay down beside me and pressed himself against the covered lump and put his arm over it as if to protect it.

We lay like that—the fully dressed police lieutenant and the lump—for a while before he spoke again.

"I think we need some help here," he said.

Under the covers, I went rigid with fear. You don't have a crazy mother without wondering, in your darkest and most private moments, whether it might happen to you, too. And there I was, prostrate and hiding in the middle of the morning, turning into a vegetable like my poor sick mother. Oh God.

"I'm going to call Marsha," Geof said, and his weight shifted on top of the mattress as he got up.

She told him to deliver me to her house after office hours.

I crawled back under the covers and stayed there in my cave.

Geof returned to work that afternoon, after seeing that the only thing I intended to do was to sleep for hours. Then he came back after me and drove me into town to the home of my longtime friend, Marsha Sandy.

Geof hugged me to him tightly, kissed me hard enough to leave an imprint, and then left me completely alone with her.

"Howdy," she said to me.

"Doody," I replied to my childhood friend.

She took my hand and led me into her den, where she pushed me down into a cushiony easy chair. Then she pulled a footstool directly in front of me and sat down on it. Marsha wore dark gray wool slacks and a cashmere sweater in a lighter shade. She looked elegant, concerned, and every bit as determined as she used to look behind the catcher's mask on our softball team in the fourth grade. I sighed and leaned back, surrendering to the inevitable.

"Geof thinks I'm cracking up."

"I do, too."

"Oh, great! That's just what I want to hear from a shrink."

"Well, tell me . . . what's up?"

"Not me, Doc. I'm all the way down."

"And nothin' looks like up to you?"

"Um."

"I heard you were looking for your mother in an obituary."

"Yeah, and she wasn't there," I said, bitterly.

"So where is she?"

"The rumor is, she's dead."

"Well?"

I sighed, and looked away from the sympathetic brown eyes focused so intently on me. "Maybe, but I'm not convinced she was ever alive. If you believed that obituary, you'd think she only lived through other people. But surely that can't be true. There must have been a . . . *her*."

Marsha clasped her hands over one knee and waited silently for me to continue.

"I have this awful feeling I didn't know *her*—whoever she was—at all. It's like I didn't pay enough attention."

"So? Children don't."

I waved off her easy reassurance. "It's like Willy Loman, you know? Attention must be paid. And it wasn't. And I didn't. And what if somebody had paid more attention? There were signs, Marsha." I turned my face to look at her again, accusingly, lumping her in with all of the doctors who hadn't explained anything to me. "She was terribly upset, and there were signs. That Christmas, she was seriously depressed, I realize that now. Maybe she could have been helped earlier. Maybe it wouldn't have happened. Oh, Marsha!" I leaned over and put my head in my hands, overwhelmed by a feeling of utter helplessness and futility. "There's so much I didn't know! And I still don't know! My father was playing around on my mother, my mother was going crazy, our business was going bankrupt. And I didn't know anything about anything at all! There I was, just blithely picking out clothes to wear back to school, and my mother's and father's worlds were falling down around them, and I was too goddamned blind and selfish to sense it! I can't bear it." Marsha unclasped her hands, and stroked my head, lightly, comfortingly, as Geof had done. "I have a master's degree in business administration, for heaven's sake, and I don't really know why our business failed. It embarrassed me and shamed me and I don't think I really wanted to know. And I know even less about why my mother's life failed. Marsha, I can't bear the thought of what she endured, without any help or comfort from me—" I was crying so hard by then I couldn't talk any more.

"Come on." Marsha's voice was gentle, but she tugged strongly on my knees to get my attention. "Children aren't supposed to have to take care of their parents, and if you didn't know what was going on, it's because they tried to protect you from it. You know that. There's something else bothering you. What else is wrong, Jenny?"

I felt cold, and it took me a few moments—I had to stop crying first —to get up the courage to finally put my worst fears into words.

"They say I look the most like her."

"Yes?"

"She was quieter than I am and God knows she was shyer, but people say we were a lot alike in other ways. And Sherry was always Daddy's Little Girl, but Mom was closer to me—"

"Yes?"

"And one day I went off to school and she was this perfectly normal woman . . . nervous, a little high-strung, but normal . . . and then the next thing I know, she's . . . nuts."

"And?"

The truth finally came blurting out. "And if it could happen to her, if I'm so much like her, why couldn't it happen to me? I want her to be *different* from me, Marsha. I'm desperate to find some difference between us! I want her to have existed as a completely whole and separate person from any of us, so that I don't have to walk around feeling terrified that it could happen to me. Geof wants to have children, and I'm beginning to think, maybe. But Marsha, I'd die before I'd take even the smallest chance of putting my children through—"

"What you and Sherry have been through."

"Yes."

"Then why don't you find out, Jenny?"

I stared at her. "What?"

She smiled at me. "You're such a hotshot amateur sleuth? Always sticking your nose into other people's business?" Her smile turned self-deprecating. "Like me. Well, here you've been going around for years helping other people solve the mysteries of their lives . . . what about the mysteries of your own life? Why did your father's business fail? Ask around. Find out! Who was the woman named Margaret Cain? Find out! Investigate your mother's life. Interview people who knew her. Maybe she'll begin to come alive for you as the separate person she really was. You might even find some clues the doctors missed that will help us to understand what happened to her." She added quickly, "I think that's unlikely, but you never know. And if it would make you feel better to try, then why not do it?"

I continued staring at her, but now it was in admiration. Tears spurted to my eyes, but this time I wiped them away, and they stopped flowing. "You did that in fifteen minutes flat," I joked. "Are you going to charge me for a full fifty minutes anyway?"

Marsha smiled again, but her tone was serious as she said, "And listen, how do you feel? Physically, I mean. Do you feel as terrible as you look?"

"Thanks a lot." I grinned foolishly, feeling eager and even a little happy. "I guess the answer is not quite. I'm tired, that's all. I want to sleep all the time, and I don't have any appetite. I've lost about ten pounds in the last five days—"

"Not good, Jenny."

"I know, but—"

"I want you to get a physical. I know you'll put it off if I leave it up to you, so I'm going to call Doc Farrell—he's still your GYN, isn't he? —and get you in to see him tomorrow. You're way too thin and you're so pale I think they buried the wrong woman. I think you'll feel better if you're put on a vitamin regimen, and that sort of advice should come from a doctor who has examined you, and not from me." Having delivered herself of those prescriptions, she stood up and reached out a hand to me. "Let's fix some hot chocolate. You're having yours with marshmallows."

I was suddenly ravenously hungry as I let my best friend help me to my feet.

"Do you feel any better, Jen?"

"I feel a lot better," I admitted, as I followed her to her kitchen. "Kind of hopeful. Less crazy and sad and helpless."

She turned halfway around and jabbed one of my shoulders with one of her fingers, hard enough to make me cry, "Ouch!"

"You're not crazy," she said, and then she faced me straight on and grasped both my shoulders with her hands. "I am a bona fide, gen-u-ine psychiatrist, and I hereby declare you not crazy. A shade neurotic, perhaps, on the subject of your mother, maybe a mite confused about the separation between your identity and hers, but otherwise every bit as sane as your average contemporary American female."

Marsha smiled at me and released me. She turned back around and continued on down the hall to her kitchen.

"Thank you," I said, hurrying after her. "I think."

But I thought of my strange visit to my mother's hospital room, of my outburst of hysteria in the funeral limousine, of my behavior at

Sherry's house after the funeral, and of leaving work in tears that very morning. Not to mention my general reputation about town as a woman who regularly got involved in trouble more often than any normal person ought to do. And I said, in words so prophetic I would have taken the next bus to Boston if I'd known the truth of them: "You'd have a hard time convincing some people."

5

AT BREAKFAST THE NEXT MORNING, GEOF MADE ME EAT CHOCO-
late chip cookies, along with a breakfast of eggs and toast.

"Are you trying to fatten me up?" I asked him.

"Fatten schmatten," my husband replied, as he fed a last bite of
cookie into my waiting mouth. "I'd be happy just to get you all the way
up to thin. I want you to eat at least two more of these, Jenny. And
drink all of your milk. The whole glass."

"Aw, Dad, you're so mean to me."

I called my assistant at her home that morning to tell her I wouldn't
be at the office that day.

"Good," Faye said. "I approve. Stay away as long as you need,
Jenny. I'll take care of everything just fine."

"I know you, Faye," I laughed. "You'll take care of everything so
'fine' the foundation won't need me anymore."

It was only intended as a joke, and I was surprised to feel my spirits
lift at the very idea. What, me? Not go back to the foundation? What an
extraordinary thought. I loved my job, didn't I? But Faye was good
enough, she could do it . . . in an emergency. Like now. Right, that
was all. Now. Temporarily. For a day or two. Of course I was going
back to my job.

As I emerged from our house that Tuesday morning, my body felt
loose and rattly in its skin, and my skin itself felt dry and itchy, as did
my throat. If I'd had to run the fifty-yard dash, I'd have been winded by
the third yard. Still, I was moving. Eating. Talking. I felt as if I were
emerging from a dark, warm, silent cave. I was a bat, blinking in the

sunlight, flapping my wings weakly, tentatively, to see if they'd still hold me up. And, deep inside, longing a bit to return to the strange, dark comfort of the cave. But I knew that Marsha was right in something she hadn't even voiced: In the process of immersing myself in the mysteries of other people's lives, I had avoided my own.

Well, no longer.

Even bats eventually fly out of their caves.

I flapped my elbows experimentally (after looking around to make sure nobody was around to see me) and then I got into my car.

I had a list. I had a plan. I had hope.

I would start at the beginning . . .

Once upon a time, a child named Margaret Mary Thorne was born to a Lutheran father and a Catholic mother in the seacoast town of Port Frederick, Massachusetts. And it came to pass that the priest who christened her, and educated her in the church, and who heard her childish confessions was Father Francis Gower . . .

He was eighty-two now, and living in retirement in a tiny, one-story brick house squeezed between St. Michael's Cathedral and its rectory. I knew him by reputation and by the vaguest memories of things I thought my mother had told me, as he was not a priest who had ever entered into the wider affairs of the community outside of his own church. When I had called him the previous night to make an appointment for this morning, Father Francis had sounded old, tired and cranky as a nun in a wool habit. "I'm retired," he'd said, in a weak croak. "I don't feel well at all. And you are not a member of my parish, so what gives you the right to bother me now?"

"I want to ask you some things about my mother," I told him, not at all abashed by his bad temper. With five elderly powerhouses on my board of trustees, I was used to dealing with those moments when their aching bones and failing eyesight and hearing made them irritable and hard to get along with. Hell, in their place, I'd have been cranky, too, and a lot more often. "I'm gathering memories of her. And I have a gift for you."

"Things! I don't need any more *things.*"

"It's food, Father Gower, cookies."

There had been a pause, full of suspicion. "What kind of cookies?"

"Chocolate chip, like my mother used to make."

"I don't believe it," he said, but he sounded as if he wanted to believe

46

it. "I hear you're a working woman. Everybody knows working women don't cook, which is the reason their husbands run around and their children take drugs."

I laughed, and sweetened the bribe: "Two dozen."

"You're sure it's her recipe?"

"Out of her very own recipe box."

"All right. Ten o'clock in the morning. Put the cookies in a paper sack, and be sure you give them to me and not to anybody else, do you understand?"

"No," I said, "but I'll do that."

"Not to anybody else!"

At my phone, I raised my left hand. "I swear it."

He grunted, and hung up.

So I had the cookies with me when I walked up his front steps. I was thinking how this man remembered my mother as a baby; it was poignant to think of her as a child, to imagine her sweet innocence, and the loss of it. I rang his doorbell.

"You bring the cookies?" he demanded, right off.

Physically, he suited his house well, as he, too, was small in height, but thick and solid-looking, like a brick, with a face of a similar flushed color. That was from high blood pressure, I deduced, which might help to account for his choleric disposition. Even wearing low-heeled shoes, I loomed over him by a good eight inches.

I smiled in reply, and held out the brown paper sack to him.

Father Gower took it, opened it, held it up to his face, and sniffed. He reached in with one hand and took out a cookie, which he stuck in his mouth while offering the open sack to me. Having already eaten three for breakfast, I declined. He crumpled up the mouth of the sack and, munching his cookie, escorted me into his little home.

He wiped crumbs from his whiskery chin. "Don't tell."

I was alarmed. "You aren't diabetic or anything, are you?"

"No, no." But when he opened the hall closet and stuffed the paper sack into a sleeve of a black raincoat, after removing one more cookie, I wondered if he'd tricked me into helping him break a diet. "No, nothing like that," he said, as he tried to shove the door to again. It wasn't easy, as the tiny closet was stuffed with a lot more than coats; I glimpsed piles of newspapers, boots, walking canes, hats, rectangles of cardboard, a vacuum sweeper, a broom, and a mop. Clearly, it double—tripled?—as a parish art supply and utility closet, too. I put my own shoulder to the task. "It's not that at all," he repeated, as the door clicked shut, catching only a bit of a sleeve in the crack. "It's Mrs. Kennedy, my daily. She's the world's worst cook with the world's most sensitive feelings. When she catches me eating some other woman's cooking, she gets her feelings hurt, and then I suffer the consequences for meals to come. Mrs. K takes it out on me by trying to impress me with strange concoctions she calls gourmet dinners, things like fried spinach turnovers." He shivered. "Awful stuff like that. You have no idea how bad it used to be back in the days when we had to eat fish on Fridays. What that woman could do to cod ought to be against canon law. I used to make her do a penance and say five Hail Marys for some of those offenses against the culinary arts. I have been at the mercy of that woman for forty-two years, and I'll keep those chocolate chip cookies a secret from her if I have to commit a venial sin to do it. Come in, come in. Sit down."

We were in his compact living room by then.

It was immaculate, thanks to the infamous Mrs. K, I supposed. A number of lurid prints of paintings purporting to be of Jesus Christ adorned the walls. Judging from them, Jesus was an anorexic white man with glaucoma and a bad barber. The room was also distinguished by a plentitude of doilies draped over every conceivable surface—on the arms and backs of the sofa and chairs, under the church magazines that were stacked on the coffee table, under the lamps on the end tables, under the candy dishes on top of the television set, under the homemade pen holder that contained pencils and felt-tip pens, even pinned to the hassocks. I could only guess that Father Gower had brought with him into retirement his collection of Christmas and birthday gifts made for him through the years by the devoted women of his parish. Or, as jealous as he claimed his housekeeper to be, maybe Mrs. K had crocheted two doilies for every one he'd been given. The room smelled strongly of lavender, as if she'd hidden sachets in every drawer, perhaps also gifts from the ladies guilds.

When he sat down, only the tips of his brogues touched the carpet. He wore baggy black trousers, belted with brown leather, and a red flannel shirt that was buttoned to his neck and frayed at the cuffs. The shirt made his complexion look even redder, so that even his ears, below a rim of white hair, looked fiery. If it hadn't been for the stern expression on his face, what with his short stature and high color he would have looked more like a retired circus clown than a retired priest. I had a feeling, however, that it would be unwise in the extreme to laugh at this man.

"Jennifer Lynn." He pronounced my name slowly, experimentally, as if trying it out on his tongue to see if it had a good Catholic feel to it. Evidently not, judging from the way his mouth pursed in distaste. "Margaret Mary's oldest girl."

"That's right, Father."

"You're not married."

"Yes, I am."

"What's your last name now?"

"It's still Cain."

"Hmmph. I suppose you work, and you don't have any children"

"That's right, Father."

"I thought as much. It's young women like you who are responsible for the decline of parishes like this one. Women are the backbone, the very mainstay of a church. When you selfishly work somewhere for money, you deprive your family and your church of the fruit of your labor and the wealth of your time."

"Yes," I agreed. "We do."

He shot me a canny look, not at all deceived by the mildness of my tone. "Hmmph. It is woman's role to serve God and man."

"How very convenient for you both." Although my words were sarcastic, I was careful to keep my tone nearly as cheerful as my stepmother's. "Tell me, Father, my mother attended St. Michael's as a child, didn't she?"

"You expect me to remember that?"

"I expect you have an excellent memory, Father. What *do* you remember about her?"

"Why do you want to know?"

Out of sheer frustration, I laughed. "Are you a Jesuit?"

"Why do you ask?"

I smiled at him. "Because *you* ask, instead of answering."

"I am a diocesan priest, not a Jesuit, as you would surely know had you been raised properly in the church. But, if you like, I will give you questions. Three of them." He proceeded to tick them off on his short, stubby fingers. "What business is it of yours to pry into your mother's spiritual life? What gives you, who never participated in my church, the expectation that I will serve your whim now? Three, your mother's soul is in the hands of God, and who are you to question the natural order of the sacred universe?"

"Is that what I'm doing?" I shook my head. "I thought I was only asking someone who knew her to share a few memories of her with me. I'm only trying to find out what kind of life my mother had before she got sick, Father. And why she *got* so sick. I'm trying to trace her life and her death, so that I can find some peace in my own soul about it."

"Our Lord Jesus is the only path to peace."

"Well, here I am, talking to a priest."

He grunted. "My memories are none of your business."

"Even when they're about my own mother?" I heard my voice rise in disbelief. I felt baffled by this hard old man, and I asked him out of genuine curiosity, "Why are you being so tough with me, Father Gower?"

He ignored the second question and answered only the first one. "Even when they include other people, my memories are still mine." He glanced dismissively around him at the doily-littered room. "Priests own nothing, not even their own souls. I came to retirement with nothing but my vestments and a change of clothing. Nothing else do I own or want to own. But my thoughts are my own, known only to God and to me, and so are my memories of other people's confessions. As a priest, I have been expected to relinquish everything else, but I do not have to give my memories away. And I will not. Not to you or to anyone. You have your own memories of your mother. Do I ask you to give them to me? I do not. I do not want them. And do not ask me to give you mine."

I stood up. "I didn't know my request would offend you."

He started to rise, too, but the effort of pulling his thick body out of his chair seemed to defeat him. I was reminded of myself, last night at Marsha's house, and I wanted to reach out a hand to help him up, as she had helped me. But I remained on my side of the wall he had erected between us, afraid of offending him even more. Father Gower glared up at me from under eyebrows that might once have been ferociously bushy and black. "Is that an apology?"

"No," I said, "I don't believe it is."

When he didn't respond, I started to leave the room, but he stopped me by asking, "Where did you bury her?"

I turned to face him again. "Harbor Lights."

"In the Catholic section?"

"No, we told you, she wanted to be buried with her father's people, and they were Protestant."

He crossed himself, and muttered something in Latin. I wanted to think it was "rest in peace," but I was half afraid it was a curse of some kind. I was glad the weather that day had kept him even from attending, much less presiding over, her funeral.

"Your mother's past is none of your business, either," he suddenly said, startling me. "Leave it alone. Leave her alone. You'll be happier that way. You think you'll find the mother you loved—and you might. But you might also find a woman you wouldn't even recognize if you passed her on the street. You might not even like her."

"I doubt that."

"You don't know," he said, angrily. "Listen to me! It's risky enough to dive into one's own past, but it's particularly dangerous to dig into somebody else's life. You don't belong in it. Get out of it!"

We were divided only by the length of a tiny living room, Father Gower and I, but it felt like a gulf we could never bridge. I didn't know what else to say to him, so I settled for, "Thanks for the advice. I hope you enjoy the cookies."

"Thank you for those," he said, grudgingly. "They're good."

"I'll tell my husband you said so. He baked them."

With which (most satisfying) riposte, I walked out—only to literally run into a woman as she was bustling in the front door. We bounced off of each other and backed away, smiling in mutual, flustered embarrassment.

"Excuse me!"

"Oh, forgive me, dear!"

I stepped out onto the porch with her, and closed the screen door and front door behind me. "I'm really sorry. Are you okay?"

"Oh, I'm fine, dear." She laughed as if I'd made a great joke. "As fat as I've gotten in my old age, it would take a Sherman tank to run me down." She had frizzled white hair that looked as if it might be on the sixth day after its weekly visit to the beauty shop, and she wore a bulky red polyester sweater over bulging black slacks. On her feet were white tennis shoes—with the laces untied—and, incongruously, those tennis socks that have little fuzzy balls on the heels to keep them from sliding down into the shoes. In one hand she held a black plastic trash bag, and in the other, a metal dust pan.

"Mrs. Kennedy?" I guessed.

"Why, yes, dear." She smiled broadly, but then tempered that by letting her expressive eyes and mouth droop into lugubriousness. I felt my own face fall in instinctive response to her. "It was a lovely funeral."

"What? I'm sorry, were you—"

"Yes, I was there, dear, of course I was, why I knew her from the time she was a tiny child, didn't I?" The smile was back, and I couldn't seem to help but smile back at her. "I remember the first time I ever saw your mother, at her baptism, and then the last time, too—" Mrs. K broke off, and pressed the open end of the trash bag to her ample chest, now looking flustered and distressed. I caught myself frowning down at her. The woman was a virtual one-act play, and I seemed to be the audience she held in the palm of her hand. "Oh, forgive me, you don't want to hear—"

"Please, I do! What about the last time?"

Mrs. Kennedy appeared to employ whatever she held in her hands, like stage props, to punctuate her sentences. "Well, she was here." The dust pan pointed to the steps. "At the rectory, I mean." The trash bag pointed next door. "Come to see Father, she was, but never too upset to stop to talk to me." The dust pan fanned the air in a kind of pantomime of "never." I felt dust drifting up my nostrils, and nearly sneezed. "So kind she was, such a lovely, lovely girl."

"You say Mom was upset?"

She had spoken in such dramatic tones that my own words came out sounding like lines of dialogue. Feeling like an ingenue attempting a tough role, I tried to sound merely curious, in a way that wouldn't scare Mrs. K away from her memories. For safety's sake, I stepped back out of the way of the talking dust pan. "Do you remember why?"

"Upset?" Now it was Mrs. Kennedy who looked upset. The Irish accent that I hadn't noticed at all when she first spoke, was by now so thick I could hardly understand some words. "Did I say that? Oh, dear, and I don't know that I meant that at all. Nervous, is more like it, you know how your mother was, dear, hurrying and scurrying about like a pretty little squirrel sometimes." She crossed the trash bag and dust pan back and forth in front of her several times, making the bag billow and the dust fly. "I'm sure that's all it was, running late for car pool or some such thing, that's all." Mrs. K's confusion suddenly focused on a

52

thought that brought tears dramatically to her blue eyes. "I'm so sorry for that bit of trouble she had, and your wee family, too."

"I thank you, I do."

She leaned toward me and whispered, looking suddenly and marvelously like an old, fat leprechaun grandmother, "What sort of mood is *he* in today?"

I smiled down at her and shrugged, struggling to retain a hold on my natural Massachusetts accent. "Normal, I'd guess."

"Oh dear. And if I don't get his bed made and get back to the rectory, the beans'll burn and there'll be heck to pay for sure."

"How have you put up with the old tartar all these years?" I asked her, out of my own exasperation with him. "Why didn't you ever just walk out?"

"Leave him?" Mrs. Kennedy stared at me as if I'd just posted Luther's ninety-five theses to the Cathedral door. "But my dear, 'tis an honor to me to serve a man who serves God!"

Hmmph, I thought, echoing the grumpy priest as I moved aside to let her enter: Reminds me of the old joke about the fellow who swept up after the elephants in the circus. "Why don't you quit?" somebody asked him. "What?" he cried in horror. "And leave show business?"

"Good day to you," she cried, as she closed the front door with a final flourish of the trash bag.

I grinned at the space where she'd been—it still seemed to vibrate—and shook my head. *And the top o' the mornin' to you, too, Mrs. K.* I was willing to bet that even the trivia of everyday life was high drama to her. My God, I thought, as I turned away, what a challenge he must be to her, and how she must get on his nerves!

At the end of Father Gower's front walk, I took a little notebook out of my purse and jotted a couple of questions in it: One, why was my mother "upset" on what may have been her last visit to her parish priest? Considering Mrs. K's tendency to overdramatize, I was a little wary of taking her word for the "upset," but I put it down anyway. And, two, what did Father Gower mean by that reference to his "memories of other people's confessions"?

I flipped back to a previous page in the notebook: Here was where I'd made my list of things to do and people to see in my (possibly quixotic) quest for the truth about my mother, our family business, and—maybe at least by inference—me. According to that list, and my watch, I had a luncheon date with Miss Lucille Grant at noon and an hour and a half to kill until then.

There was time enough to start my "investigation" into the Fall of the House of Cain Clams.

6

THE PORT FREDERICK MAIN LIBRARY, LOCATED NEAR THE downtown square, had long been a favorite place of mine, a calming port of balm and refuge where I could hide among the books and stacks. It was a wonderfully quaint and rambling building with English ivy climbing its quarry-cut stone walls, and cozy nooks and crannies inside, along with long, shining walnut tables and wingback chairs in which to curl up and read *Anne of Green Gables* or *Little Women*. It was a place where seagulls roosted in the eaves, looking as if they'd flown out of the pages of "The Ancient Mariner," and where drafts straight out of *Wuthering Heights* whistled through the cracks, and where, once, when a kid (me) knocked over a table lamp, the librarian greeted the crash with a cry of, "Hark! What light by yonder window breaks?" Pronounced "libree" around these parts, accent on the first syllable, with the second syllable cut short, it looked and smelled and even sounded the part of the quintessential New England public library, right down to the American flag at the door and the portraits of the presidents on the walls.

And that's where I walked, late on that crisp March morning, thinking I would research the bankruptcy of our family business just as if it had belonged to other people, just as if I were a graduate business student doing research on an assignment.

Subject: Cain Clams

Problem: Pinpoint the cause or causes for the apparently sudden and heretofore inadequately explained collapse of a thriving, 100-year-old family firm. Use interviews with the principals, examination of available company records, and other pertinent materials to buttress your hypothesis.

I'd kept my library card current at all times since I was five years old. It had been my mother who had taught me to use it, and now maybe I'd be using it to look her up.

"Hi, Jenny," called the librarian at the front desk.

She was a former schoolmate of mine, but I only smiled at her and didn't stop to chat, hoping she wouldn't think I was snubbing her. Hah, that was a laugh. As low as the Cains had fallen after the bankruptcy, who could possibly feel snubbed, for any reason, by any of us?

Here at my beloved public library, I'd have access to the Boston and New York newspapers, to trade journals and *The Wall Street Journal.* Cain Clams had not been significant by international standards, but it had been a "major player," as we used to say at business School, in the East Coast shellfish industry. And for at least two generations, it was Top Clam in Massachusetts.

First I looked it up in the *Reader's Guide to Periodical Literature.* It felt so strange, looking up my own name: "Cain Clams." After noting the publications in which articles appeared, I submitted my microfilm requests to the young man at the periodicals desk. He handed me a foot-high stack of films, which I carried to a microfilm projector, where I pulled up a chair and sat down.

There were fewer articles than I had expected, and almost all of them had appeared locally, with nothing more than what amounted to a few business bulletins appearing in the national press. That immediately surprised me, because I had always assumed we were bigger news than that. *Just goes to show how we inflate our own importance in the world,* I thought, feeling oddly diminished. *Guess we were a big fish in a much smaller pond than I've ever been led to believe.*

I read the headlines, because I had to, but I didn't stop to read the bodies of the stories. In fact, I literally averted my eyes from them, because I didn't want to take the chance of getting all emotional right there in the middle of the library. I felt exposed enough as it was— sitting there staring at headlines that included: CAIN CREDITORS SEEK PAY-BACK GUARANTEES, and CAIN ATTEMPTS DEBT RESTRUCTURING, and CAIN BLAMES CASH-FLOW PROBLEMS ON CHESAPEAKE POLLU-TION, POOR CLAM CROP, and CAIN LAY-OFFS ANNOUNCED. They blared off the machine at me as if they were posted in 64-point type, when they were really printed much more discreetly in a mere 14-point. Still, I didn't want passers-by reading those headlines over my shoulder; it would have felt too much like putting a scandalous family diary on public display.

I thought of my mother opening *The Port Frederick Times* every morning, dreading the possibility of facing this news. That image of her —in bathrobe and slippers, with her coffee growing cold in front of her and her cornflakes getting soft in the bowl as she read the paper—made me feel nearly as ill as I imagined she must have felt. I tried to clamp down on my imagination and to concentrate on the process of making copies of the articles to take home with me. I dropped in dime after dime to make photocopies.

When I finished the first stack of microfilm cannisters, I perused other catalogs, looking for more references to articles about Cain Clams. It took me only the hour and fifteen minutes I had available to accumulate a stack of copies about half an inch high. I rolled them up and secured them with rubber bands borrowed from the librarian at the periodicals desk.

"Making a family scrapbook, Ms. Cain?" he asked as I handed back the microfilm cannisters. I had been unaware that he'd recognized me until he spoke.

"No," I said, "this isn't the kind of family history I cherish, you know?"

"My mother kept all the articles, too."

I looked up sharply, to find him staring at me. He was about ten years younger than I, which would have made him about seven years of age when the company folded.

"She took them around with her to job interviews in other towns," he said, impassively, "to prove that it wasn't her fault that she got fired."

I felt myself flushing. "I'm so sorry."

"Yeah, well, maybe you should be," he said, taking back the cannisters and averting his eyes, as if he couldn't stand to look at me any longer.

The sheaf of copied articles trembled in my hand as I walked out of the library into a day that had turned colder while I was inside. This wasn't the first time I had been directly confronted with the bitter residue of the fall of Cain Clams, nor was it by any means the worst of those times. But it was rare for anybody to throw it up to me, especially after all these years. I was only a Cain child, after all, hardly responsible for thc disaster. Was this what my mother had endured, and much more frequently and harshly, because she was the very visible wife of the owner? Was that why she had made herself less and less visible, hiding in her house, in her room? Was this what she had faced every day on the phone, and every time she walked out of her front door? And for what reason? Was she any more to blame than her daughters?

As I walked on weak legs down the front steps to the sidewalk, I realized that for the first time in my life, I wanted to know—truly wanted to know—the real reasons for the bankruptcy, and not just the lame excuses my father made. I wanted to know who or what to blame, even if it turned out, as I suspected it would, to be him.

"Because," I said to myself. *"And so."*

If nobody else could do it for me, I would fill in the blanks of my own life. I suspected I might be setting myself an impossible task; I didn't know it was also a dangerous one. I only knew that I was supposed to meet my sixth-grade teacher for lunch in ten minutes and that I felt as if I would throw up if I had to swallow anything more than water. Having your family's business go bankrupt and throw dozens of people out of work is, I had long before discovered, like waking up with a terrible hangover: The guilt is enough to make you start drinking again just to help you forget how bad you feel about it.

I had a sudden craving for a *big* glass of beer.

That, I could swallow.

"You don't want to drink this early in the day, Jennifer."

Miss Lucille Grant, my former teacher and the only female trustee on the foundation board, smiled at me across the dining table at the C'est La Vie Restaurant down by the harbor. Since I had an unbreakable quarter-century habit of following her good advice, I reluctantly canceled my order for a Beck's Light and ordered a crab salad, instead, even though my stomach clenched at the thought of eating it.

"Your mother," Miss Grant said, continuing her narrative where it had been interrupted so that we might order lunch, "was a good little girl, as you were, although she was more conventional in her goodness than you are." There was a hint of a twitch at the corners of the old schoolteacher's mouth, and I knew she was thinking of the fact that I had wanted to drink a beer at midday. My beloved mentor was older by now than I liked to admit; her soft skin folded into countless wrinkles, her once-resonant voice wavered and trembled now, though her opinions did not. In one of the restaurant's cane-back chairs, Miss Lucille sat as straight as arthritis and a touch of widow's hump allowed her. Her large, plain hands remained immobile, reflecting the "small, still place" within her that always radiated a calming effect upon me, her perpetual pupil.

"One day," Miss Lucille said, in that wonderful, storytelling way she had of making me feel as if I were ten years old and seated at her feet again, "it had been raining off and on in the morning before recess, so that when I took the children outside to the playground there were little puddles everywhere. Naturally, I instructed them not to jump in the puddles." She smiled at me. "Of course, teachers are supposed to instruct children not to do those things that are the most fun to do. I wouldn't have minded if they'd jumped in the puddles—it is fun, isn't it, and we all want to do it, really—but it was a cool day, and I didn't want them to go through the rest of the afternoon with wet feet. I didn't want them to catch colds, or to ruin their shoes, for that matter."

The waitress set down rolls and butter, and Miss Lucille waited for her to finish.

"Anyway," she continued then, "your mother astonished me and I think she astonished herself by jumping in a puddle. I watched her stand outside of that puddle and look at it, and I could tell she was weighing the pros and cons of, by golly, just letting go and pouncing into that puddle! Well, the devil won. She jumped. With both feet. She made a great splash, and water landed on her skirt. Her little girlfriends gasped and exclaimed, 'Oh, Meg, you're in trouble now!' And then your mother jumped out of the puddle, looking pleased and frightened all at the same time.

"Well, I had to call her over to reprimand her. Frankly, I didn't want to do it, because I was so happy to see that dear good child do something wrong for a change, but the other children had seen her break a rule, and they would have thought I was playing favorites if I didn't punish Margaret Mary. So I called her name. Your mother came to me with her head down, dragging her wet feet, her little hands hidden in her wet skirt. I said to her, as gently and casually as I could, 'Meg, you know you're not supposed to jump in puddles.'

"Well, your poor mother burst into tears. Not loudly, of course, she wouldn't have allowed herself to make such a fool of herself. But her lips quivered and the tears came down her cheeks, and she whispered to me, 'I'm sorry, Miss Grant.' She stood there like a pitiful little penitent until I dismissed her, and then she ran away back to her friends, who whispered and giggled while she shushed them and cast frightened glances in my direction. I felt such an ogre! I wanted to call her back, to say, 'Meg, it wasn't such a bad thing, it was just a little petty rule you broke, something any child might do, something *I* would like to do with my great black clodhopper shoes, it's nothing so awful for you to feel so bad as all this.'

"But I didn't do that, you see, because I doubted she would believe me. Margaret Mary's little world had many rules—there were rules of etiquette and rules of polite society, there were religious strictures and rules for law-abiding little persons, there were parental rules and school rules, rules, rules. I could quite understand how she had to stay right on top of them, and try not to break any single one of them, for fear they might all tumble down around her. Children are like that, you know, unconsciously they quite expect the death penalty for the most minor infraction."

Miss Grant stopped talking long enough for the waitress to set our iced teas and salads before us and then she took a few bites of her lunch before continuing her story. I sipped my tea, and hoped she wouldn't notice that I wasn't eating. She put her fork down and dabbed at her mouth with her napkin.

"I understood how your mother felt, Jennifer, but I was frankly appalled at her overreaction to my little reprimand. Any other child would have said, 'Sorry!' and run off giggling to do it again when I wasn't looking. But your mother was mortified by this terrible sin she had committed of being childish and jumping in a puddle. She was quiet the rest of the day, and hypersensitive to any criticism, and I felt so sorry for her, but there wasn't any help for it. She was supposed to be a nice little girl and that, by golly, was what she was going to be if it killed her."

"Miss Grant—"

"Try to eat a few bites of your salad, Jennifer."

I picked up my fork. "Miss Grant, what do you think she might have been if she hadn't spent all of that energy trying to be a nice little girl and a nice little woman?"

"And a good wife and a good mother, too? I don't know, dear. I can't honestly tell you that I ever saw any particular latent talent in your mother. She was a good reader, an adequate little artist, she had a typical child's singing voice, but no Shirley Temple. I don't really believe she was a case of a frustrated writer or business executive, or what have you. She wasn't you, dear. There was only one thing that I think she sometimes wanted to do that she couldn't—"

"What?"

"Now and then," Miss Grant said, slowly, as if she were thinking as she spoke, "I think she really wanted, maybe even desperately wanted, to break a rule. Jump in another puddle. Jump in a lot of puddles! Do something mischievous. Get into trouble. Get away with something she wasn't supposed to do. But except for jumping in that pitiful little puddle, I don't suppose she ever did. I do believe I know why, too."

"Tell me, please."

"The penalty for doing wrong was too high for her to bear."

Perhaps from fatigue, my heart was beating abnormally fast and hard. "What penalty?"

The old woman—who had taught my mother, my father, my sister, my husband, and me—thought again before she spoke. "The one she paid in her good little girl's heart. Somewhere along the line, she got the idea that she was loved for being good. Unfortunately, the corollary of that idea is that a child will be hated and rejected for being 'bad.' Your mother had fine, decent parents, Jennifer, and I'm sure they didn't mean to give her that message. But give it to her they did. 'Be a good girl, Meg, and we'll always love you. But do something—anything bad, and you'll lose our love.' It was a common message to girl children in those days." She eyed me for a moment. "Perhaps it still is."

"I've broken rules, Miss Grant."

"What?" Her tone was gently scoffing. "Living with a man before marriage, is that the one you mean? You married him, didn't you? You came back to your hometown, like a good girl, didn't you? You hold a respectable, low-paying, womanly, other-serving job. You are honest and ethical to a fault, and I would very much like you to try to tell me exactly which other rules you think that you break."

"But Miss Grant, don't you live by them, too?"

"Yes." The old woman sighed. "And most of the time I don't regret it, but now and then the idea of Paris and Baghdad seem very attractive to me. Don't they to you, dear?"

I laughed. "We'll go!"

But she only straightened her back a millimeter more and shook her head. "I seriously doubt it, my child, for either one of us. And before you have time to take that as some sort of challenge, let me inquire as to a bit of more mundane business. Is everything all right down at that gallery where we're funding that outrageous display of art?"

"I thought you liked it," I said.

"Oh, I do!" She chuckled. "I'm especially fond of that parody of Degas's painting of the woman bathing, where it is a rather plump and surprised-looking man who is caught in the act of bathing, instead. But it does outrage some of the good people of our city, doesn't it? Faye has told me about those anonymous letters that we have received from MOAC. I'll admit that I'm worried about protecting the artists and their work from that kind of sublimated rage, and I do believe that we assumed that responsibility when we agreed to sponsor them, don't you?"

"Yes, m'am." I smiled at her. "I'll talk to Faye."

"Soon," she directed me. "I am truly concerned."

"Today," I agreed, but I resented it a little.

"Eat more of your salad, Jennifer. You're too thin."

I suddenly wanted to tell my beloved mentor to go jump in a puddle. But I ate the damned salad anyway. I asked her if she remembered who had stood behind her in line to sign the guest book at my mother's funeral, but she didn't. When she asked me why, and I told her, she only said, in the Delphic way she sometimes had of saying things she thought you ought to be able to figure out for yourself, "Guilt is such a confusing emotion, isn't it?"

Miss Grant had taken a taxi to the restaurant, which made me feel guilty because I knew what a budget-breaker that was for her. Because of that, I insisted on paying for lunch ("But I invited *you,* Miss Grant!") and I drove her home. After helping her to her door, and kissing her good-bye, I returned to my car and sat for a few moments with my open notebook in my hand. There wasn't really anything to write down from my talk with Miss Grant, except maybe "puddle," and that didn't exactly seem pertinent. But I thought about that little girl with the overactive conscience that Miss Grant had described to me at lunch.

"What if . . ." I mused aloud. "What if Mom believed that our family had committed a 'sin,' by putting so many people out of work? Wouldn't that be something she would confess to her priest? And it could certainly account for the fact that she was upset the last time she went to see him."

Could that guilt and shame have literally driven her nuts?

I.O.U.

Well, hell, it was as good an explanation as any the doctors had ever given me, but I wasn't satisfied with it. Not yet. Maybe I'd never find an answer to satisfy me.

"And *that* will drive *me* crazy," I said, as I started the car.

7

MY FRIEND MARSHA HAD ARRANGED A TWO O'CLOCK APPOINT-
ment for me with Dr. Calvin Farrell, the gynecologist/obstetrician I
had managed to insult at my sister's house after the funeral. As a result,
I was looking forward to this physical exam even less than usual.

Partly as a delaying action, I stopped in the lobby of the medical
building to use a pay phone, before taking the elevator to Dr. Farrell's
office.

My assistant answered the phone, sounding enormously happy as she
said, "Good afternoon! Port Frederick Civic Foundation. Faye Basil
speaking."

"Hi, Faye, it's—"

"Jenny! Oh, it's wonderful to hear your voice. How are you?"

I was tempted to kid her about her obvious enthusiasm for taking
over my job, but I thought that might cause her to feel guilty and self-
conscious, so I just replied, "I'm great, Faye, but I'm a little worried
about the New East Gallery. I just had lunch with Miss Grant, and she
thinks we ought to hire a—"

"Security guard. You bet. I've hired one, and she'll be there tomorrow."

I paused, slightly taken aback by her efficiency, which shouldn't have
come as even the least surprise to me. I loved the fact that she had hired
a woman to do it. It was wonderfully appropriate, and the artists would
appreciate her sensitivity. "Good. It sounds as if you're taking care of
business just fine, Faye."

"Well, thanks, but I really do miss you."

And I felt fortunate in my knowledge that she meant that. We discussed a few items of other business, I answered a couple of questions, but it was clear that there wasn't much I could have been doing there that she couldn't do just as well. Again, I wanted to tease her about trying to usurp my job, but I thought better of that, too, and just said good-bye, "for a little while longer."

I then rode the elevator up to the third floor.

Like Father Francis Gower, Doc Farrell was also attended by doting, bustling women. They were his lab techs, his accountants and secretaries, and his majordomo of a nurse/receptionist, Marjorie Earnshaw. A big-boned, imposing woman, she was his Mrs. K, but with a forcefully bitter edge, a woman who never missed an opportunity to tell you how *she* could have been a doctor if her parents hadn't forced her into nurse's school back in 1930 because that was considered more acceptable for girls.

"What's the problem, dear?" Marj inquired, pen poised over her appointment book, eyebrows cocked over her reading glasses. She'd worn the same hairstyle for all the years I'd known her—hair slicked up and held in place all the way around her skull by an elasticized band, with fat, stiff curls pouring down over her head. On this day, the band was white with a bold pattern of fiery orange and black poppies to match the fabric of her shirtwaist dress. She was a sturdy-looking, buxom woman of middle height, so she could carry it off all right without looking altogether like a fire engine. The orange also matched her lipstick and her stubby fingernails. I couldn't imagine how she tolerated wearing those bands around her skull all the time; in her place, I would have had to process those poppies into heroin to treat my headache. She said, reprovingly, "I squeezed you in on Dr. Marsha Sandy's special request. Are you sick? Something urgent that can't wait for a regular appointment?"

I swallowed my annoyance. As if there were a chance in hell that I was going to blurt out to her: "I'm run-down because I've been in a state of acute depression since my mother died. So what do you prescribe, Marj?" She'd have done it, too; Marj was a great one for passing out samples of pills that the pharmaceutical salespeople left behind.

"What is it that can't wait?" she repeated, narrowing her eyes, which were an unattractive hazel, and already a little squinty to begin with.

I was sufficiently on edge to let her goad me into doing a very thoughtless thing. I leaned forward and whispered: "AIDS test."

"Oh?" The hazel eyes opened to their full, if limited, width. She didn't bother to hide her disapproving surprise. "Then you'll want a blood workup first thing. Go on down the hall to the lab, Jennifer. I thought you were married."

"Yes, I am."

"You haven't had a blood transfusion?"

"Never."

"Well, then why—"

I was already regretting my poor choice of a joke, but I jumped in the next puddle anyway. Blame it on Miss Grant. "I haven't always been married, Marj."

"And neither has your husband," she said sharply, pursing her orange lips. "Have you thought of that?"

I put my hand to my heart and feigned dismay. "Oh, my. Oh, no!"

She nodded portentously, full of wisdom and doom, the heavy mass of steel gray curls dipping down, then rising again.

I turned and escaped down the hall to the lab, feeling less guilty than I should have that I'd managed to put one over on the nosy old bitch. *God'll get you for this, Cain,* I chided myself.

Nurses took my blood and urine samples and told me to wait on a bench until I was called. It gave me time to contemplate my own sins, none of which I cared to confess either to Father Gower or to Miss Grant.

An hour later, I had disrobed and rerobed in a cotton examination gown—pink with little yellow flowers—and was lying on my back on a metal table with a sheet of white paper under me. My feet were propped up in padded metal stirrups, no longer the cold bare metal ones of yore. (The world *was* making progress, or at least women were.) It was nearly time for my "yearly" anyway, so we'd gone ahead with the full shebang —breast exam, pap smear, and all. Doc Farrell, once he was finished, pushed his little stool on wheels back away from the end of the table where I lay with my legs splayed and my eyes resignedly focused on the ceiling like the virgin sacrifice in a pagan fertility rite.

"We've always misinterpreted the Victorians, Doc."

"Hmm?" he said, as he peeled off his gloves and tossed them in the trash.

"*This* is when we should lie back and think of England, not during sex."

"Very funny."

The physician beyond my knees was seventy-six years old and now delivering the babies of the "baby boomers" that he had delivered. Though he looked the part of the archetypal kindly grandfather, white hair and all, Doc Farrell was infamous for his lousy bedside manner. "You're sick?" he had once said to me when I had called with a croaky throat. "Why? You need attention? Get a boyfriend." His idea of a prescription was to tell you to "take two aspirins and if you're still sick in the morning, I don't want to hear about it. Call Marj. If she thinks you're sick enough, she'll let me know, but frankly, I've got a hell of a busy day tomorrow with people who are really sick, and I couldn't squeeze you in if you were dying, which you aren't by a long shot."

His metal speculum clattered into a metal pan as he threw it down and said, "There, that wasn't so bad, was it?"

"Well, it wasn't so good, either."

He frowned at me over his shoulder as he wheeled himself over to the sink. That was something else you could always count on with Doc Farrell: He was nearly always wrong about what hurt and what didn't. If he said, "This won't hurt at all," you knew to breathe deep and grit your teeth, but if he said, "This may hurt," you knew it was safe to relax. Once you understood that, you knew when to brace yourself. One of these days, I swore for the umpteenth time, I'm switching to a woman gynecologist.

I had never understood why he had continued to be the most popular "female" doctor in Port Frederick, or even why I had carried on my mother's habit of seeing him. I guess that was the answer: habit. As he finished and I sat up on the table while he washed his hands, I promised myself that if he was rude to me this time, I'd find myself another gynecologist next time.

He looked up from the sink and smiled like a real grandfather.

"You look just like your mother, Jenny."

Well, damn. So I was stuck with him for a while longer.

"Except that she took better care of herself."

"Thank you for going to the funeral. I'm sorry that I—"

He waved me off. "There's nothing wrong with you that time and a few good vitamins won't cure. What else can I do for you?"

"Well." If he'd been his usual curmudgeonly self, I might have coped, but this observant, brusquely gentle old man had me on the verge of tears already. My voice shook as I said, "I don't know if you remember,

Doctor Cal, but I was away at college when my mother was committed to Hampshire. My father never really explained anything to me—either he wouldn't or he couldn't—and my sister was too young to understand anything, and nobody else seemed to know, and I was too young to quiz the doctors, and then later when I did feel confident enough to ask them questions, I never got the same answer twice. And so I still want to know. I'd really like to know exactly what happened back then while I was away. Do you remember? Will you tell me?"

He frowned and shook his head as if he were going to discourage me like Father Gower. But instead he said, "I remember better than I want to, Jenny. Do you know I was the doctor who committed her to Hampshire?"

"No," I said, feeling unaccountably shocked, "I didn't know that."

"Well, I was." He glanced at the large watch on his left wrist, but seemed to decide to take the time to talk to me. "Jenny, what do you know?"

I tried to think back almost two decades ago, and to remember. "I was a freshman at college. I'd just come back to my room from lunch in the dorm cafeteria and I found a note from my roommate telling me to call home. I did, and I think I talked to my father, who told me something vague, like they'd put Mother into a hospital for tests. He didn't sound upset or anything, but then you know Dad, if it wasn't his tonsils they were taking out, he wouldn't pay much attention. Anyway, I don't remember any sense of urgency, no Jenny Come Home Immediately Your Mother Is Dying sort of thing. I don't even recall having the sense that she was even very sick."

"He didn't want to frighten you."

"Maybe not."

"Did they tell you which hospital?"

"No, and of course it didn't occur to me that it might be anything but an ordinary one. I suppose I did ask what was wrong with her, at least I hope I did, but all I kept hearing was that she was going in for tests. I don't suppose he ever said what kind, and I must have assumed he meant, I don't know, blood tests, or whatever. I don't think I was even particularly worried about it."

"You didn't go home?"

"No. As I said, he didn't give me any sense of urgency."

Doc Farrell was quiet for a moment, playing with the stethoscope that dangled from his neck. "It was pretty urgent, Jenny."

"I'll bet it was. What was really going on?"

"I'll tell you that, but first, finish your story. When did you finally come home? When did you find out the truth?"

"I didn't come home until school was out. By then it was essentially all over but the shouting." (My shouting? Memories, awful ones, flooded me, including one of me weeping and yelling horrible things at my father, only my father wasn't there. I was yelling in an empty room. My room. When nobody else was home. How could I have forgotten all of that fury?) "Until this moment, I had forgotten how angry I was at my father for not telling me everything. I was heartsick. I would have come home earlier, immediately, right then. I would have helped. I could have seen her." My hand went to my heart involuntarily. "Oh God, it still hurts to think that she might have wondered where I was, maybe she even thought I didn't care enough—"

"I doubt it."

His astringent tone helped me.

I managed to smile at him. "All right. Then when did I learn the truth? I guess when I got home and I told Dad I wanted to visit Mom at the hospital and he told me it was Hampshire Psychiatric."

"What did he tell you was wrong with her?"

I shrugged. "You know Dad. A nervous breakdown, I think he said. I had to ask her psychiatrist, and he wasn't able to tell me much more than that, either." I felt a ball of self-pity—and pity for my mother—rising up my esophagus. "When you come right down to it, nobody's ever given me any better explanation than that."

Still seated on his rolling stool, Doc Farrell leaned back against the sink; he folded his arms over his chest, and sighed. "She did come in for tests, Jenny, and we found rampant endometriosis, fibroids, and cystitis, and after that it was a routine hysterectomy. Everything went swell. But your mother never recovered from it emotionally or mentally. I'll swear to this day I don't know exactly what went wrong, although I suspect that the hormonal changes, combined with her essentially fragile nature, are what did her in."

He paused, as if to give me a chance to comment, but I was silently reeling from the word *hysterectomy*. *What* hysterectomy? I wanted to shout, but I couldn't bring myself to do it, and thus admit to him the depth of my apparent ignorance and, worse, the extent of the failure of trust and communication in my family.

He said, "I don't suppose it helped her state of mind, or her physical well-being, that your father was in the middle of the bankruptcy proceedings, not to mention—" Doc Farrell shifted his weight against the sink. "Well, I guess I should not mention it."

"Doc, I know he was unfaithful to her."

"Well, I'm sorry you know that," he said gruffly. "It's not the sort of thing that daughters ought to know about their fathers."

"He's never been exactly discreet."

"Hmm. When your mother fell apart, your dad couldn't cope. No surprise there. So I did what had to be done. I convinced him to commit her to Hampshire." He cleared his throat, and looked away from me. "Jenny, I didn't dream she'd still be there when she died. I don't believe it was my fault, it was such a routine operation, we had such good people working it, but I'll swear I've never been more sorry about anything in my life. She was a lovely woman." He turned back to me, and frowned forbiddingly. "And you are the image of her. Or you would be if you didn't look so scrawny and worried. You haven't been eating or sleeping well since she died, have you? Well, that's natural, I'd expect that. But I don't want to have to worry about you, Jenny." He winked at me. "I'm too busy for such nonsense. Here." He reached out a long, white-clad arm and opened a drawer, pulled out from it a plastic bottle and threw it at me. "These are super-duper make-you-feel-better multi maxi vitamins. Take these home and *take* them, one a day."

"Thanks, Doctor Cal."

He clapped his hands, signaling the end of my appointment, and his voice turned familiarly gruff again. "And listen here, if you don't take care of yourself, and you make yourself sick because of it, don't call me. I'll have no patience with you."

Through teary eyes, I winked at him as he walked out of the examining room. I dressed quickly, then stopped by the front desk to pay my bill.

"You seem very tense, Jenny," Marjorie Earnshaw informed me as I wrote out a check. "Understandable, of course, under the circumstances, but it won't help matters to be upset about them." She, too, reached into a drawer and brought out a plastic bottle. "These are Valium. It won't hurt you to take one now and then when you can't sleep or when you can't eat for worrying."

Rather than argue with her, I put the pills in my purse along with my checkbook. "Marjorie, would you please send copies of my mother's medical records to me?"

"Those are confidential, Jenny."

"Well, it won't matter to her now."

"If she were going to another doctor, I could send them to him, but I can hardly turn patient records over to just anybody who wants them."

"I'm not just anybody, I'm her daughter."

"It's irregular."

"Do you want me to get Dr. Farrell's approval?"

"No, that isn't necessary."

I waited for her to tell me what was necessary. When she didn't, I said, "They are part of her estate, which now belongs to Sherry and me." It was a bluff, since I didn't have any idea what my legal rights were to them. I faked a laugh. "Are you going to make me sue you to get them, Marj?"

"Why in the world do you want them?"

"Because I do!" I was damned if I would explain to this obstreperous woman that I had an insatiable curiosity about my mother that wouldn't quit until I'd tracked down every bit of her history I could lay my hands on, medical and otherwise. "Will you do it, please?"

"I'll check with Doctor," she said grudgingly. "By the way, that was quite a nice turnout you had at the funeral, considering the weather."

"You were there, Marj? I'm sorry, I didn't notice you."

It was an outright lie, of course. I had seen her with Doc Farrell at my sister's house, but I wasn't about to give her the pleasure of letting her know that I'd paid her the slightest notice. Damn, if the woman didn't bring out the worst, most perverse side of me!

"Yes, I was there." She looked offended, which pleased me. "I know this may sound odd to you, Jenny, but I feel that attending that sort of occasion is part of my duty to our patients. I help to usher them in and to—"

"Usher them out," I said, dryly, and handed her my check. I patted my purse where her "prescription" lay. "Gee, I've always thought you should have been a doctor, Marj."

"I would have been, too, if only—"

A ringing telephone distracted her, and delivered me from my own evil ways.

8

OUT IN THE HALL OF THE MEDICAL BUILDING, I SOUGHT OUT A bench to sit down. There, between a woman in a leg cast and a man with a bad cold, I took my notebook out of my purse. As I wrote down the words, I tried to digest what they meant: one, that my mother's mental illness had appeared after a hysterectomy that nobody had ever before mentioned to me; and two, that her obstetrician had thought of her as a woman with an "essentially fragile nature."

I closed the notebook.

My own nature felt a shade fragile at that moment.

I stared down into my purse at the vials of vitamins and Valium sitting on top. Maybe Marj Earnshaw had given me the tranquilizers to take the edge off my concern about my AIDS test. To paraphrase Doc Farrell: How very amusing, Jenny. I opened the cap of the vitamin bottle and shook out a beige pill. My throat closed at the sight of it. I slid it back into the bottle, and returned the bottle and the notebook to my purse. *Later. I'll take a vitamin later, I promise, Doc.* I dug a quarter out of my billfold, and got up to locate a pay phone.

With shaking fingers—I was getting more and more resentful as the minutes passed—I dialed the home of my mother's old friend, the woman who was supposedly also *my* old friend, Francine Daniel.

"Francie," I said without preamble, "I never knew Mom had a hysterectomy. Did you know she did?"

"Well—"

"So you did. All right, so neither you nor anybody else ever saw fit to tell me or, I presume, Sherry. Talk to me now, Francie. What was the matter with her that she needed one? Just how sick was she? Why didn't you or anybody else ever tell us about it? Was she depressed about it? Is that what set her off into mental illness?"

"Oh, Jenny." For a long moment, Francie didn't say anything else. When she finally spoke again, she didn't sound defensive, as I expected her to; rather, she sounded nervous, and nearly as depressed as I felt. "You have to understand—"

"I want to!"

"—there were so many difficult things going on in her life at that time. Your dad was driving her crazy—well, maybe I shouldn't put it quite like that, I didn't mean that literally. The bankruptcy was incredibly traumatic for her. You were at college, so there's no way for you to know what it was like for her on a daily basis. The world was collapsing around her, Jenny. Your dad was coming home every night—when he came home—with tales of woe. And then there were the newspaper articles. And the rumors. Oh, my lord, the rumors!"

"What rumors?"

"Oh, about fraud, mismanagement, you know—"

"I don't know!"

"And the angry phone calls. She got simply desperate phone calls from people who were losing their jobs, and they begged her to do something, to help them somehow. And there wasn't anything she could do, and Jenny, you know what a sweet-hearted woman she was. It killed her, it just killed her to listen to them and to feel responsible somehow. Well, I don't mean it actually killed her. And of course there was Sherry, she had to deal with your sister, too. It was humiliating for Sherry at school. And all over town, people that your parents had been friends with all of their lives began to snub them, and even to accuse them of all sorts of—" Francie took a deep breath. "You just don't know how bad it was, Jenny."

"Accuse who? Mom and Dad? Of what?"

"It was just so awful, there's no way you could know."

"That's what I want to know. Everything. Please." I tried not to beg, and I also tried to keep the growing anger out of my voice although I felt as if it were about to choke me, but I didn't succeed at either aim. "What else do you know that I don't, Francie?"

"All right, Jenny!" For the first time, I heard some spirit, maybe even some matching anger in her voice. But when she spoke again, she had her voice under better control. "I'm home, if you want to come on over. We'll have a talk that maybe we should have had a long time ago."

My hand was shaking even harder as I hung up from that call.

I was infuriated that she and my father had kept this information from me as if I were a child who had to be protected from "loaded" words like hysterectomy. *"What's a hysterectomy, Daddy? What's a uterus, Daddy? What's it for, Daddy? But how does the baby get in there, Daddy?"* I was also frightened about what lay ahead of me in the next hour or so, and I was thinking: *Now what have I done? Am I pushing Francie into telling me things that I don't really want to know? Maybe Marj Earnshaw—and even Father Gower—were correct, and I don't have the right to dig into the confidential records and memories of my mother's past. Didn't my mother have a right to privacy, even from her own daughter?*

Of course, I drove to Francie's anyway. I was exhausted, I was nervous, but I was also full of stubborn determination to uncover, at last, some of the mysteries of my own and my mother's lives. There is a phrase to describe well-intentioned resolves like that; in fact there are two of them: one is looking for trouble; and the other has to do with the road to hell.

Francie and Duke Daniel still lived in the neighborhood where I had grown up. Their house was rambling and roomy, a three-story, wood frame Colonial, straight up and down, with shuttered windows that looked like friendly eyes gazing benignly out at the neighborhood. Inside, the house was comfortable with cushions and chintz and fireplaces. Duke was something of a collector of marine artifacts, and Francie collected Sandwich glass, so the windowsills were chock-full of ships in bottles and vases that caught the sun and cast fruit-colored shadows on the floors. There was an iron fence, painted white, around the house and a matching widow's walk on top of it. I'd been in and out of the Daniels' home frequently as a kid, playing with their children while our mothers talked about us; and again, several times as a grown child needing the companionship of the only one of my mother's friends who had ever seemed to really understand. It felt like a second home to me.

When I parked in front of the Daniels' old white Colonial home, I was surprised to see no welcoming smoke curling from their chimneys on this afternoon that begged for a crackling fire.

Francie worked part-time these days as a receptionist at the Harbor Lights Funeral Home, so it was no surprise to find her home on a late

Monday afternoon. But Duke, her husband, was still a full-time archi-tect with offices downtown, so I was startled when he opened their front door.

"Duke? Hi. I didn't expect to see you, too."

"I'm working at home this afternoon," the big man said. His nick-name derived from his slight resemblance to the late actor, John Wayne. I'd always thought it was wonderful that Duke's big, meaty fingers could execute such detailed drawings. Now, however, he held one of those massive hands palm-out toward me, as if to ward me off, as if I were an evil spell or a Jehovah's Witness. "Sorry, Jenny, but Francie's not going to be able to see you after all. She came down with a flu bug or something, right after you called. That's really why I'm home, to take care of her."

"Is that right?" I said, with what sounded even to me like a deadly calm. I looked past his shoulder, and thought I saw movement on the cranberry carpet that covered the darkened front hall and the central stairs. If he was home working, why weren't the lights on? Had they wanted somebody to think they weren't at home? "Did your house-keeper quit, Duke?"

"No, no, I just thought Fran needed me to come home—"

"Really." I didn't bother to hide my skepticism.

He flushed a little. John Wayne never could tell a good lie, either. "She'll give you a call when she feels better, okay?"

I hated standing on the bottom step, staring up at him. It made me feel even more like a child or a supplicant.

"Came on pretty sudden, didn't it, Duke?"

"Yes, well—"

The invalid herself suddenly appeared at his left shoulder, looking so pale that I could almost believe his story.

"What's the matter, Francie?" I asked her.

"Your mother was my dear friend," she said in a voice so soft and trembly that I had to move a step closer to hear her. "I still miss her, and I love you like a daughter, but you have to stop all of these ques-tions! It upsets me to think about it, and I wish you'd just let me alone about this." She was starting to cry, and dabbing at her nose and eyes with a worn tissue. Duke stared down at me as his wife cried. She said, "I wish you'd just let your poor mother die!"

"I'm sorry," I said, coolly.

"She got like this," Francie whispered as Duke reached back to put an arm protectively around her. "Like you are now. So obsessed and frantic. She got so thin, like you are now, and we couldn't get her to eat anything, and then . . . please don't get like that, Jenny, dear God in heaven, don't get like your moth—"

I turned and walked away from them.

"Jenny! Please try to understand—"

Duke called out, "Jenny, don't go away mad at us—"

Just go away, I thought, bitterly.

Behind my back, one of them, I wished I knew who, closed their front door quietly. I stalked to my car and got into it. Then I sat behind my steering wheel, fuming. *Old friends. Loyal friends. Some friends. Won't talk to me about my own mother. Won't tell me what I have every right to know. Sick. Right. Sure, Francie's sick, all right. Sick of me bugging her. Sick of my family. Sick of all of us, doesn't want anything to do with us anymore. Well, all right. If that's the way she wants it. All right. All* right!

I stormed out of my car again, threw open their white iron gate again and ran onto their lawn. In front of one of the tall, wide windows on the first floor, I screamed, "I'm sorry you're sick, Francie! I hope you get well, Francie! Not like my mother! Remember her? Your dear friend, the one you won't talk to me about anymore? Do you want me to go away, Francie? All right, you'll get your wish. I'll go away. Permanently!"

Tears choked off my screams, so I turned and stumbled back to my car. With fumbling fingers, I turned the key in the ignition and pulled away from the curb. I tried to ignore the Greek chorus in my head—(or was it my mother's voice?)—that was whispering, "This is how you treat an old friend like Francie? You ought to be ashamed of yourself."

"So should she," I muttered. "So should she!"

I drove home, and crawled under the bedcovers again.

When Geof arrived home from work, he came upstairs and said, "Uh oh, and I thought we were making progress." I heard him cross over the carpet to our bed. "Scratch that, I ought to know better." Once again, I felt his weight sink the mattress as he sat down beside me. "I guess recovery from grief is not a short, straight line, is it?"

"No," I mumbled, and then poked my head out. "I did a terrible thing today, Geof."

"Good," he said. "That always makes life more interesting. Where would I be if people didn't do terrible things? Out of a job, most likely. What did you do? Strangle your sister? That's not so terrible—at least it's justifiable. Beat your stepmother to a bloody pulp? I could buy that. Wait, don't tell me, I know—you drowned your father, and not a minute too soon, if you ask me."

He almost had me laughing. "Geof—"

"Well, if you think I'm going to arrest you for any of those offenses, you're wrong. Those are only misdemeanors. I'm not even sure they should be against the law. A small fine, a short probation, and we'll have you back in the streets in no time. Hell, if it's your dad you drowned, they'll probably give you a ticker-tape parade downtown."

I placed my hand on his mouth to shut him up.

"What happened was, Francie Daniel refused to see me when I went to her house this afternoon—at her invitation—so I did the only intelligent thing. I stood on her lawn and brayed insults at her like the total jackass I am."

He removed my hand from his mouth. "I will listen to the rest of this story only on the condition that you get out of bed. Get dressed. Come downstairs and sit with me at the kitchen table like a normal person." He got up and gazed down at me. Lord, he was handsome. I hoped I wasn't responsible for the two or three new gray hairs above his ears. "By the way, you *are* a normal person. I keep telling you to remember that, and you keep forgetting."

Faye Basil's phrase popped into my head. "It's the Alzheimer's of grief."

"What?"

"Doc Farrell—Dr. Calvin Farrell, you know?—told me something today that I'd never heard before. My mother had a hysterectomy right before she cracked up. That's all I wanted to ask Francie about. I'm not sure what that has to do with the Alzheimer's of grief, but I seem to be losing my mind because I can't think of anything but grieving over my mother. So maybe she cracked up out of grief for her lost fertility . . . ?"

He looked doubtful, but game to take my word for it. "If you say so. Maybe that's it. Come on downstairs and tell me the rest of it, all right?"

I cupped my hands around my coffee mug and complained to Geof, "Why wouldn't she talk to me?"

"Why do you think she wouldn't?"

I made a face at him. "You've been hanging around my friend Marsha too much. Now you're throwing my questions back at me. Okay, I think she's probably having her own tough time dealing with my mother's death—maybe even having a delayed reaction like mine—and dealing with me is more than she can handle at this time."

"Sounds reasonable to me," Geof said. "How does it sound to you?"

I thought it over. "Not good enough. Still, I should apologize."

"How are you going to do it?"

I noted his unspoken agreement that I should. "Well, I thought maybe I'd rent a truck and a loudspeaker and drive by her house shouting, 'Forgive me, Francie, I'm sorry!' "

"Either that, or a billboard would be good."

"A note?"

"Yeah," he said, and reached for the coffee pot to refill my mug. "And maybe flowers, followed by an abjectly apologetic phone call. And speaking of flowers, I don't have anything for you on the flowers that kook sent to your mother's funeral, or on the message in the guest book. I'm sorry. You haven't had any other strange communications, have you?"

"Not in regard to my mother, although there's a group calling itself Morality in Our Arts Committee that has sent the foundation little notes warning us we're all going to burn in hell for sponsoring that show down at the New East Gallery. You ever heard of MOAC?"

"MOAC? Sounds like a macaw. I'll ask around."

"Geof?"

"Yo?"

"What would you think if I took a leave of absence?"

"From the foundation?"

"Well, not from you."

"Do it," he said, instantly.

I stared at him, suspicious of his quick reaction. "You don't harbor a secret wish for a sweet little housewife, do you?"

He didn't laugh, but only put down his coffee, and laid his hands on top of mine. "I harbor a secret wish for you to be happy, that's all. I want you to do what you want to do. Remember that time when I was fed up with police work and I was going to quit? You stuck by me then, didn't you, and we weren't even married yet. And if I had quit, you'd have been there, helping me to write my letter of resignation. So now it's your turn, and mine."

I remembered. I also remembered how worried I had been about him —and about the effect of his mental state on us—at the time.

"I love you," I told him.

He smirked. "Wise woman."

I crossed over to him, sat down on his lap and squeezed his face in my hands. "Take back that smirk, you smart alec."

"Make me."

I kissed the smirk away. "I would carry you upstairs," I murmured, "only you're bigger than I am. I am but a weak, fluttery little woman with hardly enough strength left in my poor emaciated body to screw your brains out."

"I'll grab your hair," he said, "and haul you up the stairs."

I put my hand to the back of my head, and winced. "God, can you imagine how that would hurt?" I sat up on his lap. "But listen, do you mind if I finish my coffee first?"

"Nope." Geof pushed me off his lap. Of such was marriage, as compared to courtship. "In fact, I wouldn't mind finishing off that cheesecake you brought home from Sherry's." He leered at me. "To build up my stamina." And that was the nice part about marriage—there wasn't any hurry, because it felt as if we had all the time in the world to be together.

I felt such a rush of affection for the man that I hurled myself back into his lap and his arms. On second thought, we agreed a few minutes later, the coffee and cheesecake could wait. As for getting up the stairs to the bedroom, we helped each other. This time, when I crawled under the covers, I had company.

Geof was called back to work later that night on a homicide, which, for once, didn't involve me or anybody I ever knew; what a relief. I felt lonely without him, and wandered back downstairs to our living room to read. I pulled from our bookshelves the only medical reference book, a thick, beige tome, ten years out of date, that I could also have used for building muscle tone. I hefted it over to Geof's favorite chair, turned on the reading lamp and sat down with the book covering my lap.

"Cysts . . . breast, ovarian, testicular."

No, definitely not the latter, and probably not breast, because why would that require a hysterectomy? Must have been ovarian, although

Doc Farrell hadn't specifically said so. Page 362. I stuck a finger there and then another finger in "Endometriosis, page 412." And in "Fibroids, page 410." I thought I knew what they were, those familiar-sounding disorders of the female reproductive system, but I quickly discovered that my laywoman's knowledge didn't begin to cover the subjects.

"Surgical removal of cysts may be necessary if they are suspected of originating in a tumor . . ."

"Endometriosis . . . produces cysts . . . menstrual discomfort . . ." *(Discomfort, ha! I thought. Must have been written by a man. Bet what he means is red hot aching pain.)* "More prevalent in women who marry and conceive late in life . . . surgical removal of tissue or administration of steroids . . ."

Or had Doc Farrell said "Endometritis?" instead of "Endometriosis?" The one came right after the other in my medical tome, and now I couldn't remember which he had said. "Endometritis . . . bacterial infection causing inflammation of the lining of the uterus . . . lower back and abdominal pain." *(Jeez, if the writer comes right out and calls it pain, it must be unbearable!)* "May require dilation and curettage (D and C)."

Moving on alphabetically . . .

"Fibroids are uterine tumors, usually benign . . . appearing more often in black women and childless women . . . abnormal bleeding is the most common symptom . . . hysterectomy rarely required except for large or multiple fibroids."

Doc Farrell must have performed the hysterectomy due to endometriosis and ovarian cysts, I decided, and maybe fibroids, because nobody'd ever mentioned Mom suffering the sort of acute pain that seemed to be indicated by endometritis. On the other hand, nobody'd ever mentioned her having a hysterectomy, either. It was funny, though, that I didn't remember my mother ever complaining about difficult periods, which she should have had with endometriosis and cysts. But then maybe her generation was more circumspect about "female complaints" than mine was. Certainly, *some*body in my family was embarrassed by the word *hysterectomy,* and it might have even been Mom, herself.

Well, I thought as I shoved the book back into its place on the shelf, if I got those medical records from Marjorie Earnshaw, I'd find out for sure, although why I wanted to do so, I couldn't precisely say. "But then," I said aloud to the empty room, "if we always knew exactly why we did the things we do, we'd be so appalled by our own motives that we wouldn't do half of them."

On which profundity, I went to bed, although once again I had trouble sleeping. Sadness, depression, restlessness, and unfocused anger came in separate waves through the long hours that Geof was gone, so that by the morning, I woke up feeling disoriented, like a traveler with jet lag. For a moment, as I rubbed my eyes, I could have sworn it was only the horrible night that was real, while the sunlight was but a dream.

"These days," I said, on the verge of tears already, and it was only seven o'clock in the morning, "have got to get better."

9

THE MINUTE I STARTED GETTING DRESSED, THE DAY DID APPEAR to brighten. As I plucked my pantyhose into place around my knees, it occurred to me that if I took a leave of absence from my job this might be the last morning for a long time that I would have to dress up. That astonishing thought prompted me to walk over to my closet, throw open the door and stare at the contents within: suits, silk blouses, proper little business dresses with proper little jackets, low-heeled pumps (so I wouldn't tower over short benefactors with big egos). And how would all of that look, I pondered, if it were shoved over to make room for sweat suits and sneakers? And what about my dresser drawers —with their bras and silky slips pushed aside for T-shirts and cotton socks?

Not to have to wear pantyhose every day?

Oh my. I sat on the edge of the bed, overcome with the sheer bliss of the idea. Later, in the bathroom as I brushed on eyeshadow and blusher, I thought: *Hey, maybe I won't have to do this every morning from now on. Maybe I'll wear less makeup or even—oh my!—none at all.* Could I go cold turkey on mascara?

I was laughing to myself—at myself—as I walked downstairs to where my personal computer was set up on the dining room table. There, I composed a letter to my trustees, requesting a leave. I struggled over the phrase "one month," because my fingers wanted to type "three months" or "six" or even "one year." The rest of the letter came easily.

In the wake of my mother's death . . .

I tried to be as frank and specific as possible.

. . . I find myself wanting to answer lingering questions in my own mind in regard to her life, her illness, and her death. I also want to satisfy my curiosity about the reasons for and the consequences of the collapse of our family business. I do not believe I will be able to attend adequately to the foundation's business until I have taken care of this pressing personal business.

There was more, but of a less personal nature. I mentioned my uninterrupted years of service and (trying not to sound martyred) I counted the vacation days and holidays I had not taken. I thanked them profusely for their understanding and I begged their kind forebearance. I recommended highly Faye Basil's ability to assume my responsibilities in my absence. I started to offer myself for "consultation" during my month off, but, at the last minute, left that out. Finally, I made five copies on our home copier and sealed those letters into envelopes for my trustees: Peter Falwell, Lucille Grant, Edwin Ottilini, Roy Lelad, and Jack Fenton. As I tucked them into a side pocket of my purse, a subversive idea sneaked into my mind: A month didn't seem like a very long time.

I was ready to go . . . and yet. Some cautionary voice within me said, "think about it," at least for a couple of hours. I didn't want to heed it, but, on the other hand, I had all day to do this task, and no other particular plan in mind.

"Okay," I capitulated to myself. "I'll let it simmer."

To use the time, I took the sheaf of newspaper articles I had obtained from the library the day before and carried them with me into the kitchen to peruse while I worked up to my caffeine quota for the morning.

Over the first cup of coffee, I saw that the first article to appear in *The Port Frederick Times* had been a two-paragraph announcement of what a Cain Clams company spokesman termed "cash-flow difficulties." Ah yes. I smiled grimly to myself. The infamous, all-purpose excuse for anything—cash-flow difficulties. I would have expected big headlines, given the company's importance to the city, but the story was positioned in the back pages by the want ads. The difficulties were blamed, by Vice President Cecil Greenstreet, on "poor clam crops, clam bed pollution, increased competition, and new and costly pollution control

83

requirements." *What?* I wondered, *no mention of terrorist attacks in Lebanon?*

Now, Jenny, I chided myself, *don't be cynical.*

At least, not yet.

Two weeks after that first article appeared, I learned in the business pages of *The Port Frederick Times* that Cain Clams had fired—"released" was the euphemism employed by the vice president—one-third of its employees "in an effort to solve our cash-flow problems." Sitting in my kitchen, reading this sour mash, I thought: *thereby creating unbelievable cash-flow problems in one-third of its employees' homes and families.*

Why wasn't this bigger news at the time? I wondered.

Next, I learned from the newspaper, Cain filed for a voluntary Chapter II bankruptcy, which would, essentially, allow it to reorganize without having to pay its bills. Cecil Greenstreet, the VP, was quoted in that article as saying "they"—whoever that was—"are holding meetings on restructuring." (Greenstreet, Greenstreet . . . where had I seen that name lately? Oh, right, in the guest book, he'd signed it at the funeral.) The paper concluded with the observation that small creditors were filing suits, and large creditors were trying to help restructure the debt load to keep Cain Clams afloat. And my question, as I poured myself fresh coffee, was: Do dead clams float?

Cynicism, I decided, was a great defense against pain.

"Greenstreet!" I said, in the manner of "eureka!" Of course! His had been one of the signatures sandwiching the anonymous words, "Forgive me." That's why his name nagged me every time I saw it mentioned in the paper. Damned nice of the man to have come to the funeral, I thought, considering that we'd probably done him out of a pretty good job.

I picked up the articles again and read through the middle of the pile, learning in a series of brief business page announcements that the top executives of Cain Clams, including my father, had resigned, and were replaced by a court-appointed management firm. The first thing the new managers did was to halt all new construction at the plant. The second thing they did was to go looking for short-term loans to pay short-term bills.

At that point, I came across the first—and evidently the only—*Port Frederick Times* editorial on the subject. In it, Samuel Hayes, Sr. (father of the current owner, publisher, and editor), basically opined as to how it was a bad day at Black Rock. I shuffled through the pile, looking for the other editorials I assumed would be there, but didn't find any.

This was very odd coverage, indeed. My father, I decided, must have had more influence, at least at the time, than I would have suspected. Otherwise, why such discreet reporting on such a major economic calamity?

The paper next reported that the construction company slated to build Dad's new addition had filed mechanic's liens to get its bills paid, and then there was news of a foreclosure order by a U.S. judge, meaning that secured creditors could foreclose on their collateral to get their money back. The next thing I read was that Port Frederick Fisheries had bought all remaining assets, assumed all remaining liabilities, and planned to proceed with new construction to "modernize the century-old Cain canning facilities."

Port Frederick Fisheries. PFF.

"It's a Pretty Fine kettle of Fish you got us into this time, Ollie." I sighed, thinking of my father.

I pulled the phone over to call him.

"Dad," I said, "do you remember Cecil Greenstreet, who was a vice president of your company?"

You'd think, of course, that naturally he'd remember, but you could never be sure with my dad. This time, however, I got lucky, although I had to ask the question several different ways, and follow many different conversational detours with him before I got my answer. "Well, of course, I remember him," Dad told me at last, sounding insulted that I would even imply that he might not. "Greenstreet was a fine fellow; I hated to lose him." He made it sound as if the man had quit a thriving concern, rather than jumped a sinking ship. "The last I heard he was with Downeast Marine, Inc., out of Boston, you know."

What I knew was that Downeast Marine was another canning company. I got their number from Boston "information," and I called Mr. Greenstreet, whose secretary passed me over to him after a fairly lengthy wait on "hold."

"I'm Jimmy Cain's daughter," I told him, by way of introducing myself. It was always risky to start off on that particular foot, but I couldn't see an alternative. "I'm calling to thank you for the lovely flowers you sent to my mother's funeral. My father and the rest of the family and I appreciated them so much."

"It was the least I could do," he said. "How is your father?"

"The same," I said, figuring he could interpret that as he chose. "I'm afraid I have a favor to ask of you, Mr. Greenstreet."

"I would be honored," the deep voice intoned.

You would? I thought. *How kind of you. But why in the world should you be?*

"I am taking a leave of absence from my job," I said. That part was true; it was only the next part that was pure fabrication, or at least, I was pretty sure it was. "And I'm going back to school to get a doctorate in economics. I have decided to take as my initial research effort a study of our own family business. Would you agree to let me interview you about it?"

"Interview me?" Greenstreet sounded taken aback. "About what?"

"Well, frankly, about what happens when a family business fails. You were there, you saw it all, and I wasn't around for any of it."

He cleared his throat. "Ms. Cain, while I respect your father enormously—"

You do? I thought, incredulously. *You really* are *a nice man, even if you do sound a shade oily.*

"—this is not a subject for which I feel a great deal of nostalgia. Still, if you need this for a school project . . ." *(What did he think I was, sixteen?)* "What sorts of questions will you ask me?"

"Oh, like what were the factors leading up to the collapse, why did it happen, who were the principle players in it, how might it have been avoided, that sort of thing."

"Well, all right, I'll certainly help you if I can."

Once he had committed himself, Greenstreet seemed to want to get it out of the way quickly, and asked me if I could meet him for a late lunch that very afternoon at his office near Boston Harbor. I checked my watch, saw that I would just have time to deliver my letters and make the drive, and said, "I'd love to, thank you."

Then I made one more phone call.

"Port Frederick Times."

"Sam Hayes, please. Jenny Cain calling."

Sam came on the line, sounding like a not-very-much younger version of his stuffy old dad. He said, "What have we done to offend you now, Jenny?"

Oops, not a good start. Guess Sammy-boy was still mad about my objections to his precious obituary of my mother. Make nice, Jenny. "Nothing, Sam," I purred, "in fact, I thought your editorial was especially well-thought-out this morning." Of course, I hadn't read it yet, a fact that became all too clear with his next comment.

"Really? I wouldn't have picked you as a fan of forcing welfare mothers to work part-time in the Head Start program."

"I didn't say I *agreed* with you." I tap-danced fast. "I only said it was well-thought-out. Uh, Sam, I'd like to see you. I've been reading through some old articles about my family's bankruptcy, and I want to ask you about them. How about five-thirty, in your office?"

"I'll put you down," he said, pompously. If I hadn't known for a fact that Sam Hayes lacked a sense of humor, I would have suspected a little joke at my expense.

I rolled the copies of the newspaper articles back into a sheaf and carried it with me into the dining room, where my purse—with its five letters—sat in the table beside the computer. Well? I'd given my letter time to simmer . . . had my enthusiasm for this idea of a leave of absence boiled away and evaporated?

"Nope."

I grabbed my purse, stuck the articles under one arm, and left the house feeling lighter and more invigorated than I had since my mother died.

Miss Grant wasn't home, so I slipped her copy under the door of her apartment. I left copies for Jack Fenton, Roy Leland, and Edwin Ottilini with their secretaries. But when I dropped off a copy for my board president, Pete Falwell—at his office at Port Frederick Fisheries where he was chairman of the board—I asked for an appointment.

His secretary, Paige Lorimer, checked her calendar. "Four-thirty?"

She was another one of those "ladies of a certain age," like Mrs. Kennedy and Marj Earnshaw, who was "married" to her boss's job, having been Pete Falwell's right-hand woman for at least forty years.

"Fine," I said. "I should be back from Boston by then."

She looked up, smiling. "Boston? Lucky you, and on such a pretty day. Business or pleasure?"

"Neither, really." I smiled back at her. She had a way of "nosing" without offending. "I'm going to meet a man," I said, teasingly.

"Lucky you, indeed!"

"I don't know about that. He used to be a vice president of Cain Clams . . ."

We both suddenly discovered a reason to look away from each other.

It was, all of a sudden, awkward and embarrassing to stand there in the heart of Port Frederick Fisheries, where Cain Clams used to be. And although I'd done this many times—visited Pete at his office—these awful moments came and went with some regularity. Usually, I tried not to look around me very much, or at least not to dwell morbidly on the fact that PFF was decorated like a virtual museum of maritime history, a lot of it Cain history.

There were wharf barrels and lobster pots and, in some corners, picturesque humps of netting in bright colors—red, yellow, blue, and brown. There were walls hung with green nets with red bobbers, and there were paintings everywhere of schooners and clippers and sailing vessels of every description, and bronze statues of the "men who go down to the sea in ships." A blue swordfish pointed the way to the men's room and beautiful seashells were as plentiful as lint.

A whole lot of that quaint decor had decorated my father's administrative offices. I had loved it all; it had been one of the enticements of "going down to the plant to visit Daddy." (Another had been the employee's lunchroom, where the line workers tended to spoil the boss's daughters with soft drinks and candy bars from the vending machines.) Pete had hauled it all on board when he cast his own corporate net and caught Cain Clams.

Ms. Lorimer, bless her, was exquisitely sensitive to these moments when past and present intersected painfully. She said, quickly, to help me over the hump of my own lack of tact, "Cecil Greenstreet?"

"You knew him, Ms. Lorimer?"

"Oh, yes." I wondered later if she would have spoken so freely if she hadn't been rushing away from that other delicate subject. "He was in and out of here a lot in those . . . days." Too late, she realized she'd wandered back to the bankruptcy. Again, she rushed where maybe she ought to have paused. "When Mr. Greenstreet first came to town, Mr. Falwell took him under his wing, they being in the same business and all. It was nice to see him again at your mother's funeral, which was so beautiful, by the way."

"Thank you." I was so distracted that I didn't even respond courteously to the implication that she must have attended the funeral, too. Another one of the invisible women, like Mrs. Kennedy. Out of the context of their offices and the men they served, they were sometimes damned hard to recognize. "Well, I've got to run if I'm going to make it to Boston on time. See you at four-thirty, Ms. Lorimer."

Walking back to my car in the PFF parking lot, I was thinking furiously: "Those days?" *Which* days? The ones before, during, or after our bankruptcy? The days before, during, or after Port Frederick Fisheries bought out Cain Clams? Why was our vice president hanging out with the president of the competition, the eventual owners, in fact? I wanted to assume that Greenstreet had only helped to facilitate the transfer of assets and the assumption of liabilities or that his friendship with Pete Falwell had been purely social—a golf or tennis or Rotary Club friendship, maybe. But as I slid behind my wheel, the inevitable questions nagged me: *What if "those days" were before the bankruptcy? What was the vice president of Cain Clams doing at the office of the president of PFF?*

I recalled Geof's advice: Calm down, don't jump to conclusions.

And Marsha's advice: Find out.

"I am calm," I said, as I turned toward downtown Port Frederick in order to catch the expressway into Boston. "I am not going to jump to any conclusions. But I am going to find out whatever there is to find out."

My route took me past the New East Gallery where the controversial exhibit was showing. The gallery, which was on a quiet side street, was open only after 2 P.M. on weekdays, so I was surprised to see several women gathered on the sidewalk in front of it at this hour. I slowed down, and then I saw the reason for the commotion: Somebody had affixed cardboard placards all over the plate glass windows in the front of the store and over the glass in the front door, completely blocking the view that anyone standing outside the gallery might have of the interior.

"Damn," I thought, "we needed that guard yesterday!"

No, wait, that wasn't fair to Faye. She'd acted quicker than I would have; it wasn't her fault if the security company couldn't provide a guard until today.

I didn't have to crane or squint to read the grafitti, which was bright red and more simple and straightforward than any I had ever seen before. "MOAC," the signs said in big, neat, block letters that looked as if they had been carefully outlined, using stencils, and then filled in with red markers. That was all, no obscenities, no vulgarities; this was an extraordinarily tasteful and conservative sort of protest. But effective, nonetheless, at least until the artists took down the signs, which they were starting to do.

Even with the signs down, the protestors had made their point—and they'd probably *win* points for being relatively respectful of private property, for showing restraint by not going to unpleasant extremes about it. That would make them look good, in many people's eyes, compared to those "wild-eyed radical" artists.

Damn, I thought again. *Better find a place to park.*

No, wait.

You're on leave, remember? I reminded myself. *Faye's in charge, and you said yourself in your letter that she could handle it. If you step in now, you'll undermine her authority and your own recommendation. This is not your job today. It's hers. So shut up, go away, and let her do it.*

Well, shoot, and it looked so interesting, too.

Nevertheless, I pressed on the accelerator and drove on toward Boston.

10

MY STATE, MASSACHUSETTS, LOOKS TINY ON A MAP, BUT IT TAKES
a long time to get from here to there because of our traffic and our
twisty roads. Any way you go, Boston is not just a pleasant little day
trip from Poor Fred. There's no direct train, so it's usually a nerve-
tearing odyssey by car, whether through stalled traffic in backwater
towns (like ours!) or bumper-to-bumper on the highways. (There's a
reason, you see, why Americans in states west of the Charles River
rarely ever see Massachusetts license plates: Our traffic is so bad we
can't get out of here.) So, our major city seems a lot farther away than it
really is, a distance I tend to measure in culture as well as in miles.

I always find it downright startling to go from a small, quiet city like
Poor Fred to noisy, colorful, chaotic Boston. It really is a great place to
visit—trust me—but I really wouldn't want to live there, no offense.
When I drive into the city, as I did that day at about a half hour past
noon, I tend to think of it as Jenny Goes to the Big City. And when I
get home again, I always add with a sigh of relief: And Returns Alive to
Tell the Tale.

Funny, I don't feel that way about Manhattan.

It must be because I don't drive there; that's the difference, and they
don't have cobblestone streets that make me fear for my tires, my align-
ment, and my U-frame.

Downeast Marine, Inc. was headquartered in a renovated red brick
warehouse at the edge of the harbor. The pretty, young receptionist in
the lobby of the canning company didn't even have to check a list when
I gave her my name, but smiled brightly and said, "Good afternoon,

Ms. Cain. Mr. Greenstreet is expecting you. I'll ring his assistant to come down for you."

Soon, brass elevator doors opened to emit another young woman, who introduced herself only as Mr. Greenstreet's assistant. She led me smilingly up ten floors to the executive dining room. When the doors opened again, she stepped back to let me through. I found myself walking directly into the dining room. It was empty except for the two of us and a mammoth round table, surely big enough for an entire board of directors to dine with plenty of elbow room. Floor to ceiling windows lined the water side of the room, affording a spectacular view of the harbor. A plush, forest green carpet covered the floor like moss. The enormous table was covered in lime green linen, and set with china, crystal, and silver, for two.

"Mr. Greenstreet will be right here," the nameless young woman assured me. "As busy as he is, he always tries to be prompt. Such a considerate man. I know he is especially looking forward to talking to you. He has told me so many fine things about your father, who must be a wonderful man. Would you like something to drink, a glass of wine or a cup of coffee?"

I searched her face for signs that she was putting me on about Dad. "White wine would be nice," I said.

And why not? I thought. *After all, I'm on leave!*

She walked to a door discreetly set into wood paneling, and opened it to reveal a beautifully stocked liquor cabinet with several shelves of crystal ware. I watched her select the wine, open it and pour me a glassful. She was wearing a black suit, black pumps, a white blouse, and a red string tie, and she appeared, with her neat brown hairdo and her quiet makeup and brown glasses, to be another Ms. Lorimer in the making. Add thirty years and a pension plan, and she could pass. She depressed me. The servile receptionist downstairs depressed me. I thought of Mrs. Kennedy at the rectory, and of Marjorie Earnshaw at the doctor's office, and of Paige Lorimer at Port Frederick Fisheries, and now this young woman. I wanted to shout at all of them until the dirt flew from their dustpans and the papers rattled in their typewriters: for God's sake, stop borrowing his life, and get one of your own!

Morosely, I was lifting the wine to my lips when an awful thought came into my head: *And aren't you a fine one to talk, Jenny Cain, you with four old men on your board to cater to and cajole and manipulate into doing it your way? And how often do you get to do that? And haven't*

*you spent most of the last decade doing exactly what they asked you to
do?*

I emptied half of the glass before I realized I had drunk it.

Not anymore, I won't.

I realized I was full of conviction and wine, and either one can make
you dizzy. I stepped away from the young woman in order to gaze out
of the wall-length windows at the harbor. Boston's a funny-looking
town in a way, I always think, an uneasy mix of the past and the future.
There are the lovely, old, red brick buildings with pretty white trim—
like the old and the new Statehouses and the townhouses on Beacon
Hill; and right beside them you'll find the stark metal and glass of
modern buildings, like the Prudential and the John Hancock. Every city
has those contrasts, I suppose, but they seem more dramatic in Boston,
because there's so much more of the past left standing than there is in
most other American cities. From atop Downeast Marine, I could see
the frigate *Constitution,* "Old Ironsides," moored dockside. I watched a
tug maneuver a barge into the harbor. *You're the tug, Jenny. Your board
is the barge. And you're tired of pushing them along in the right directions.*

"Jenny!" I turned to see that the assistant had vanished and that a
tall man was approaching me with outstretched hand and a hearty
smile on his face. He was in his mid-fifties, and a sartorial vision in
wool, cotton, and silk, and Italian shoes. "Welcome!"

I took the soft, fleshy hand, and shook it.

"Cecil. Thank you!"

I tried to return his smile, but it wasn't easy. His own smile ended at
his big white teeth, never making it as far as his eyes, which were the
greenish brown of pond scum.

Algae, I chided myself, *algae.*

I had rarely taken such an immediate and violent dislike to anybody
as I did to Cecil Greenstreet, former vice president of Cain Clams.

Our lunch, too, was heavily into watery greens. Watercress salad. Red
snapper with a pesto sauce and spinach pasta. Lime sherbet with chocolate mint cookies. All served on that green linen tablecloth with those
matching napkins. Could it possibly have been coincidence? I wondered. Or was this man Greenstreet on some kind of bright green ego
trip? But he wasn't wearing anything green. So maybe it was his staff,
currying favor. Or having a risky joke at the boss's expense? Or maybe
it was only an unconscious pun on everybody's part.

I'd never know, but I couldn't wait to tell Geof.

The food was great. Green, but great.

"Where will you take your doctorate, Jenny?"

I smiled, and pointed to my face, thus indicating that I couldn't talk with my mouth full. It was a ruse, intended to give me time to think. When I couldn't stall any longer, when that snapper was chewed to the consistency of mousse, I swallowed and said, "Harvard." What the hell, if you have to lie, lie big.

"My MBA is from Harvard Business, Jenny. If you need an alum reference, let me know."

There was a not-so-hidden invitation there, a clarion come-on. *Call me. I'll squeeze out some of my influence for you. And then we'll see what you will do for me.* Like many people in positions of power, Greenstreet appeared to me to have an overabundance of libido that couldn't be channeled only into sex or only into power, but spilled over into everything he said, every movement he made, from the constant directness of his gaze and the half-smile on his face to the nearly lascivious manner in which he enjoyed his wine and his meal. He'd been flirting with me, the ex-boss's daughter, all through lunch.

I thanked him for his offer, and then quickly changed the subject. "Cecil, did you come into Cain Clams as a VP?"

"Yes, I did, Jenny."

"I'm sorry I can't recall how long you were there."

"No reason you should. Two years was all."

"Until it folded."

"Unfortunately. Yes."

"What went wrong?"

He sighed, and pushed himself away from the table. "Do you smoke?"

"No."

"More coffee, a little more wine?"

"Nothing, thanks."

"You're like your father," he said, an unlikely statement that managed to alarm me considerably. "You only take what you need. You aren't greedy."

I though that was a remarkable extrapolation from one little refusal of something to drink. And were we talking about the same father I knew? The Jimmy Cain I knew took all of life's luxuries he could get his hands on, and then usually complained they weren't enough. Not enough money. Not enough women. Not enough Hermes stores in cities around the world. Not enough sunny days to play golf. It was my experience that there wasn't enough of anything, anywhere, to satisfy him. I thought about telling Greenstreet that it wasn't true, what he was saying about me, and that I wanted many things I didn't really need, but I was afraid that he would read a sexual message into that, so I shut up and let him canonize me. Maybe he'd cool down a bit if he thought he was dealing with St. Jenny, daughter of St. James.

"People blamed Jim for wanting that new addition to the plant," Cecil continued. "But he only wanted what he needed. Granted, I argued against it, but in hindsight, I can see that he was right."

"If he was right, how come it threw us into bankruptcy?"

"I know that is the popular view of what happened, but that does not take into account the fact that there was, coincidentally, a pollution scare on the Chesapeake Bay that devastated the shellfish market the previous year. As a result, the EPA demanded stringent new regulations, really outrageously expensive pollution control devices and procedures, that we would have had to implement in our existing operations as well as in the new addition. On top of all of that, there was also a civil war in South America that disrupted tin production and transportation and consequently sent the price of cans through the roof. Your father had no way of predicting or controlling any of those factors. It was bad luck, plain and simple."

Straight from the pages of *The Port Frederick Times.*

He sounded as if he were still the loyal spokesman for Cain Clams.

Greenstreet didn't seem to hear the ironic contradiction of his own explanation: Blame pollution on the one hand, and then blame pollution control on the other. *That,* I thought, *is called having your excuse and eating it, too.*

"But," I said, "if the bottom dropped out of the shellfish market a whole year before Dad planned the addition, he had time to trim his expansion plans accordingly. Why did he try to go ahead with it, in the face of so many negative economic indicators and a down market?"

"I'll admit that I argued against it at the time, Jenny, but as I also said, in retrospect, I think your father was right—it was just his timing that was off."

"I think that was my point, Cecil."

"Well, look, the market came back up within eighteen months."

"You call that slightly off?"

He cleared his throat. "It was a tough call. He had the drawings, he had the contractors and unions lined up to do the job, and he had the loans in place. It was go or no go, and we went, based on your father's best judgment, which I respected then and I continue to respect to this day. I think the proof of my contention that your father had the right idea is that after PFF took over, they went ahead with your father's expansion plans, and look where they are today."

"Yeah, catching golden fish with golden bait. But Cecil, Pete Falwell *didn't* proceed immediately."

"Well, no, not for a couple of years."

"Not until the market improved?"

"That's true."

"So you might say his judgment was considerably better than my father's."

"His *luck* was considerably better."

"My dad is certainly fortunate in one way, Cecil."

He looked curious. "How's that?"

"To have a loyal friend like you."

He smiled, all the way up to his cheekbones.

I said, "I guess Pete's a pretty good friend of yours, too?"

He cleared his throat again. "Who's that?"

"Pete Falwell," I said. "The retired president and present chairman of the board of Port Frederick Fisheries. Didn't I hear that you and he were pals?"

"No, I hardly know the man," he said, with every appearance of honesty. "I'm not even sure I ever met him."

"Oh, well." I smiled away the "misunderstanding," and stood up, holding out my hand. "One other question. I'm trying to send thank-you notes to everybody who attended the funeral and there are a couple of signatures in the guest book that I can't read for the life of me. You didn't happen to notice who was standing in front of you before you signed it?"

"No, sorry, must not have been anybody I knew."

I waved the subject away. "Thanks so much, Cecil. For your time. For lunch. And for being so kind to my father."

Greenstreet stood, too, and grasped my hand in both of his, pulling me a step closer to him. "I'm not just being kind, Jenny."

"But you lost your job, too." I allowed him to hang onto me as I gazed sympathetically into the intensely focused coldness of his eyes. *Frozen pond scum?* "It must have been rough. Where'd you land after Cain's folded, Cecil?"

He smiled ruefully as he finally released me. I stepped back out of range of the heaviest cloud layer of his cologne. "I'm a little embarrassed to admit that one of the benefits of being a devil's advocate is that you see the writing on the wall before it's even written. As I told you, I argued against the expansion. When I saw your father was hell-bent on going ahead with it, I started socking some of my salary away."

"You thought you might soon need your savings?"

He nodded, so that his well-fed jowls met his shirt collar. "Yes, even though I still say that I think your father was right. But it is true that the financial cushion that I provided for myself gave me the luxury of looking around before I took a new position."

I smiled, and opened my arms wide to encompass the spectacular view of Boston and the harbor outside his windows. "And now you can look around in every direction."

"Yes," he said, "I've had good luck."

An unusually modest man, I thought wryly, as I rode the elevator back down to the first floor. I knew that psychological studies indicated that most men ascribed their success to their own talent, while women tended to credit their success to luck. And yet Cecil Greenstreet . . . he of the green carpet and the green linens and the green food and algae eyes . . . humbly attributed his rise in the shellfish industry to good fortune.

Yeah. Right. Maybe

11

BY ONCE AGAIN SKIPPING THE SCENIC CIRCUITOUS ROUTE, AND keeping to the expressways, I managed to make it back to Port Frederick and to Pete Falwell's office by the appointment time of four-thirty. I was feeling awfully tired by that time, the consequence of too many difficult days and nights in a traumatic row. I felt like a Vermont maple tree in the fall after its sap has run out.

With luck, I thought as I hauled one foot after another on the sidewalk leading up to the front door of Port Frederick Fisheries, with any luck, Pete will pat me on the shoulder and say, "We understand perfectly, Jennifer; you take all the time off you need."

Two years, Pete? Would you go for three?

I was smiling wearily to myself as I walked past Ms. Lorimer, who waved me into the inner sanctum.

"Come in." Pete stood up behind his mahogany desk and gestured to a green leather library chair in front of it. He had a fancier office now, as chairman, than he'd had even as president. "Sit down."

In his semiretirement, he favored golf attire like the black and white checked trousers he wore on this afternoon, with a white Polo shirt topped by a yellow golf cardigan. Pete's thinning white hair was slicked back over his deeply tanned and liver-spotted skull, and his neck and hands displayed par-5 tans, as well. His casual attire contrasted strongly with the peremptory tone of his words and with the stern, unsmiling expression on his rather good-looking face. My own smile wavered as I got the first inkling that this interview might not proceed as amiably as I had imagined it.

Of all of my trustees, Pete Falwell came the closest to being exactly what he appeared to be: a country club capitalist who was so Republican and conservative that he made William F. Buckley look like Cesar Chavez. Pete and I could talk business with ease, but we tiptoed around each other's politics. I liked Pete all right, and I respected his business savvy, but of all of my bosses, he was the one with whom I had the coolest, least personal relationship. And, judging by his demeanor, it was getting cooler and more impersonal by the second. Feeling some trepidation, I crossed the red and green plaid carpet and sat down. Should I take the lead, I wondered, or wait for him to—

"I'll tell you up front," Pete began even before he was fully seated again behind his desk, "that the other trustees are amenable to your request for a leave, but I am not. I hope to convince you that it would be a serious mistake for you and a disservice to the foundation, as well as a disservice to Mrs. Basil, who is not experienced enough to handle the projects you have on deck."

I attempted to give every appearance of listening respectfully, but I was thinking: Four votes to one, he can't make me stay.

Pete picked up a brass paperweight made in the shape of a tennis racquet and tapped it on the edge of the desk as he made each of his points. "I know you're upset about your mother's death, and I sympathize. I've known your mother and father forever. Once upon a time, I was even in love with your mother . . ." He smiled a little. "Bet you didn't know that, did you? It was in eighth grade. She was the sweetest girl in the class, and of course I was smitten." The smile vanished and he tapped the paperweight again. "So, of course I sympathize. We all do. But dropping out is not the way to deal with your problems, Jennifer; you'll be much better off if you keep yourself busy with familiar things, especially your job. Go to work every morning. Concentrate on your responsibilities there. Wear yourself out in that sort of good and proper way so that you can sleep more easily at night. That's the way to deal with grief. Quitting, thinking too much about your mother, that's not the way. If you do that, you'll only depress yourself. Not healthy. Not at all. Stay on the job, Jennifer, that's the ticket."

"I appreciate your concern, Pete," I said, leaning forward, "and while I agree that might be good advice for some people, I don't think it is for me. I know what I'm doing. I know that what I need is to step back from my usual responsibilities for a while. And then, I hope, I'll come back to work rejuvenated, and ready to go again."

Liar, I thought, shocking myself with the truth: *You'll never be ready to go back.*

From the skeptical expression on Pete's face, I saw that he recognized bullshit when he heard it, too. He didn't say it in so many words, but his tone proceeded to get tougher, and his arguments escalated into ones that were harder and harder for me to rebut.

"Mrs. Basil isn't ready," he said, bluntly.

"I think she is, Pete."

"She has neither your experience nor the confidence of the entire board."

Meaning him, I guessed.

"However," I countered, "she has the advantages of greater maturity and fewer personal problems to distract her. She can handle it, especially for only a month."

"Not situations like this, she can't." He tossed me a thick, white, business-size envelope. I withdrew from it a wad of paper, folded over twice to fit inside. Each page featured a photo of a famous painting of men at war—except that on top of the muscular, masculine bodies of the victors, somebody had pasted photos of women's heads snipped out of magazines. They stood arrogantly—their swords bloodied, their pistols drawn (depending on the particular painting)—over slain bodies of vanquished men. The whole thing had a title page: "What Women Really Want." And there was a credit: Morality in Our Arts Committee. MOAC. It was all as neatly and painstakingly executed as the placards in the gallery windows had been. The exception that proved the rule of this little exhibit was an untouched photograph of a painting of Salome being offered on a silver platter the bloody, decapitated head of John the Baptist.

I responded in the only appropriate way: by laughing and tossing the envelope back across the desk to Pete. "Faye will know how to handle this—by refusing to take it seriously." I spoke with more confidence than I felt, since it did appear that MOAC was escalating its protests; this one was still quiet and relatively low-key, but it displayed a level of paranoia that the plain letters MOAC, lettered onto cardboard, did not. If the letters to my office were step one in their campaign, and the signs at the gallery were step two, then this was step three, and I had to admit to myself that I was a little worried about what steps four and five would be, and whether it was fair to teach Faye to swim by throwing her into his pond. "You don't take it seriously, do you, Pete? In a couple of weeks, the exhibit will be over anyway."

"You got us into this, Jennifer."

"And Faye will get you out of it."

You, I had said, not *us.*

"I must say I'm disappointed in your attitude."

Well, I thought, *you'll get over it.*

"I'm sorry to hear that, Pete." I spread my hands in a show of openness and sincerity. "But you see? I'm distracted. I'm disappointing you already. I'd be better off taking a leave of absence, for the good of the foundation." *Nicely done,* I congratulated myself: *Throw his own arguments right back at him.*

But then the old golfer hit a clean, straight, fair one right off the tee and into the bucket.

"Your contract forbids it," he reminded me.

I stared at him, not believing what he was doing.

"Perhaps you have forgotten, it's been so long ago, but your original contract of employment forbids any unpaid leaves of absence. So I regret to tell you that regardless of our sympathy and regardless of the kind intentions of the other members of the board, you have no alternative but to stay on the job."

"You would hold me to that, Pete?"

He nodded. "For the good of the foundation, I will, yes."

"No matter what the other trustees say?"

"A contract is a contract, and yours is quite clear."

I didn't even feel angry at him, but only exhausted, as I said, "There is an alternative, Pete, and I guess you're going to force me to use it." I breathed deeply, let it out. "I quit."

"No. You can't. Your contract says—"

"So sue me," I said, wearily.

Pete's reply to that was frozen silence, which continued as I got up from the chair and made my way back across the plaid carpet to the door.

But there were a couple more questions, which I turned around to ask—

"Pete, why'd Cain Clams go under?"

He was in no mood to spare my feelings. "Because your father was a poor businessman."

101

"Pete, what if . . . what if he hadn't tried to build that addition to the plant? What would have happened to Cain Clams then?"

"It might have held steady, but without any growth."

"That would have been fine," I said softly, more to myself than to him.

But he brought my head up with his sharp retort. "No, it wouldn't. Not for this town or the state or the industry. Look how we've expanded and grown with it since then, Jenny, look how we've diversified, look how we've increased shareholders' profits, employment and wages, and you tell me, which outcome was better for Port Frederick in the long run?"

"Maybe. How long have you known Cecil Greenstreet?"

He was already staring at me, so his expression didn't change when he said, "Years. Why?"

"He told me today that he doesn't know you."

Pete didn't hesitate. "That was stupid of him." His voice held a controlled but intense anger that I suspected was really aimed at me.

Outside of Pete's office, I stood for a moment behind Ms. Lorimer's back, while she talked on her phone, and I took it all in. Here was the elegant front office that was located in just about the same spot where line workers used to stuff seafood into cans for Cain Clams, here were the high walls that rose on the site of my family's business, here were the plush carpeting and muted telephones, the indirect lighting and music floating out of hidden speakers. And of course, the maritime gimcracks: the figureheads from old ships, the glass cases filled with scrimshaw, the collections of ship's porcelain, and all of the rest of the seafaring memorabilia that made my heart ache with longing for what might have been.

I was filled in that moment with a bitterness and a regret so sharp that I tasted it as bile on my tongue. What a funny child I'd been, that clever girl who thought she'd get to run the "ancestral firm" one day. What a laugh, how I'd kept on pedaling, through my prebusiness courses, then through an advanced degree in business, long after the object of all of that ambition was gone, but still acting as if there were some point to all of that specialized learning. And look where it had led me: back here, to the company I would never run, being pressed to the wall by the man who took it over, and finally facing the fact that it wasn't *business* I'd loved at all, it was *the* business. This business. Old salts and salt air and salt water. The business that was ours, the one where I cared about the welfare of the people who worked for it, the one that gave our family pride of place in the community, the one that I had fantasized about perpetuating into a fourth generation.

The rush of exhilaration I'd felt the moment I quit faded, leaving behind it a hollow fear—now I didn't have either this business or my job. Now what?

It wasn't money that worried me. Between Geof and me, at least one of us still had a job and we were both among the lucky ones who had family money to fall back on. No, it wasn't the money, it had never been the money, except in the sense of wanting to earn it instead of just inherit it. It was: What now? Without the foundation, what would I *do?* My life revolved around my job. What would I do, literally *do,* with the hours of my days and the days of the weeks? Who was I without it? Ready or not, it looked as if I was going to have to find out.

I walked on past Ms. Lorimer as she talked on the phone. She smiled and winked at me. A second red button lit up on her console, and I wondered which of the other trustees Pete was calling first to report the news of my resignation. From a coffee table, I picked up a copy of the latest Port Frederick Fisheries annual report. I stared at the cover, which was a cartoon of a fat, smiling, prosperous-looking clam peeking out of its shell, and I thought: *What the hell, the wound's already raw, I might as well grab this salt and rub it in.* I carried the annual report with me back out to my car.

It was five o'clock.

I was supposed to see Sam Hayes at *The Times* at five-thirty.

Instead, I drove to The Buoy Bar and Grill and went inside.

I got lucky and snagged one of the old wooden booths just as another couple abandoned it. I thought about the fact that I hadn't eaten anything since lunch in Boston, and it had been pretty light food, but I ordered a Beck's beer anyway. So what if my head got fuzzy? So maybe I'd take a cab home, or call Geof to come meet me. So I didn't have to be at work the next day, or any day from now on, so who cared?

"Cheers," I said to the empty place opposite me.

As I slowly emptied my beer, more than a dozen people I knew waved or nodded hello to me, but nobody came over to sit down and chat. Recent death'll do that, I've found; it'll shoot your charisma all to hell. I figured people were afraid they'd say the wrong thing or, worse, that they'd walk over to ask, "How are you, Jenny?" and I'd tell them.

I peeled strips off the label on the Beck's bottle, like pulling petals off a daisy: My dad was an idiot who mismanaged the company and made it possible for Pete Falwell to benefit from his mistakes; my dad was a victim of circumstances beyond his control; my dad was both an idiot *and* the victim of circumstances, or possibly even of collusion between his old friend and my boss, Pete Falwell, and his old employee, Cecil Greenstreet. I preferred the second scenario.

I ordered a second beer.

As I drank that one, I stripped the label off of it, too: My mother was so distraught about having a hysterectomy, that it drove her crazy; my mother, like a lot of women, was a victim of an unnecessary operation, and *that* drove her crazy; my father drove my mother crazy; the combination of the hysterectomy, the hormonal changes, and the emotional overload of the bankruptcy combined to drive my mother crazy; my mother was crazy to begin with, and I'd never noticed, because in my family, who could tell?

I laughed, and ordered a third Beck's.

I considered pulling out my notebook, but thought, the hell with it. The notebook was stupid, merely a silly way to give me the illusion of accomplishing something. Hah. What was there to write down, anyway —that Pete Falwell had loved my mother in the eighth grade? What if she'd fallen for Pete instead of for my dad, then Pete could have been my father. Now there was a chilling thought. On the other hand, we'd still have a business. And on the *other* hand, he probably never would have considered allowing a daughter to run it. Pete had always had enough trouble just living with the idea of a woman running the civic foundation. I had always wondered if he had been outvoted when they hired me.

Not that it mattered now.

When the beer came, I opened my purse, fumbled around for the bottle of Doc Farrell's magic vitamins, poured one into my hand without even looking at it, and washed it down with a swallow of beer. With any luck, the B-complex would help to counteract the hangover I was sure to have in the morning. I didn't drink much anymore; three beers in a row was unusual for me. But the whole day, in fact the whole last several days, had been the most unusual and upsetting of my life, which, considering my life, was saying something. I couldn't figure out why I couldn't "adjust." So my mother died. So everybody's mother dies. *So come on, Jenny, get with it; it's been almost a whole week.*

I laughed again.

"Ready for another beer?"

I shook my head at the waitress. No, definitely not.

Checking my watch, I saw that it was nearly six o'clock. I gathered my purse and put out enough money for the drinks and a tip. I stood up and slid into my coat, and then weaved my way between the tables to the pay phones out front.

"Sam?" I said, when I reached the publisher of *The Times.* "Listen, I'm sorry, but I got held up, and now I won't be able to make it tonight. How about tomorrow?"

"Are you at a bar? It sounds like it."

"How about I'll buy you lunch tomorrow, Sam?"

"Where are you going now? I want to talk to you."

"Now? Home, I guess. Why do you want to talk to me?"

"I want a statement on why you quit the foundation."

Oh, shit. I had forgotten about this part of it. In a city this size, with a foundation this important, it was already news. "Personal reasons."

"Come on, Jenny, give me more than that."

"Have lunch with me tomorrow, Sam, and maybe I will."

I heard him sigh, but he said, "Noon. Meet me here."

He hung up before I did. I fished out another quarter, inserted it and dialed Geof's extension at the police department.

"Hi," he said, "how are you?"

"A little drunk, I think. Geof, I quit my job."

"Did you say quit?"

"That's what I said. Any chance you can drive me home?"

"Honey, I can't right now. Where are you, at The Buoy? I wish I could meet you there, but I'm right in the middle of something. Why don't you call a cab? I'll be home as soon as I can. I want to hear all about it."

"Okay, love you."

"Love you, too," he said, and hung up.

I searched my billfold, and then the bottom of my purse, for another quarter, but came up empty-handed. "Oops. Can't call a cab without any money," I said. I felt so funny, all of a sudden, so loose-limbed and happy, and I couldn't imagine why I thought I couldn't drive home perfectly safely. Why, I was a good driver. I didn't need any old cab to deliver me, like some old drunk. I'd just drive on home myself, and be there in a jiffy, and crawl right into bed to wait for my husband to celebrate my new freedom. What a lovely, fuzzy feeling I had around the edges of my head and my body. My, how my fingers tingled and my toes, enough to make me giggle a little. Life wasn't so bad, life was good and rich and full, and I could survive anything, sure I could, sure I would, just watch me . . .

Outside, it was cold as midnight. I rolled down all the car windows so the freezing air would keep me awake, but by the time I turned off the two-lane blacktop onto our dark dirt road, I was so drowsy and soft-limbed that I felt as if I could have sleep-driven the car the rest of the way home. Oh, it felt so good to want to sleep so bad. To know that my eyes would seal shut and my brain would shut down the minute my head hit the pillow. Sorry, Geof, we'll have to wait to celebrate in the morning. I sighed, looking forward to deep and dreamless, drowning sleep.

I mumbled a song blissfully to myself as the car bounced along the dirt road. "Pack up all my cares and woe, see them go, goo-ood niight, Jen-ny." And then a chorus of "Lullaby of Birdland," and "Rockabye Baby" . . . "Rockabye Jenny in an Accord, when the car stops, you'll fall on the floord." I giggled sleepily at my own nonsense. And even that felt good, so good, to be silly for once instead of so damned serious and somber all of the time. I sang as I pressed the button on the garage door opener, and as I waited for the double door to rise.

Oops, I'd forgotten it didn't work.

"Outta batt'ries."

The door was already open, just as I'd left it that morning.

"Come on along and listen to the Lullaby of Jen-ny, the hiphooray and wallaby, the Lullaby of Jen-ny." Driving into the garage, I miscalculated and banged into the trash cans. "Oops again." Feeling befuddled but good, so good, I stared at the cans, wondering what in the world I should do now. "Leave'm," I decided, and then I sang some more. "When a Poor Fred baby says good-night, it's early in the morning, Fredricans don't sleep tight, unless it's liiiight! Goooodniiight, Jennnnny, policeman's on his waaay . . ."

I opened my door, but didn't move to get out.

The car was still running as I reached for my purse. Ah, there was the Port Frederick Fisheries annual report under my purse. I picked it up and flipped through it in slow motion. Huh? What was this, under

I.O.U.

the heading "subsidiary companies"? The amazing, disturbing words doubled and fuzzed and pinwheeled and cartwheeled in front of my eyes. I was suddenly so tired that all I wanted to do was to drape my arms over the top of the steering wheel and rest my cheek on them and go to sleep.

And so I did.

I never heard the sound of footsteps on the garage floor.

I didn't see the hand that lifted the PFF report as it slid from my lap, or hear my car door close. And I didn't hear the garage door come down and shut me inside with the car engine still running.

12

"JEN? HONEY? *JENNY!*"

A face with a halo around it floated in front of me. My, they had handsome angels in heaven. But oh, how I wished it would hold still. It made me so sick and dizzy just to look at it. I closed my eyes again.

"Jenny!"

Ohhh. I was going to throw up.

"Here, honey, here's the pan, do it here."

"Ohhh. Goddd."

I remembered a time when I was a teenager and a couple of friends and I had decided it would be a great adventure to cross the United States by Greyhound bus. And of course it was. Except that the bus fumes made me sick. Regularly. There had been one time in particular when we were all three standing outside of the L.A. downtown bus station waiting for one of our relatives to pick us up, and he'd been late and the bus fumes had been as thick as—

"Oh, God, I feel so incredibly sick."

Smog flu, he'd called it.

"Your system's full of carbon monoxide, that's why."

Is that what I had this time, smog flu?

One of the voices I'd been hearing in heaven—the deep, worried, gentle one that I took for St. Peter—was, I realized now, my husband's. He was the one saying honey and Jenny. The other one was unfamiliar to me, a woman's that was sharp and high-pitched, and when I opened my eyes again I discovered her to be a nurse. A nurse? I was lying in a hospital room? Must be one hell of a case of smog flu. Over a horrible new wave of nausea, I asked her, "Why'ssyt'mfull'oxide?"

She didn't respond to my question.

I heaved into a gold plastic, kidney-shaped pan again, and she helped me to wash off my lips and chin. Only then did I open my eyes once more, focus them on my husband's face, and try like anything to smile at him, though I pretty much failed to do it. One thing I definitely didn't want to do was to breathe on him. Love has its limits, and I thought that might breach his. The room, I managed to see, was painted a bilious mauve. Geof was leaning toward me from a chair made of chrome and vinyl that was a sickening brown color. The television set, which stuck out of the wall opposite my feet, was turned on to an afternoon Western adventure. Even with the volume turned low, the sound of every bullet pierced my eyes and made me feel like Wyatt Earp's last name. The nurse returned from the bathroom where she had taken my gold pan. *Give me back my pan!* She set it next to me on the bed. I felt so relieved to have it back.

"I wish I were dead."

Geof nodded sympathetically.

But the nurse retorted, senselessly, it seemed to me, "No, you don't. You're a very lucky girl to be alive at all. I don't want to hear any of that silly talk. We've worked too hard on you to put up with that kind of ingratitude now!" She patted my hip (even that light touch on a far extremity made my gorge rise, and I closed my eyes on the misery), and then I heard her leave the room.

I squinted at Geof.

"I wish I were dead."

"I'll bet." He reached a hand toward me.

"Don't touch me, or I'll throw up."

Quickly, he withdrew his hand.

"What happened to me?"

"Do you remember anything?"

"Stop that." I tried to laugh, but that also made my gorge rise. "Will you stop being a cop? I remember driving into the garage—oh, listen, I'm sorry, but I smashed the trash cans—and I think I remember being *in* the garage, and that's it. What happened?"

"Do you remember what else you did yesterday?"

Yesterday, I thought. *Thank God.* I'd lost only a day, maybe even less than twenty-four hours. Not days, weeks, or even years. Like my mother. "I had a beer at The Buoy." I paused a long time between sentences, forcing myself to think back, and trying to breathe past the sickness in my sore throat. Why was my throat so sore? "Maybe more than one. That was just before I went home. Oh, do I have to do this? I'm so dizzy and sick. I met with Pete Falwell before that. I think I quit my job." I glanced at him to see if he looked surprised. He didn't, so I gathered that he already knew. "I went to Boston to talk to a man named Cecil Greenstreet. He was a vice president at Cain Clams right before it folded. What else? There's something. Oh, I can't think—"

"What, Jenny? What are you remembering?"

I started to raise my right hand to rub my forehead, only to discover I was attached to an IV. I put my arm back down on the bed and tried to focus on the wispy thought that had floated in behind my eyes and then out again. "Something . . . I don't know, it hurts to think. Please tell me what happened to me."

"You passed out," Geof lied, trying to spare me for a while.

I believed it, as far as it went, because I knew all too well that I had been abusing my poor body—not feeding it well, not resting it properly. No wonder it had collapsed on me. Served me right.

Then a smidgen of logic sneaked past the nausea.

"But why do I have this terrible headache, and why am I so sick to my stomach?"

"Gas fumes."

Oh, I hadn't turned off the ignition before I passed out. But wait. Another snippet of logic was trying to creep in, trying to make some point about how there was something wrong with that explanation . . .

"Go back to sleep," Geof said, softly.

That sounded like a fine idea.

"Who's been here?" I mumbled, as I closed my eyes. "Besides you?"

"Your father. He kept going to the window and remarking on what a beautiful view of the harbor you have. Randy came with him. She kept trying to soothe your fevered brow with little pats and kisses—"

I grimaced, and pulled the gold pan closer.

"—which I knew you'd hate, so I made them leave. Your trustees sent flowers, and Faye and Marvin did, too." (Marvin Lastelic was our part-time accountant at the foundation.) "You've got a separate bunch of flowers from Miss Lucille Grant, apart from the ones the trustees sent, and a big bunch from Francie and Duke Daniel, with a card saying they love you." He paused, to let me register that fact.

"That's nice," I managed.

"Marsha Sandy has been by several times, but I've kept everybody else out. So mostly, it's just been me."

"My sister?"

He didn't answer, and I was drifting away again.

"You're going to be fine, Jenny."

Away, away, drifting away.

"I'll tell you about it later, Jenny."

"Much . . ." I murmured, ". . . later."

And it was much, much later when I willingly opened my eyes to admit the world again. Until then, I kept them closed every chance I got, not wanting to talk to anybody, not wanting to encourage anybody to talk to me. If I talked, I threw up. If I listened, I threw up. Silence was as precious as oxygen to me. Still, I heard things. Frightening things. Even though the swish of a nurse's slacks made my brain feel as if the frontal lobes were rubbing together, even though the mere pop of a plastic cap being pulled off a fresh syringe caused little bubbles of pain to burst in my neck, and so I tried to block it all out with sleep, sleep, sleep—still, I heard things that made me feel even sicker, but now with fear. I was like a drunk waking up with the world's worst hangover and beginning to get a terrible, nauseating, humiliating glimmer—from little things she overheard people say—of exactly what she had done with the lampshade the night before. More than ever, I began to wish that somebody would just shoot me and put me out of this misery.

That evening, the night after it happened, I was able to sit up in bed and let Geof tell me the story of what happened to me. Even before he began to talk, I was filled with such dread that I was already on the verge of tears, and trying to hide it from him.

Was he going to confirm my worst fears?

Please God, no.

"I got home that night," he said, as I endeavored to look him in the eye, and to sit calmly with my hands in my lap. The two of us were alone in the hospital room, with the door closed. "The garage door was down. The house was dark. To make a long story short, I found you unconscious and pulled you out of there and called the dispatcher for help."

I closed my eyes, feeling tears starting behind the lids.

"Jenny? Do you remember anything now?"

The horrible truth was, I didn't. For all I knew, I had tried—even if unconsciously—to kill myself. That's what I was so afraid of. On the face of it, it seemed entirely too possible. At my mother's funeral, hadn't I morbidly fantasized about my own death, and about the "rest and comfort" of being cradled by a being of light and love? If that wasn't a death wish, I didn't know what was. And the day before, after seeing Pete Falwell, hadn't I felt run-down, stressed-out, and screwed-over? Manic one minute, despairing the next, I sounded like a perfect candidate for suicide. How selfish, how humiliating. I couldn't open my eyes. I was too frightened and ashamed to look my husband in the face. I felt the tears rolling down my cheeks, faster and harder, and I brought my hands up to hide them.

"Jenny?" Suddenly Geof was holding me and I was trying to burrow my head into his chest, so he couldn't see me. "Honey, I'm sorry, I guess it's too soon to talk about—"

"Just like my mother—"

"What, Jenny?"

"I flipped out, didn't I?"

"What?"

"Just like my poor crazy mother and my nutty father. Like mother, like father, like daughter. I'm sorry, Geof, I'm so—"

"Stop it."

But that only made me cry harder. Geof literally shook me, and said, "Jenny, stop it! It isn't true. Don't you know yourself better than that?" He laughed a little. "If you think you tried to kill yourself, you're wrong."

I looked up at him, finally, hardly daring to hope.

"Prove it," I whispered.

"All right," he said. "Listen to me! The official finding is going to be that it was an accident, that you fell asleep at the wheel after you put the garage door down and before you turned off the ignition."

I felt a lifting of hope. Could that have happened?

"But think, Jenny, what's the problem with that theory?"

I didn't want to think of a problem with it. I liked it. I wanted to keep it. Shit. The dread crept back into my stomach again. "My opener doesn't work," I mumbled. "Dead batteries."

"Yes, it has dead batteries that I promised to replace for you two weeks ago. So it wouldn't have mattered if you had *sat* on the god-damned button, it couldn't have closed the garage door."

"Do the cops—the other cops—know this, Geof?"

"They know the batteries were missing from the garage door opener when they found it." A wry, weary tone entered his voice. "They know I claim to have taken them out two weeks ago when you discovered the opener was dead. They also know that I could have removed the batteries last night, to protect you. You see, attempted suicide is unlawful, but it's not a prosecutable offense in Massachusetts. If you tried to kill yourself, you couldn't go to jail, but you could lose your insurance over it, and you'd certainly suffer a loss of reputation. So the department thinks it's doing me a favor by calling it an accident."

I thought so, too, and was starting to cry again.

"*Stop* that, and listen," Geof said, as if he were impatient with me. "So the department thinks I removed the batteries last night, to make it look as if you couldn't have lowered the garage door. How they think I managed to call for help and to give you CPR and to remove the batteries all at the same time, they haven't told me."

"I could have gotten out of the car," I whispered, arguing against myself. "I could have manually pulled down the door myself, and then got back into the car."

"That's what they said, too. There's only one thing wrong with that. You had your seat belt on."

It took a minute for the implications of that to sink in. And then I sat up and grabbed him as if I'd been shot through with lightning. *"What? What did you say?"*

"That's right, Jenny, you were still wearing your seat belt."

"Then I never left my car!"

"Nope."

"Don't the other cops know that, Geof?"

"They didn't find you. I did. And I had to unbelt you to drag you out of there. So it's my word."

"Isn't that good enough?"

"I'm your husband, what are they going to think?"

Neither of us spoke for a moment, and then I voiced the most chilling thought of all: "So who shut the garage door, Geof?"

"That," he said, grimly, "is what we're going to find out."

"Oh Geof." I began laughing and crying all at the same time, and I grabbed him again and started covering his face with kisses as I blubbered on. "Thank you, thank you, thank you! I was so scared I had gone off the deep end! But you know what! Of all the ways I could choose to kill myself, that's the one I'd never pick! Really, I never would. And you know why? I spent my childhood getting carsick, Geof! When I was a kid on family vacations, I threw up in every state between here and Hawaii. Even today, if I get caught in traffic behind a bus or even a diesel Mercedes, I get nauseated. So I might shoot myself. Or slit my wrists. Or even put strychnine in my coffee. But I would never, never, never lock myself in a garage with the car turned on, because more than anything else in the world, I hate to throw up."

He laughed, as he held me and let me blubber into his shoulder. "It may not be the most convincing argument I ever heard, but I believe it."

Better than that, he believed in me.

I was alive, and so lucky.

Better than that, it was true: I wasn't crazy. I hadn't plunged so far into grief and guilt and depression that I had lost my mind and tried to kill myself. I wasn't my mother.

"I want to go home," I said, a little while later, as I sniffed up the last of my tears.

"Tomorrow," Geof assured me.

"Geof, you told me that Dad was here, and Randy was here, but what about Sherry?"

He hesitated before he spoke. "Lars has called me several times since last night. He's quite concerned about you, he sends his love, and the children's. Sherry sent those flowers." Geof pointed to a modest potted plant that sat on the window ledge. I asked him to hand me the card attached to it, and when he did, I read this message: "Get well soon, the Guthries."

I looked up. "Get well soon? The Guthries?"

He shrugged. "As I said, Lars calls. He wants to come by to see you, but I've discouraged him from doing it."

"Lars is not my sister."

"You'd be better off if he were."

"Flowers," I said. "Do you think—"

"Do I think that the attempt on your life was related to those flowers that were sent to the funeral? And to the message in the guest book and to what happened to you at the grave? I don't know yet, Jenny. It could even be connected to those letters you got at the foundation."

"From MOAC?"

"They were threatening, weren't they?"

"Yes," I admitted, and added, "I am suddenly all tuckered out."

"You sleep," he said, comfortingly. But when he got up and I saw that he meant to go, I clutched at him. "You're not leaving?"

He patted my hands, before gently disengaging them. "Only for a few hours, because there's something I have to do at home. Don't worry, I've got somebody posted outside your door. A retired friend of mine. Starting tomorrow, I'm taking time off to keep an eye on you."

"They'll let you do that?"

"No." The sudden coldness in his smile was not directed at me. "They won't let me do that. But they can't very well argue if I suddenly come down with a raging case of the flu, can they?"

"Geof, your job—"

"Is not as important as your life." He bent down and kissed my mouth. As he walked out of the room, I smiled tearily to myself, and said, "Great exit, Lieutenant."

Before I could fall asleep, Dr. Calvin Farrell dropped by.

"Your cousin almost didn't let me in," he complained.

"My cousin?"

"Wanted proof I was a doctor, for heaven's sake." Doc Farrell flipped his stethoscope at me. "What the hell's he think I am, a car mechanic?"

He was wearing a rumpled suit and shirt and his great shock of white hair was a mess, as if he'd been running his hands through it all day. He looked tired, and every one of his years.

"Oh," I said, finally remembering that Geof had stationed "somebody" outside my room to guard me. "That's Clyde, on my mother's side. He's a little strange."

Doc Farrell stepped to my bedside and lifted my wrist. "How we doin'?"

"Checking to see if I have a pulse? I think you could now light a match under my nose without fear of explosion."

He dropped my hand back onto the bed. "I'm going to consider it a personal insult if it's true that you tried to kill yourself, Jennifer. I worked damned hard helping your mother bring you into this world. Suicides are a waste of my valuable time."

"I didn't," I said, with as much dignity as I could muster lying there on my back with an IV sticking out of my arm.

"Really?" His great eyebrows lifted. "Well then, what were you doing mixing alcohol and tranquilizers?"

I stared at him. "What?"

"Valium," the Doc said. "You had traces of benzodiazepine in your blood, along with whatever you'd been drinking."

"Beer," I said. "Oh, damn, you know what I'll bet I did? I thought I was taking one of your vitamins, Doc, but I must have taken one of the Valiums that Marj gave me. I had both bottles in my purse, and I was tired, and I didn't look closely to see what I opened. It's no wonder I passed out."

"Doctor Marjorie Earnshaw and her goddamned prescriptions!" Doc Farrell exploded. "One of these days . . ." He suddenly focused his anger on me. "And by the way, what the hell were you doing telling her you were in my office for an AIDS test?"

"A bad joke," I confessed.

"It certainly was. Poor Marjorie was not amused when I told her it was poppycock, and I didn't find it funny myself. You wouldn't, either, if you were treating the AIDS babies I am."

In order to defend myself, I would have to disparage his loyal receptionist and tell him what a nosy, presumptuous old bitch I thought she was, and I couldn't do that, so I just said meekly, "I'm sorry."

"I'm really going to have to do something about that woman," Doc Farrell said. "But she's been with me forty years and if I fire her now, well, I can't fire her now, how could I fire her now, after so many years?" He blew out a great breath that swelled his mottled cheeks. "I can't do it. But throw those damn tranquilizers away, Jenny. If I think you need them, I'll see that you get them." His coattails flew as he turned to leave.

"Doc? Can I see my mother's medical records?"

He stopped to glare at me. "What the hell for? This is getting to be an obsession with you, this business about your mother, and it's not healthy. No, you can't have your mother's medical records."

"Why not?" I said, indignantly.

"Because I said so," he declared, and started to stalk out of the room.

"Please!" I called after him.

"Oh, all right," I heard him mutter as he, like Santa Claus, flew out of sight. "I'll tell Marj to take care of it."

Satisfied, I finally rolled over, and closed my eyes.

13

WHILE I SLEPT, GEOF DROVE HOME.

He had already walked the half-mile length of the gravel road leading to our house, searching for some trace of the person or persons who'd either preceded or followed me home that night. He had also been over the garage itself carefully, looking for traces of something, anything. But it was a terrible disadvantage, working alone, without the detectives and technicians who normally would have gathered evidence. Because the department was determined to "help" him by labeling it an accident, there was nobody to make casts of tire prints or footprints, if any such evidence existed, and there was no lab available to him to analyze them if it did.

He was on his own, as he told me later, a policeman turned amateur sleuth, and he hated it. He wanted the other cops around him, thinking of all of the possibilities he might miss, picking up traces he might not have the special expertise to find. He wanted a normal, everyday scene of the crime investigation, that was all. He would have settled for that, not even any special treatment because the victim was his wife. But the Port Frederick police didn't think our garage was a crime scene, so he didn't have help. They thought there was plenty of reason to believe that his wife was off her nut—wasn't the whole town talking about how she'd behaved at her mother's funeral, and hadn't she suddenly up and quit her job for no good reason, and hadn't she thrown some kind of conniption fit out on Duke Daniel's front lawn, and didn't her family have a history of mental illness? What Geof didn't tell me, what I didn't learn until much later, was that he had even been instructed to leave it alone. "There isn't anything to investigate, Bushfield," was how his

Captain had put it to him, attempting to be both blunt and kind. "You'll do your wife a bigger favor if you forget this imaginary killer, and try to get her some help. I think she needs it, Geof."

"That's bullshit," had been my husband's reply.

As a consequence, he was working alone and unsanctioned, and trying to believe the old axiom that "murderers leave tracks," which he thought he ought to be able to find, even by himself. He tried to believe it, tried not to think of all of the other murderers who apparently had left *no* tracks, or of the tracks he had fruitlessly tried to follow in other cases.

Because he had already searched in daylight, and found nothing, he decided to try it once at night, even though it didn't make much sense. After all, who could see anything on a country driveway in pitch blackness? But it was night when the crime took place. And he was stubborn, my husband, and worried, and, God knows, he was the sort and always had been who'd try almost anything once.

It's a sharp left turn off the blacktop county highway to our road. Geof pulled in just past the stand of fir trees that marks the end of county property and the beginning of our acreage, and parked his BMW in the darkest shadows of the trees.

He pulled his flashlight out from under the seat where it was attached to the bottom by a plastic sling. It was a truncheon of a light, eighteen inches long, sheathed in black rubber, capable of casting a beam of thirty feet. It could, he claimed, blind a burglar at twenty paces. Once outside the car, he used the light to look at the little thermometer attached to the zipper pull on his black ski jacket, and discovered that the temperature had dropped another ten degrees. Shivering, he stuck the flashlight between his thighs while he zipped and buttoned his jacket, pushed up the collar, and pulled the flaps of his black cap down over his ears. He felt like a farmer going out into the back pasture to check on Flossie. He didn't put on his gloves, which he carried but rarely wore. He liked to be able to use his hands in an emergency without having to stop to remove his gloves or to fumble through leather.

He used the flash to guide his feet to the gravel, but then he turned the light off. That didn't make any sense, either. How could he see anything without sun or flashlight? But he wasn't going by that kind of logical sense, he was going by his other senses, the intangible ones that cops—and mothers—develop over many years, the ones that whisper in the back of your brain, prick your fingertips, raise the hair on the back of your neck, burn your gut, guide your feet and your eyes and your ears and hands when you'd otherwise feel blind and deaf and paralyzed.

He started walking up the half-mile drive to our cottage. Slowly. Quietly in his rubber-soled boots. Crunching a little on the rocks, but going fairly noiselessly for a man who was nearly six feet three and who weighed 185 pounds. What did he expect to see? He didn't expect anything. He just walked, alone, the night closing in behind him as the fir trees cut off the passing car lights on the county highway.

It was a very cold, very clear night, just the sort we'd moved to the edge of the ocean to find. The Milky Way looked so clear, so close that he thought he could hear the stars move in their orbits—swish, swish. But that was only the swish of the tree branches rubbing against other branches.

He felt the ocean under his boots, although it was a full mile away— the half mile to our house and another half mile down the rocky slope to the beach. He could hear it, another swish, of surf upon rocks. And he could smell it, in the clear night air, along with the sharp tang of balsam, and a faint whiff of dead fish.

We had moved here for peace and solitude and love.

It was he who had found the cottage and given it to me, and the gift had felt to me as if he'd poured fragrant oil on my body and softly, smoothly, soothingly stroked it into my prickly skin and my bunched muscles.

This property was ours. Our refuge.

He was angry beyond words that it had been breached. Invaded. Violated. He felt as if our property had been raped and nearly murdered, as if the home he had presented to me as a private offering of love had been penetrated by a rapist who, in breaking and entering our domain, had left it stained with a secretion of evil. Semen. He felt as if he were looking for a rapist's semen. His spoor. His inevitable trail, as if it were blood and DNA, as if it would glisten in the moonlight, like a slug's trail, and as if he could follow it to its source.

Geof continued up the driveway, finding nothing.

Our garage was detached from the house, sitting ten yards to the south side and about the same distance back. Big enough for two cars and a few implements, it was constructed of the same fieldstone and timber as the house, although it was built fifteen years later than the house, which dated from 1940. Looking at the garage as we drove in, we saw fieldstone walls, a peaked roof of variegated slate and, if it were closed, a double door of wood, painted gray.

Geof had stuck an orange wind sock at the very peak of the gable on the garage. (I'd tried to talk him into one of those quaint iron jobs with an iron man astride an iron horse, riding tail to the wind, but he'd said he was "the one who had to carry the damn thing up there on a ladder, and nylon's a hell of a lot lighter than iron. You want quaint, Jenny, you carry it.") So now we had an orange nylon wind sock, which, by the time Geof looked up and saw it on this night of increasing cold and wind, was completely filled with air and sticking straight out to the south like a fat orange erection, meaning there was probably one cold sucker of a storm on its way down from Nova Scotia.

He looked up at it and felt a pang of regret that he hadn't given me one of those damn quaint iron directionals, if that's what I'd really wanted. He lowered his gaze from it—the wind was already biting the outside edges of his eyes—and stared at the open maw of the garage. He'd opened and closed it twice since he'd found me, working with excruciating care, not wanting to take the chance of screwing up even the slightest bit of evidence that might have adhered to the door, to its handle, to the rope that manually pulled it down, or even to the cement floor where the intruder would have stepped inside. He had dusted for fingerprints, photographing and then lifting what he found on the pertinent surfaces. He had slipped those to a friend on the force who would run them through the computer for comparison with Geof's own fingerprints and mine, which they already had on file (but those are other stories).

So far he'd found nothing substantial, no sign, no spoor.

He figured the bastard had worn gloves. It was winter, after all. The temperature the previous night had been 17 degrees Fahrenheit, with a wind chill factor of minus one.

Now, looking into the dark garage, he regretted that he hadn't fixed my door opener the first day I'd mentioned it to him. He'd known it wasn't the sort of thing I would ever manage to get done for myself, he'd known that if it was ever going to work again, he'd have to be the one to replace the batteries. He knew that about me, that while I might change a light bulb at work two seconds after it expired, it might take me two months to change a bulb at home, where I was more relaxed—

to a fault—about my responsibilities. He had known that about me, and still had procrastinated. All perfectly normal and natural and human. Only now he hated himself for it.

The driveway was so dark, so empty, so lonely.

Jesus, he berated himself, why didn't I ever install spotlights that Jenny could activate as she drove up? Or fix them so they'd come on automatically at twilight, and stay on until one of us turned them off?

Why was I satisfied with locks and bolts on the house and not with an alarm system on the whole goddamned property? he furiously demanded of himself. *Why didn't my wife, a cop's wife for Christ's sake, have a two-way radio in her car, an alarm of some kind, a way to reach me if she needed me . . .*

He thought of his wife driving up here by herself at night, and his heart turned over in his chest. Why hadn't he ever realized how isolated and vulnerable she'd be? Why had he ever bought this goddamned lonely outpost of a place? Why didn't he just take her and put her out in the Klondike somewhere, like some goddamned gold miner's wife, and leave her exposed to the elements and to whatever evil passed by, while he went off with his gun and his badge and the security of his height and his strength, like some goddamned Canadian Mountie . . .

He was unforgiving of himself.

Until he heard the sound of his wife's voice inside his head. She was laughing at him, and saying, "Oh, knock it off."

The guilt that had been tearing at his breastbone like a serrated knife every time he breathed, dulled a little. Geof smiled to himself. But it was a close-lipped smile. He didn't want that cold wind on his teeth.

He walked up to the garage.

It had become important to him to know whether the intruder had arrived before me or had followed me home. If the former, then the intruder would have had to hide and wait somewhere, either in the garage itself or in his own car, which would have been hidden somewhere, probably close by, on the grounds.

For this search, he switched on his flashlight.

Again, he walked our yard around the garage, still searching for some sign that a vehicle had parked there. But there was no broken grass, no faint track in the frozen dirt, no freshly broken gravel that Geof could detect, no oil or antifreeze drippings, no easy, overt sign. By the time he abandoned that search, Geof was glad to enter the comparative shelter of the garage. It wasn't warm, but at least he was out of the wind.

He switched on the overhead light, but, since it didn't reveal every corner, he kept his flashlight on, as well. Where could a person hide in this garage? Behind the lawn mower? Behind the snow blower? Behind the empty gasoline can? There was no place to hide here. None at all, none, none, goddamned none. Not on the cement floor, not in the ceiling, not on the walls, not in a window well. No place to run, no place to hide.

If there'd been somebody waiting inside here, Jenny would have seen them in her headlights, he thought. But if there'd been a car hiding behind the garage, he wouldn't necessarily have found any track of it.

Had he followed her home?

Wouldn't she have noticed headlights or an engine?

Not if the headlights were turned off, she wouldn't. And she wouldn't have heard anything if she had her windows rolled up and the radio turned on. Although it hadn't been turned to "on" when he found her. She'd been singing at the top of her lungs, she'd said. Idiot. He smiled at the thought of it.

Maybe the bastard waited at the turnoff long enough for her to drive a ways up the gravel road. Then turned in, his headlights off, keeping his foot off the brake, maybe driving in second gear. Or maybe he only drove partway up the drive, hid his car off the road there, and walked the rest of the way. But that would have been taking the chance that Geof might have come home and caught his car—and him—dead in Geof's headlights.

No, Geof thought, he had to have preceded her.

Parked outside, somewhere beyond her vision.

Silently got out of his car.

Quietly closed his door. Or he'd already unscrewed his interior lightbulb so it wouldn't shine if he left his door open.

Walked toward the garage, avoiding the gravel, keeping to the dirt.

Sneaked into the garage, where Jenny sat in her car.

No. That wouldn't work. Couldn't logically work.

She'd have looked up. Moved. Fought. Struggled. Run away. But when he, Geof, had found here, she was lazily slumped over her steering wheel, her hands limp beside her, her hair falling neatly to the sides of her face. Nothing mussed. Nothing awry. Just Jenny, fallen gently forward to sleep.

Oh, shit, he was forgetting the beer.

She could have fallen asleep with the engine running. Must have, in fact. And so maybe the bastard walked in on her, saw an opportunity, and took it.

Or . . .

When the last idea came to Geof, he felt as if the wind from Nova Scotia had whipped into the garage and snaked into his clothes, chilling him all over, turning him to gooseflesh.

"Jesus," he whispered. "He could have been in the car."

The bastard could have ridden home with her, could have been in the car with her all along, lying on the floor of the back seat.

No, because then how would he get away from here? Maybe somebody else drove after him and picked him up. No, that was getting pretty complicated and the more complicated it got, the more unlikely it felt.

Feeling frustrated and impotent, Geof walked back out of the garage and glared at the sky: "Come on. Give me an answer. Give me something."

He glanced over at the cottage, where we always left enough lights burning to fool almost anybody into thinking we were home. The front door knocker, a brass seashell that had been a housewarming/Christmas gift from my sister, gleamed dully under the scudding clouds. It was pretentious, according to our taste, but we had felt we almost had to put it up. He glanced away from it, and then looked back again, puzzled. Was he seeing an optical illusion? He walked toward the circle drive in front of our house and then up our front walk. He hadn't used this door since the morning he'd come home to find me prostrate in bed, and he knew I couldn't have used it at any time past Tuesday morning. And anyway, we wouldn't have knocked at our own front door.

And yet the brass door knocker, stiff in its newness, was half lifted off its base, as if in mid-knock. He knew that if you didn't push it down, it wouldn't fall into place of its own weight, because it was still too new, too resistent. Somebody had knocked at this front door, recently.

He backed away and then carefully made his way back down the walk to the circle drive. He hadn't previously paid much attention to this part of the property, because he had assumed the would-be murderer would have tried to hide his presence at the house. It had not occurred to him, before this moment, that the person might have parked out in the open, and maybe even have openly knocked at the front door. Geof ran his flashlight beam over the expanse of gravel driveway that lay before him, and almost immediately picked up in the beam a glimmer of plastic. He moved closer to find it was a cup, the kind that comes with coffee or tea that drops out of vending machines, and just the kind of detritus that falls unnoticed out of cars when their doors are opened.

He walked, restraining himself from running, back the length of the long road to get his car—with its evidence envelopes and fingerprinting kit—but his heart was pounding with the surge of adrenaline that always accompanied a break in any murder case. A plastic cup and a lifted knocker weren't much. But maybe they'd lead somewhere, to someone.

When he finished with his camel-hair brush, his dusting powder, camera, and tape, Geof put on the gloves he kept in his pocket but seldom wore, and returned one last time to our garage. By then, fully frustrated by the awkwardness of having to perform evidence-gathering that he wasn't used to doing, his feeling of euphoria had disintegrated into hopelessness. He was cold, he was tired. He was pissed at everybody as he jerked open all the doors of my car.

He shone his flashlight inside, examining the floor carpet quarter inch by quarter inch, growing increasingly annoyed with me for the fact that I hadn't bothered to vacuum my car for what looked to him like the last six years. (Unfair—I'd only had the car a couple of years.) He found a few coins and gum wrappers, a week-old newspaper, folded in half, and a plastic rain hat. He found one mitten stuck down between the front seats. A plastic box for a cassette tape. A pencil that needed sharpening. A parking ticket, six weeks old. (Of course, that really frosted him.) He gathered them all in a sack and brought it all back to the hospital that night. Then he walked into my room . . .

And gave me hell.

14

"CHRIST, JENNY, HOW COULD YOU?"

Geof's fingers were trembling with anger and cold as he placed the brown paper bag in my lap. He held another, smaller brown bag in his other hand, but he kept hold of that one. At first he stood over my bed, looming large, and then he paced up and down in front of me, coming as close to yelling as you can in a hospital room without bringing a nurse on the run. He'd awakened me, none too gently, and then he'd exploded.

"I told you to take a cab! Hell, if I'd known you were going to drive, I'd have dropped everything and picked you up. Why the *hell* did you drive when you *knew* you'd had too much to drink?" (It didn't seem like the best time to mention the Valium.) "How could you just blithely drive home, knowing you were loaded, knowing you could wreck the car, maybe kill yourself or somebody else? Were you sleepwalking? What in God's name were you thinking of to—"

"I guess I wasn't thinking."

"That's pretty damned obvious!"

"I was very tired, Geof."

"I don't give a shit if you were asleep on your feet, you were an *idiot* to—"

"I made a mistake, Geof. I'm sorry. There were extenuating circumstances. You know what my life has been like in the past week, you *know*. I was exhausted. I wasn't thinking straight, I probably wasn't even walking straight. The booze affected my judgment. That's what booze does! I didn't realize what bad shape I was in. I'm sorry I was careless. But you have to stop yelling at me. You have to stop yelling at me!"

His jaw was so tight it looked wired shut.

He walked over and threw himself into the chair beside my bed. But he wasn't through with me.

"It's goddamned freezing outside. I parked the car by the highway and I walked the whole length of our drive and I stood there outside our garage and I tried to figure out how it happened. How come, if he followed you, I couldn't find any place for him to hide? How come, if he got there first, I couldn't find any sign that he'd been there? The damned wind sock was sticking straight out, the wind was blowing so hard I thought my ears would freeze and drop off my head." He held out his red, raw fingers for me to see. "It was cold, Jenny. I'm still cold. If somebody hadn't already tried to kill you, I think I might do it myself. Christ, how could you be so *stupid?*"

I knew what this was all about. It was about love and anxiety and guilt over something as small as not changing a battery in a garage door opener. But even understanding him, I didn't see any reason why I had to take this. Just because your two-year-old loves you, doesn't mean you have to laugh it off when he throws his blocks at you.

"Don't talk to me like that," I said.

He looked up, saw in my face what I felt, and deflated a bit. He let his breath out. He bent his head, and rubbed his poor, raw hands on his jeans. When he looked up again he appeared just slightly embarrassed.

"Not for any reason," I said. "Not ever."

"I'm sorry."

"Believe me, I am, too." I indicated the brown paper bag he'd dumped on my lap. "What's this?"

Instead of answering me, he opened the mouth of the smaller brown bag and held it forward for me to look inside. "What's *this?*"

"A brown plastic coffee cup with a white rim?"

"I found it on the gravel in our circle drive. Could it be yours?"

"I don't see how. Looks like one of those cups that comes out of those vending machines you find in company lunchrooms. You know? The kind where the cup comes down and then hot water comes out of one spigot and instant coffee comes out of another? We don't have anything like that in our building."

"Do you have any idea who might have come to visit us since yesterday morning? Somebody who would park in the circle and walk up to the front door and use the brass knocker?"

"No. You know as well as I do that we get very few Fuller Brush men out there. Are you telling me that's what this person did who tried to kill me? He had himself a cup of coffee, and then he just strolled up to the front door?"

Geof shrugged. "The knocker was pushed partway up, and this cup was in the drive." He pushed himself up from the chair. "Don't open the other bag yet." He strode toward the door, saying, "I'll be right back."

I sat on the bed, staring at the bag, until he returned—carrying a long box of aluminum foil. "A nurse found it for me in their lunchroom," he said, as he began to roll out a long span of foil, which he tore off. "Lift up the bag." After I did, he spread the sheet of foil on my lap on top of the blanket. "I'm leaving, but I want you to *carefully* empty that bag onto this foil. Don't let any of it fall on the bedcovers or onto the floor."

"What's in here, Geof?"

"The contents of your front and back seats."

He made a face, as if he'd just touched old bubble gum left on the underside of a table.

"No editorial comments, please," I said.

"Don't touch any of it. Identify everything you can. Is it yours? Have you ever seen it before? Where'd it come from and how long has it been there—a week, ten days, three generations, since the last Ice Age—"

"Ahem."

"Then wrap it all up inside the foil and put it back into the bag without touching anything but the foil. Can you do that?"

I widened my eyes. "Gee, I don't know, Lieutenant, it may be beyond my simple powers of—"

He leaned very close to me, until I could smell orange Life Saver on his breath, and he said in his most threatening cop's voice, "Do not give me any crap, Jennifer Lynn. I am the one who is going back out into the fucking cold again. You are staying behind in this nice warm bed. I deserve for you to be especially nice to me. If you so much as say one smartass thing, I will tell the first nurse I see that the patient in room 1242 needs an enema."

"That's coercion," I said.

He leaned even closer, and kissed the top of my head. "Well, just don't say you haven't been advised of your rights."

"That's your version of the Miranda Warning?"

Geof pointed a finger at me as he turned to leave the room, taking the smaller bag with him. "*You* have the right to remain silent. There'll be somebody outside this room to watch out for you. Goodnight."

It wasn't actually all that easy to funnel the contents of the bag onto the foot-wide strip of foil that Geof had spread on top of me. A few coins fell out first, followed by a pencil that wanted to roll over my legs. I stopped it in the nick of time by raising my knees to make a valley of the blanket and foil. One by one the other items tumbled out, with the exception of the folded newspaper, and I managed to keep it all off the bed covers. If any of this was evidence, I knew that Geof didn't want my blanket or clothing fibers mixing with it to confuse the lab technicians.

Then I set about trying to identify the stuff.

I was delighted to see the mitten, a black one with metallic silver weaving, that matched a twin in the pocket of one of my coats at home. So that's where the little sucker had gone, fallen down between the seats, most likely.

The coins added up to forty-six cents and although I couldn't really identify them as mine I guessed they had probably bounced out of the console tray where I kept loose change for bridge tolls and for buying coffee at drive-through restaurants.

There was a plastic rain hat—one of those ugly transparent jobs that's pleated to fit into a little pack and that has ties for fastening under your chin. (The kind you can never find when it's raining and you just had your hair done, but which you're most likely to be wearing when you run into an old boyfriend you haven't seen in sixteen years.) I recognized it as the one I'd frantically searched my purse for one night when the heavens opened just as I was about to get out of my car to meet Geof at the theater.

The plastic cassette box was probably the one that held the Joni Mitchell tape that was probably still inserted into my car's tape player. I hummed a few bars of "Carey" ("you're a mean old daddy, but I love you"), as I considered the lineage of the pencil that needed sharpening, the newspaper folded in half, the gum wrappers and the . . .

Oops, an overdue parking ticket.

I hoped Geof hadn't noticed the date on it. Cop's spouses are supposed to be more law-abiding than I was about parking tickets. He found it annoying to get an inter-office memo informing him that there was going to be a warrant put out for the arrest of Jennifer L. Cain if Ms. Cain didn't pay her latest ticket within the next ten days. The reason he found it annoying was that he usually went in and paid it himself, rather than trust me to do it on time.

The newspaper was probably mine. Couldn't prove it, but it probably was. I tended to take the morning paper to the car with me so that if I should get stuck somewhere in my car that day with nothing to read—God forbid—I could pull out the paper and read Sam Hayes's latest editorial fulminations.

The pencil? Could be mine, maybe not.

The gum wrappers, from sugarless bubble gum, were definitely not mine. They were definitely my nephew Ian's, from those alternate Wednesdays when I drove him to soccer practice with two of his chomping, smacking, bubble-blowing buddies. I'd get them for this, those ungrateful little brats, for daring to leave a mess of paper and foil in the back seat of my immaculate car. And I knew just how I'd punish all three of them: I'd make them chew with their mouths closed. Oh, shit, what was today? Wednesday? My turn to drive? *Darn it, yes, I'm sorry, Ian.* I glanced over at the potted plant that looked as if it had come from the produce section of a grocery store: *Is that why you're neglecting me, Sherry, because I missed car pool?*

So that was it. Evidence examined. Most of it (fairly) positively identified, everything but the pencil. I stared at it, thinking what an unlikely "clue" it was. I mean, how threatening is a killer who leaves the stub of a yellow No. 2 pencil behind?

Suddenly I felt as if ice water had dribbled across my shoulders. I hunched violently forward with the chill of it, nearly spilling my treasures out onto the blanket. My hands went ice-cold, too, and my feet and the end of my nose, as if somebody had opened a window, letting in a blast of frigid air. I was shaking so that I could barely manage to fold up the "evidence" inside the foil and then place it all back in the paper bag.

I dropped the bag onto the floor beside my bed.

And then I used the button to lower my bed to a prone position and I crawled deep inside the covers with only the top of my head—my eyes and my forehead and hair—showing. I lay under there and shivered with the worst fear I'd ever experienced. I felt like an earthquake victim who had lived through the worst, main shock, only to feel terrorized by the mild aftershocks that recalled memories of the big one.

He'd been waiting for me.

Maybe even by the time I left The Buoy.

While I drove. While I sang idiotic songs to myself. While I traveled further and further from the lights of the city, while I entered the dark, two-lane blacktop highway, while I drove and drove, my headlights picking up the bare trees at the sides of the road, meeting other cars coming in the opposite direction, and none of those drivers knowing that I needed help, that there was somebody waiting for me who wanted to hurt me, who wanted to kill me, who waited until I was inside the garage, who walked in quietly and pulled the garage door down by the rope, with his hands . . .

I stuck the blanket and sheet and my own fist into my mouth and screamed and screamed, a thin, high little shriek that nobody else could hear, screaming, screaming as I would have screamed that night if I'd known what he was trying to do to me.

All the fear I didn't feel then, I felt now.

Oh, God, I almost died, somebody almost killed me.

Into my hospital sheet, my blanket, my fist, I screamed and screamed and screamed, until my throat shrieked with pain and my eyes felt as if they were dammed with backed-up tears, and then the screams turned to sobs and I cried and cried for myself, for a lot of people, for a lot of reasons, for a long time. The only comfort I felt was that my horror was final proof that I would never have tried to kill myself, because I wanted too much to live.

Finally, I fell asleep.

When I woke up in the morning, I felt cold, and clear, and awake. And I knew that the evidence that Geof sought was not lying on the tinfoil on the floor beside my hospital bed. But it should have been. It should have been there. The Port Frederick Fisheries annual report. That I had picked up and started to read before I fell asleep. The report that had shocked me with its revelation that Downeast Marine, Inc., whose president was Cecil Greenstreet, was a wholly owned subsidiary of PFF, whose chairman was Peter Falwell.

The first thing I did that last morning in the hospital—before going to the bathroom, before brushing my teeth, before eating breakfast—

was to phone my husband at home and ask him to pick up a copy of the PFF annual report before he came to get me.

"Please bring those black slacks of my mother's, too," I requested. "And her black turtleneck. And see if you can find any black loafers in my closet, I think I've got an old pair that are presentable. I'll need some thin socks, and you'll find those in the third drawer in my dresser. Oh, and look for a hair-holder-backer in my drawer in the bathroom, will you?"

"A what?"

"You know, those fat fabric things I use to tie my hair back sometimes. Get the red one if you can. Um, and something gold for earrings, in my jewelry box."

I was going home.

"Did you bring it?" I asked Geof when he arrived.

He held out a small suitcase containing, I presumed, the clothes I had requested, but that wasn't what I meant.

"No, I mean the annual report."

"It's in the car."

Geof was dressed more casually—in jeans, waffle stompers, and blue plaid lumberjack shirt—than he would have been if he'd been going in to work that day. I hoped none of his fellow (or sister) officers saw him, because apart from looking tired, he sure didn't look like anybody with a "roaring case of the flu."

It only took me about three minutes to dress. I'd already showered and washed my hair, in an attempt to scrub off the hospital smell, and done my makeup. (After a two-day stay in the hospital is no time to go cold turkey on blusher.) While I tied back my hair, Geof placed the flowers I had received on a metal cart he had borrowed for the purpose.

"Ready?" he inquired.

"Yeah."

I glanced around, checking to make sure I hadn't forgotten anything, and then preceded him out of the room. The "flower lady" with the real flower cart was making her deliveries to patients on my wing, and she stopped me as I came out the door.

"Hello," she said, brightly. "Are you 1242?"

"I was," I said.

"Um." She bent over to read the outside of a little white envelope propped against a long-necked vase which held a single white carnation, and then she peered up at me again. She had white hair and a gray uniform in about a size 16, and I was reminded of a chubby little silver squirrel that sometimes dug for acorns in our yard. "Jennifer Cain?"

"I am."

Still am, thank God.

"Oh, good, I'm glad I caught you." She tried to hand me the vase with one hand and the envelope with the other. "This is for you."

I started to reach for it automatically, but then paused, as my mind raced to catch up with my hand before it could grasp the vase. A single flower. Odd. And a carnation at that, the bargain basement of florist's choices. A *white* carnation. Like those in the floral arrangement that was sent anonymously to my mother's funeral. I heard myself give an almost imperceptible gasp, and I drew my hand back as if from a spider.

I looked back at Geof, who was already removing a white cotton handkerchief from his pants pocket. Under the curious eye of the flower lady, he managed to take both the vase and the card from her with his hand that held the handkerchief.

"Thank you," he said, when she seemed inclined to linger, but then when she started to roll her cart away, he said, "No, wait." She looked back at him, then at me, her left eyebrow raised inquisitively. Geof said, "Did you see anybody put this on your cart?"

She shook her white head, no.

"Would you mind waiting another minute, please?" He set the vase on the floor and, using his handkerchief, opened the card. After reading it, he looked up at her again. "There's no florist's logo on this card or on the envelope. Do you have any idea who could have put this on the cart?"

"Nooo," she said, drawing the vowel out, as if she wanted to give this crazy young man the answer he needed, but she didn't know how to do it. "This cart just stands against the wall in the lobby and the florists' delivery people come in and place their deliveries on it, and then we—the volunteers—come by at our scheduled time and take the flowers around to the rooms." She glanced at me. "Is there anything wrong?"

"No." Geof said it for me, and then smiled reassuringly at her. "Not a thing. It's just that there's no name on this card, and I'd like to know who to thank. That's all."

Her glance dropped to the handkerchief that separated his fingers from the card and envelope, but she nodded and then quickly pushed her cart on down the hall, away from us.

"Probably thinks we're germ freaks," I said, when she was out of hearing. "Let me see the card, Geof."

He turned it so that I could read the typing on it:

LIVE FOR TODAY.

"What the hell?" I said, angrily. "What the hell's that supposed to mean—"

"Jenny—"

"—live for today because tomorrow I'll die? Or live for today and stop nosing into the past? Damn them! Whoever! It's a good thing you're holding that thing, because I'd tear it to pieces and then I'd hurl that goddamn vase against the wall!"

As if to forestall any such unwise and precipitous action on my part, he quickly bent over to retrieve the vase, and started back into my room with it.

"What are you *doing,* Geof?"

He glanced back at me. "Calm down. I'm only going to empty the water out, and find something to put all of this in, so I don't have to carry it out of here in my handkerchief."

"Calm down!" I muttered sarcastically to his back, "Sure, right. Calm fucking *down,* Jenny!"

I was ready to give him hell when he came back out, but he forestalled me. "I'm sorry," he said, "I shouldn't have said that. Sometimes I forget you're not a cop."

That mollified me, by making me laugh a little.

He held my gold plastic vomit pan in his hands, and the vase, flower, envelope, and card lay inside it.

"Nicely symbolic," I said. "And it lends verisimilitude to your claim that you're the one with the flu. Let's go pay the bill. I'm tired, and I want to go home."

15

BUT FIRST GEOF HAD TO CARRY HIS STRANGE PACKAGE AROUND the lobby of the hospital, inquiring whether anybody had seen someone come in with it or place it on the flower cart. He asked the volunteers at the information desk, he asked patients in wheelchairs and their family members seated on benches, he asked the waitresses and the hostess in the coffee shop that had a view of the flower cart, he asked a couple of doctors passing by. But nobody could help us. The hospital was too busy, the lobby was too crowded, and everybody there had their own personal concerns that were much more pressing to them than any question about floral deliveries.

And then, before we headed home, we had to sit in his BMW, in the hospital parking lot, letting the cold car warm up while we studied the Port Frederick Fisheries annual report. My sister's potted plant leaned against my right pants leg, on the floor of the car.

"Here it is." I handed the booklet to him, and pointed. "Here's where it says that Downeast Marine is a wholly owned subsidiary of PFF. That means that Cecil Greenstreet is, in effect, an employee of Peter Falwell. Does that strike you as suspiciously coincidental?"

"What are you thinking, Jenny?"

"That Greenstreet colluded with Pete to wreck my father's business, so that PFF could buy it cheap, and that this was his reward," I said, bluntly. "Now you play the devil's advocate. Tell me where I'm wrong."

He thought a moment before saying, "Experienced canning company executives are probably not exactly a dime a dozen in this world. Maybe Pete saw the opportunity to hire one, and so he did. Moving from vice president of one canning company to the presidency of another seems like a pretty natural corporate climb, doesn't it?"

"Yes," I admitted, "it does, but then why in the world did Greenstreet deny knowing Pete Falwell?"

"He did?"

"He told me he didn't know Pete, yes. But Pete told me that he's known Greenstreet for years."

I related for him as much of my conversations with the two men as I could recall. Geof thumbed his fingers on the steering wheel before saying, "The devil ain't got no advocate for that one, Jenny."

As he started the car, I paged through the rest of the report, starting at the back and ending at the list of directors at the front, and there I found several familiar, local names, including my dear old trustee Jack Fenton, who was also the chairman of the board of First City Bank, and Samuel Hayes, Jr., publisher of *The Port Frederick Times* newspaper.

Once the car was moving, I stopped reading, so I wouldn't get carsick. If I didn't throw up again for another fifty years, it would be too soon. But I kept my thumb in the page with the names of the men on the PFF board of directors, and I mused, for several blocks, about their presence there.

The storm that Geof had expected to blow down from Nova Scotia had not materialized, but there was a pretty, glittery frosting of ice on the trees, bushes, and dead grass. The streets were dry, having already been warmed and melted by the traffic, so they were passable. The temperature was in the low 20s, but the wind was still blowing about twelve miles an hour from the north, so it seemed much colder to me than the temperature gauges indicated, especially after leaving the hothouse warmth of the hospital.

I looked at my watch: 10 A.M.

"Geof? I don't want to go home yet. I want to stop by the newspaper to talk to Sam Hayes, Jr."

"What about?"

"I've been reading the articles that *The Times* published about the bankruptcy, and I'm puzzled about them. When Cain's failed, we were the biggest employer in town, and so it must have been the worst economic disaster to hit this area since the death of the whaling industry. But *The Times* covered it as if it were about as important as a Saturday garage sale."

"Do you know why?"

"No, that's what I want to ask Sam."

"You sure you're up to this?"

"No," I confessed, "but what the heck, if I faint in Sam's office, it'll just be more grist for the local gossip mill."

"It's good of your family to supply so much of it."

I reached over and hit his arm.

"Sorry," he laughed. "Speaking of fishy situations, what killed the whaling industry?"

I groaned. We shared an embarrassing habit of committing puns that were so terrible they ought to be illegal. "Somebody discovered oil in Pennsylvania."

My family had not been whalers. Neither had they been part of the "Codfish Aristocracy"—like the Cabots and the Lowells—those fantastically rich New England families who had fattened on the "China Trade," with merchant ships that opened new lanes to the Orient after America's traditional sea commerce was killed off by the Revolutionary War. We Cains sailed along later, after whale blubber was no longer needed for lighting lamps, and we'd made our relatively modest fortune on the shells of mollusks instead of the backs of whales. I recall this, not as a point of pride, but as a point of fact: which was that my father didn't have Pennsylvania to blame. Only pollution and the EPA and the cost of tin. But now I wondered, as Geof made a right turn leading to the newspaper, instead of a left turn leading home: Was it possible that my dad had somebody much closer to blame, somebody whom he might even have called a friend? Or maybe even *friends?* It was a sickening idea, especially considering how subserviently grateful I'd been to some of those friends—my esteemed employers—for my job at the foundation.

Geof turned in between two vertical parking lines out in front of the newspaper building. "I'm going in with you," he announced. "I'll sit in the lobby." I didn't feel it was necessary to ask why he, a most independent cuss, suddenly wanted to stick so close to me. I started to get out of the car, but he stopped me by putting a hand on my arm. "Listen," he said, catching my glance and holding it. "There's something you should know. I don't really think you're in any immediate danger. It wasn't premeditated, that's what I want you to know. I've been thinking about it a lot, and I've decided that it couldn't have been premeditated, it wasn't even possible for it to be. For it to be premeditated, he'd have to have known about the dead battery in your garage door opener.

I think it was a crime of opportunity, and I think he's horrified at what he almost did, and he's lying low, praying nobody will ever discover anything that leads us to him."

"Still," I said, although I was mighty happy to hear his professional opinion of my safety, "he had to have some reason—"

"Yes, and that's what we're after."

"—and, Geof, he still *has* that reason—"

"But right now, he's paralyzed with fear—"

I laughed a little. "Like me?"

Geof squeezed my shoulder. "I understand. But I'm telling you that he's paralyzed with terror at what he nearly did to you and what that could have resulted in for him. He's picturing himself in prison. He's seeing himself being executed. The needle. The gas. The chair. He's imagining himself behind bars, probably being beaten and raped by other prisoners. His fantasies are running away with him, and he's scared shitless. While it's true that we're not going to take any chances for a while, neither is he. If you want to, you can picture him trembling and panting and hiding under a chair—"

I faked a cower. "Like me."

"—like a cat being chased by a dog."

Oddly enough, I found that homely little image convincing. I smiled at Geof and reached across the car to kiss him. "Thank you."

As I got out of the car, and then as we forced our way through the bitter wind, up the salt-scattered concrete steps to the newspaper office —I felt perfectly safe. Except, that is, for that creepy suspicion you tend to get, after somebody has tried to kill you, that there's a rifle with a high-powered scope leveled at the center of your back at all times. Or, as the bad old joke goes, "Apart from that, Mrs. Lincoln, how was the play?"

"One more thing," Geof said, putting a hand on my arm before I opened the door to *The Times.* My skin crawled involuntarily, and I fought the urge to step fully in front of him, in order to hide my back from view. "I guess I ought to say this, too. When he recovers from the immediate terror, he's going to realize that he got away with it. He'll feel unbelievable relief. He won't want to tempt fate by calling any attention to himself. So he won't make any other attempts, unless—"

"Ah, there would be an unless."

"Unless his relief turns into a feeling of invincibility. That could happen. Or unless another opportunity presents itself. If I'm right that

137

it was strictly a crime of opportunity, then opportunity is the key. And we don't want to hand him that key."

"But we don't know—"

He pulled me to him for an instant, and pressed me into the warmth and protection of his own body, just as I had wanted to do for myself. "I know, honey. Since we don't know who he is, and we don't know where you might encounter him, we don't know what might constitute an opportunity for him, and what wouldn't. We'll try to be careful, that's all we can do until either he makes a mistake or we get smart."

"Or lucky."

I slipped quickly, regretfully, from his embrace into the shelter of the building.

Samuel Hayes, Jr., the owner, editor, and publisher of *The Port Frederick Times* newspaper, had one of those offices that seemed to me to be tailor-made for paranoids and exhibitionists: From floor to ceiling, it was glass on three sides. Never ones to waste a penny on amenities, the Hayes family had supplied themselves and their staff with strictly utilitarian gray metal desks and plain swivel typing chairs. The file cabinets were the same green metal ones that his father's reporters and advertising staff had used, and some of the telephones were still dial models. I'd once had a good friend on the reporting staff, but Lewis Riss had gone on to bigger and better things, which, no reflection on Lew, wasn't too hard to do when you started out at *The Port Frederick Times.*

"I was sorry to hear of your misfortune, Jenny."

"Thank you, Sam."

He flicked a glance over my shoulder, where I knew he could see my husband seated in the modest little lobby. Sam, Jr., was the picture of old-fashioned propriety in his trademark suspenders and bow tie. On this day, the suspenders were black and the tie was red. When Sam blinked, behind his wire-rimmed glasses, it was an oddly slow and deliberate-looking movement, like an owl. Hard to believe this 1890s-looking man was younger than me. As I studied him, puzzling over how the same generation of parents could have produced the two of us, he said, "We had to run something about it, of course, but we tried to keep it vague."

"I appreciate that, Sam."

"You saw the article? We mentioned the fact that earlier that day you quit your job at the foundation."

"No, I didn't see it."

"Oh. Would you care to make a statement about that?"

"What? About quitting my job?"

"Well, yes, and about—uh, the other."

"The other" was a euphemism, I gathered, for trying to kill oneself.

"Okay, here's my statement." I cleared my throat, and sat up straighter. "I have enjoyed my years at the foundation. I am grateful to the trustees for the faith they have shown in me during all of those years. I believe they can look forward to many years of excellent service to the community under the stewardship of the woman I hope they will select as their new director, my former assistant, Faye Basil."

Sam looked sour around the mouth, as if my "statement" was far too bland and inoffensive to sell any papers. Before he could interject any questions whose answers might get me into trouble, I said, "As to the . . . *other* . . . it was an accident, Sam. I was tired and fell asleep in my car before I turned off the ignition. Fortunately, my husband arrived home in time to rescue me. It was a close call, and I feel lucky to be alive."

Geof and I had agreed that was the story we would spread, and that we'd be safe in doing it because all the police were saying publicly was that it was "accidental." It would be better, we thought, if the person who had tried to kill me could be led to believe that nobody was looking for him, because nobody suspected the truth.

Sam appeared to be sucking on a sour cherry ball, but except for a hard glance up from his notes, he didn't try to challenge me.

"Sam?" I shifted my weight, and the subject. "The reason I want to see you has nothing to do with any of this. I've been studying the articles that appeared around the time of our bankruptcy, and I'm baffled by them. Can you explain them to me?"

He cocked his head, looking more owl-like than ever.

"You may not remember those stories—that was way back when you were still in high school with Sherry—but I'll tell you that this paper covered those events as if they were less important than the high-school football games. And I'm wondering, Sam, what sort of grade that coverage would have received in journalism school." I gave him a nice, bland, inoffensive little smile. "I think maybe it would have been an F. For failure to fully investigate and report, for failure to properly place it on the front pages where it surely belonged, for failure to take an editorial stand on the events of enormous magnitude that were happening in this town."

"Now, Jenny, that was my father's—"

"I know it was, Sam, and that's why I can talk so frankly to you, since it wasn't your responsibility." I gave him another nice, bland, inoffensive little smile. "Let me explain why I think this coverage was so—if you'll pardon the expression—piss-poor. Cain Clams was the town's major employer, right?"

He nodded, with apparent reluctance.

"And it was going belly-up, right?"

Again, he had to nod in agreement.

"But what kind of coverage did the town receive from the only newspaper in town? A fistful of little bitty stories, that's what, and most of them in the business section. This story should have been trumpeted all over the front pages, Sam. There should have been interviews with the principals, there should have been frequent and lengthy analysis of exactly what was happening to the business." I shook my head, in real bewilderment. "This was the most pitiful coverage of a major civic event that I've ever read. If your reporters turned in stories like that—if PFF were going under today, for instance—you'd fire their asses."

I took a perverse pleasure in saying crude things to Sam. Like his father before him, he regularly used his editorial page to inveigh against "creeping vulgarization" in the arts. His editorial against the exhibit at the New East Gallery alone had set a whole new standard for advocating censorship. But I knew that, like his father before him, he had a mouth as foul as Richard Nixon's when he was alone with the boys. (This I knew from various other "boys" in town, including my own Geof, who played racquetball in the court next to him.)

"Jenny, I can hardly defend an editorial policy that existed when I wasn't even involved with the paper," Sam protested. "And I must say that I don't understand your attitude. I would think you would feel grateful that my father *did* keep the story on the back pages, and that he *didn't* turn it into major, front-page news."

"Why didn't he, Sam?"

"It wouldn't have been good for the town," he said, in tones that implied, *you dumbshit.* "Better to downplay these things, better to accentuate the positive, get the town back on its feet as soon as possible."

"Wouldn't have been good for which part of town, Sam? Not the part that depended on Cain Clams for their livelihood. They needed to know what was going on, they deserved to know, it seems to me. So who was it good for?"

"I don't know," Sam said, defensively. "I wasn't here."

"You're on the board of PFF, right?"

He looked puzzled, wary, at this apparent change of topic, but he said, drawing out the word reluctantly, "Yes."

"Did you inherit that position from your father?"

He chewed on that question for a moment, obviously looking for some trap beneath it. The trap was there, all right, but I didn't think he had sufficient moral principles to see it. Any journalist who would serve on the board of any entity on which he might have to report was not worth the parchment in his J-School degree. Finally, Sam said, "I guess you might say so, yes."

I smiled at him. "So, your father was probably a member of the board of directors of Port Frederick Fisheries at the same time that Cain Clams was going under and PFF was buying the plant, is that right?"

"I guess. What's the point of this, Jenny?"

Sam was not only unprincipled, he was stupid, I decided. With him in charge, it was no wonder we had such pitiful local news coverage.

"Was there some sort of cover-up, Sam?"

"A cover-up of what, for God's sake?"

"Of the truth about what was going on at Cain Clams, Sam."

"I resent that! On behalf of my father, I really, really resent that, Jenny!"

I was really, really impressed by his vehemence.

"Do you remember anything your father said about it at the time?"

"No, no I don't!"

"And you wouldn't tell me if you did, Sam?"

And then I suddenly realized: Why should he? Why should he tell me anything? It wasn't Sam who was stupid, it was I. I'd handled him all wrong, ruffling his owl-feathers and putting him needlessly on the defensive about his father. And all because I didn't like his tie? I searched for the motivation for my blind aggression toward this man. It was because . . . because I didn't like *him* . . . because . . . because . . . . I was still ticked off about my mother's obituary? *Great, Jenny,* I thought with self-disgust, *so you insult his father to get even because he insulted your mother.* Self-awareness is a wonderful thing: It allows you to realize in humiliating detail exactly how you have made a complete ass of yourself.

141

"Sam, I'm sorry, it wasn't your doing—"

I started to get up to leave. There was no need for me to stick around the newspaper any longer that day; I'd gotten the one piece of information I'd sought—which was that his father had been on the board of directors of PFF at the crucial time, thus providing a motive for a journalistic cover-up—but basically, I'd blown it.

"Jenny?" Sam leaned forward on his arms, and stared at me with his slow-blinking gaze. "What do you think *you're* doing? It was over, years ago. A lot of people have helped you and your family through those times and in the years afterward, and you ought to be grateful, instead of accusing us of covering things up. You'd better stop whatever it is you think you're doing, or you might end up hurting some of the very people who've helped you the most. You'll certainly hurt yourself and your family." He smiled, his eyes as cold as an owl with a mouse in sight. "And frankly, right now I don't think your reputation can stand any more damage, do you? Everybody knows you quit your job because Pete Falwell tried to hold you to your responsibilities and you couldn't handle it. You folded. And if you think anybody's buying that accidental asphyxiation story, you're crazier than your mother ever was. In this city, at this moment, your word's about as reliable as a two-week weather forecast. You say anything to disparage my father or any of the other fine businessmen in this town, and you know what the reaction's going to be? That you're crazy. Flipped out. Bonkers. You want to know what your word is worth on the open market in this town, on this day, Jenny? It ain't worth shit."

I stood up. "May I quote you on that, Sam?"

"I could print all that, Jenny. And don't think I have to have anything as bothersome as the truth to do it. A little article here, an editorial there, that's all it takes to ruin somebody." A hint of self-knowledge and maybe even self-hatred showed for a second in his eyes. "Believe me, I know how to do it. I took lessons from my father, who was a master at it. Maybe you're right, maybe he did that to your dad. Print a little something incriminating here, don't print a little something exonerating there. A little bit of the truth, a little less than the truth. Story placement. Type size. It all adds up to an impression, Jenny, an image made, a reputation ruined. And before it's over, Jimmy Cain—or somebody else—is o-u-t out, a has-been, a nonentity, which, in my opinion, is exactly what your father is best suited to be. So if my dad did have a hand in your father's downfall, I'm not going to cry about it, or apologize for it. Your dad didn't deserve to run that business. He wasn't smart enough. He never could have turned it into what it has become under PFF and Pete Falwell."

I made an educated guess:

"Your family owns stock in PFF, does it, Sam?"

"Yes we do, goddammit, and so do a lot of other good people in this town who are plenty happy that things turned out the way they did."

"I guess that doesn't include our former employees."

"They found other jobs, big deal. Listen, you go causing any more inconvenience to my friends, let me tell you right now that I will kill you in print. I will paste you to the pages of my newspaper so tight that for the rest of your life you won't be able to peel off the things I write about you."

He leaned back in his chair, and tapped a pencil on the arm of it, appearing suddenly to feign nonchalance. "You're fucked, Jenny."

For once in my life, I had no smart reply. I turned and left his office with my face burning and my hands shaking. In the lobby, Geof asked me what was wrong, but I grabbed his arm and forced him out the door with me. Once outside, where the frigid air cooled my cheeks, I turned and said to him, "Even if we catch the person who tried to kill me, there will always be some people in this town who refuse to believe it, won't there? People who think the police are covering up to protect your wife, or people who want to believe the worst, or people who never hear the truth."

"Jenny—"

"What do I do now, Geof? Every time somebody looks at me, I'll be wondering if they know who I am, do they think I'm crazy, do they think I tried to kill myself? What a funny thing a reputation is," I said with a self-mocking laugh, "you don't even know you have one—and God knows, you don't know how much you value it—until you lose it."

"What in the world happened in there, Jenny?"

"I'll tell you on the way to the bank. I want to see my dear old family friend—" I felt my mouth twisting in bitterness. "—Jack Fenton."

143

16

"HOW ARE YOU, JACK?"

The old gentleman sat with me on a sofa in his office, leaning onto his carved walnut, brass-headed cane. He nodded, as if to say, "Okay," but it was obvious that he wasn't okay at all. His lean, aristocratic-looking face was nearly as pale as the white between the navy blue stripes of his beautiful shirt, which he wore with a navy blue silk tie and a dark blue suit with the thinnest, most elegant of red pinstripes. The nattiness of Jack's attire contrasted painfully with the inelegant beads of sweat I saw on his upper lip and forehead. The problem was arthritis: His proud posture was curling in upon itself with the pain and crippling of rheumatoid arthritis. For the last year, I had watched in dismay at board meetings as Jack grew more quiet and participated less in our debates, which had once been enlivened by his quick wit and steadied by his innate good sense. Jack Fenton was my compassionate capitalist on the board, but lately, as he withdrew increasingly into himself, I had counted on him less frequently for the supporting voice or the deciding vote that came down on my side of an issue. He'd been a dear family friend and financial advisor for many years, as well, and now seated so near to him, I was having a hard time remembering my anger. Of all of "my" old men, I had expected Jack to age the most gracefully, because that was how he had moved through his life. But he'd fooled me, damn him. I missed Jack Fenton, banker and wit, and he wasn't even dead yet.

"I'm more concerned with how you feel, Jenny," he said, in a voice that sounded like any old man's, and not at all like his resonant, familiar one.

I had closed his door behind me after I gained admittance to his office, leaving Geof out in the lobby again, but this time he was using the time to place a few phone calls to a couple of pals at the police department.

I recalled that I was looking at a man who thought I had tried to kill myself.

"You've quite upset us," he continued in the quavery voice that lacked its previous cynical edge and authority. "Miss Grant is simply heart-stricken, as you may well imagine. Roy Leland is furious at Pete for refusing to grant your leave of absence. And I do believe you have aged Edwin Ottilini and me a good ten years that neither of us can afford to give up." He took a breath, and shifted his weight, as if it hurt him. "But I must tell you, and this may surprise you, Jenny, that of all of the trustees, Pete Falwell is taking this especially hard. I do know, Jenny, and I know this direct from Pete, himself, that you quit when he claimed that he wouldn't release you from your contract. You must know it was only a bluff. He never dreamed you would call his hand. Pete realizes, belatedly, how stubborn and wrongheaded of him it was, and he feels a painful and acute personal responsibility for what you have done." It seemed to me that Jack laid a rather heavy emphasis on those last three words. "If you really want to know how I feel, Jennifer Lynn Cain, I will tell you the truth." I was shocked to see tears come to Jack's blue eyes, and I reached out impulsively to place my hands on top of his. "I feel quite shattered by this suicide attempt of yours. Quite shattered."

He sagged on his cane, looking ill and precariously balanced, even seated. I quickly moved closer to him, put one of my arms around him, and took both of his hands in my other hand. It was an act of intimacy I never would have attempted before this, so great was his natural dignity. But age and attempted murder had bridged our emotional reserves, so that I felt compelled to embrace this old man who appeared to care so much about my well-being. I was suddenly furious at the person who had tried to kill me and who, in so doing, had also caused pain to people I loved. And yes, I discovered at that instant, I did love them, and they were still innocent of any damage to my family until proven otherwise.

"Will you help me, Jack?"

He blinked away the wetness in his eyes. "Of course. Tell me how."

"You can tell me the truth, old friend."

145

He looked genuinely puzzled. "When have I ever not?"

"Never," I assured him, hoping it was true. I shifted away from him again, so that he could regain his dignity and I could see his face. "But this time, it's about the failure of my father's business. I want to ask you some uncomfortable questions, and what I hope is that you're going to feel so sorry for me that you'll give me the whole truth and nothing but the truth."

He must have noted a glint of humor in my eyes, because he cocked a white eyebrow at me, and he leaned forward on his cane, clearly intrigued by the turn of our conversation. He said, "The straight scoop, as my grandchildren would say?"

"That's right, the straight scoop."

"Fire away, Jenny."

"All right." I took a breath, and ran my fingers along a seam in my mother's slacks before I looked up at him again. "Who provided the financing for the improvements that my dad made at the plant before it folded?"

"We did," Jack said promptly. "First City."

"Who was going to provide it for the new addition?"

"Several lending entities."

"Who was the major one?"

"We were."

"Compared to you, Jack, were any of the other lenders of any significance?"

"Not really; most of the money was coming from us."

"How was it secured?"

For the first time, he hesitated. "Well, it wasn't a loan so much as it was an extension of your father's line of credit."

I stared at him for a moment, before I said, "For how much?"

He sniffed, looked me in the eyes and said, "There wasn't any actual limit on it, although I suppose we tacitly assumed we'd go to two or three million before we cut him off."

"No limit?" I fought to keep my voice low and neutral, but some of the astonishment I was feeling crept into it. "And your loan committee just *assumed* . . ."

Jack sniffed again. His lower jaw was getting a bit stiff as he admitted these loose, to say the least, banking practices to me. "We had been doing business with Cain for a very long time, Jennifer. My father lent money to your grandfather, and my grandfather to your grandfather's

146

father. It was a relationship built on three generations of trust, my dear."

"My father is not my grandfather," I pointed out, dryly. "And even less is he my great-grandfather."

"I know that," Jack retorted sharply, "but he had never defaulted. We never had so much as a narrow miss on a loan with your dad. Cain Clams wasn't what you would call thriving under his stewardship, but it was maintaining a certain position well enough, in our view."

I was beginning to feel as outraged as I was astonished, and so I let him have it in a volley of distinctly rude interrogatories:

"I don't suppose my father or anybody else at Cain ever filled out any actual, official credit applications for the money, Jack?"

"We usually waive those for old customers—"

"How about credit and loan evaluations? Anybody at The First actually work on one of those? Or did you just take my father's word that he needed this new addition and sure, there'd be no problem paying for it?"

"We had no reason to doubt his word, Jennifer."

"So you're saying, no credit or loan evaluation?"

"I suppose not, not really."

"How about collateral?"

"All right. I am embarrassed to admit to you that part of the loan was secured, but part of it was not. We would have lost our shirt on that, but Port Frederick Fisheries assumed all liabilities as well as all assets when they took over, and Pete Falwell was meticulous about repaying all past debts."

"Were you on his board of directors then, too?"

Jack flushed. He opened his mouth, closed it, then opened it long enough to say, "Yes, I was, but—"

"So even after paying all of my dad's debts, Pete still made out like a bandit."

Jack smiled, grimly, his face still looking flushed. "I believe it is more commonly called doing good business, Jenny. Your father gambled and lost, Pete stepped in and won. It's done every day, and there's nothing invidious about it."

"Oh, no? What about the role of your bank in all of this? What about the fact that The First violated every tenet of good—and legal—banking practices by making unsecured loans, without proper application or evaluation? That's not invidious? I do believe it might be illegal—"

"Jenny, you know it's done every day all over the world—"

"And what about the fact that The First, by making the loans, in effect actually encouraged my father to overextend himself? What *do* you think is a bank's responsibility in all of this, Jack? You make the loan and one way or another you get your money back, plus who knows how much interest. You're free and clear. But my dad and my family go down the tubes, along with a lot of other families who worked for us. How's that for invidious?"

"You're being naive," he snapped.

"That's what Sam Hayes called me the other day," I said, with equal heat. "But I'll tell you something, Jack. Naive, I'm not. What I am is angry. *You* were naive. Or at least I hope that's what it was. Naive to trust my father. Naive to make loans that a simple evaluation should have shown to be in trouble from the start. And you were greedy, weren't you, my dear friend, because you must have suspected, all along, what the result could be. And there you sat, all along, on the board of the company that would buy our company when the inevitable happened. Your bank risked, at the very least, censure. And that brings up a point, Jack; why wasn't there any federal banking investigation of these loan practices?"

"There was," he said. "It was quiet; we were fined; that's all there was to it."

"And you still made money on the deal?"

"Yes." This time he merely sighed, and said, wryly, "Yes, we made money on the deal, as you put it."

"Why wasn't any of this in *The Times?*"

"Any of what?"

"Your bank's role as major lender to the project. The banking investigation, the judgment and fines?"

"Why should there be? Sam Hayes—senior, that is—determined that it was a matter of rather arcane banking procedure that would not interest the average local newspaper reader."

"My lord." I stared at him in disbelief. "And the next thing you're going to tell me is that he was also on the board of directors of this bank."

"Well, yes, although now it's Sam, Jr."

"Jack," I said, then I spread my hands pleadingly. "Jack!"

I followed his glance, which settled on his hands. They were trembling slightly on top of his cane. I said, with a sort of hopeless-sounding laugh, to his bent head, "Jack, Jack, and you call yourself a Democrat?"

His head came up, his neck remained stiff. I was not going to reach him on this, he was too far entrenched in custom and pride and the old-boy network. "It is standard operating procedure, Jenny. We did nothing that any other bank might not have done in similar circumstances. I accept no responsibility for your father's bankruptcy, because that responsibility is not mine. It is his, totally his. You do him and yourself no favor by trying to push it off onto innocent parties—"

"Innocent!"

"Yes, innocent parties."

"I thought your bank got fined."

He blinked and, for a moment, seemed to falter in his stout defense of his morally indefensible position. But then he rallied. "A slap on the hand."

"Meaning, I gather, that the practice of encouraging people to assume debt loads that are greater than they can possibly afford is a mere minor flaw in the system?"

"A system that has worked well for generations."

"Generations, yes. But well? Perhaps yes for the bank owners. Perhaps no for the overextended debtor who got that way because the banks made too much money too easy to get? Hmm?"

We glared at one another. Then, using his cane, Jack suddenly pushed himself back into the sofa, and gave a dry, quavery hoot of laughter. "I'd say you are feeling fine, Jennifer. To think I worried for a minute about you. Suicide! You! Impossible. How could I ever have thought it? Besides, they'd never let you into heaven—you'd try to argue St. Peter out of his 'discriminatory admission policies'!"

I found myself laughing, too. Here was a man who had sprinkled money in my father's path, dancing him down the road to ruin, if you will. Here was a situation that probably represented, in microcosm, many of the ills of the world's banking system. Here was a man, decent, likable, and well-respected, who probably represented the best and the worst of traditional bankers, and who couldn't, or wouldn't, acknowledge his quite direct role in the debacle. Jack Fenton had, with open eyes and open palms, willingly cooperated in the events that led to the bankruptcy of Cain Clams. He was close to eighty years old now. Was I going to change him? I wasn't. It was too late for Cain Clams anyway

. . . but what about the others who came later, unwisely looking for money they'd never be able to repay—

"Jack, do you evaluate all loan applications now?"

He nodded, smiling a little. "Yes, yes, it will please you to know that as a direct result of your father's bankruptcy, we had to tighten our loan policies, even for longtime customers."

"Well," I said, "at least there's that."

But he gave me the old cynical eye. "Won't last."

I sighed, tacitly acknowledging the truth of what he was saying. What could I do? I hated the system, I hated what it had done to my family, but I had loved this old man for too many years to suddenly start hating him now. It was time to let him off the hook, emotionally, even if he didn't deserve it: "You're right, Jack. I didn't try to kill myself. It was an accident."

I rejoined Geof in the lobby, only to find him still on the phone, a pay phone. "I'm listening to our messages on the machine at home," he explained. "A lot of people have called, asking about you, including your sister. She sounds pissed."

"How can you tell?" I asked.

He smiled, and held up one finger as a polite way of telling me to shut up. After a minute, during what must have been a long, boring, inconsequential message from somebody, he said, "I had a friend of mine run Cecil Greenstreet through the computer, but we came up empty on any sort of police record. I suspected we would, but I had to ask. I also called Chart's Flowers, but they didn't send over the carnation. So I started calling every other florist in town, but so far no luck—" He broke off, to listen more closely. "Your sister, again." He started to grin, and then broke out laughing. "Oh shit, those little devils—"

"What?" I demanded. "Who?"

He held up that infuriating finger again, so that he could hear the remaining messages, and then he hung up. He was still grinning, as he grabbed my elbow and started walking me rapidly out the door of the First City Bank. "Come on!"

"Where are we going? I'm tired, Geof. I really do want to go home this time."

"We will," he said, and started chuckling again. "But on the way we have to stop by the Harbor Lights Funeral Home. It seems that the reason Sherry is so mad at you—and me—is that our niece and nephew have developed this strange little habit of collecting obituaries from the newspaper."

"What?"

"And today she found out from a friend of Ian's that he and Heather plan to attend a funeral this afternoon at Harbor Lights. And of course, Sherry says you and I are to blame for this macabre little habit of theirs, and she's ready to kill us and to haul them off to a psychiatrist. And she wants us to go get them and straighten them out, because she's too mortified to do it herself." He looked down at my astonished face and chided me. "Oh, come on, Jenny. You can figure it out. One guess."

The light dawned as I looked at his grin—and recalled two other impish little grins in the doorway of the kitchen at Sherry's house. They'd been eavesdropping, those two little twits, and now—

"They're playing detective, Geof!"

"Bingo," he said.

17

THERE WERE TWO FUNERALS BEING CONDUCTED IN DIFFER-
ent "chapels" at the same time that afternoon at Harbor Lights, and we
couldn't be sure which one Ian and Heather would pick. We figured
they'd probably try to cover both. First we looked in the chapels themselves, to make sure the children hadn't already arrived and taken a
seat. They hadn't. So then we arranged ourselves as inconspicuously as
possible behind a ficus tree in the front lobby, Geof commenting that he
was spending a lot of time in Port Frederick lobbies on this day. And
then we waited. Luckily, the funerals weren't for anybody we knew, but
that didn't mean that we wouldn't know some of the people attending. I
stood behind Geof, so my blond hair wouldn't attract attention, and he
attempted to disguise himself as a leafy branch.

Mourners trickled in.

"Oh, God," I muttered, upon glimpsing an architect we both knew,
"there's Webster Helms. Quick, turn to me and pretend you're talking."
Geof turned his face toward me and began moving his mouth, with no
sound coming out. I put my hand over my own mouth to stifle a fit of
giggles.

The little, red-haired architect kept on moving down the corridor. We
watched him sign the guest book that lay on a pedestal in front of the
first chapel, and then he walked on in.

The children came in a few minutes later.

"Ohhh," I whispered. "Don't they look sweet?"

"Little shits," Geof whispered in reply, but he was smiling, too. Our
niece and nephew did look adorably nervous. They'd dressed in their
finest Sunday-go-to-meeting clothes, just as their mother would have

required them to do if she knew they were attending a funeral—which they didn't know she knew—and just as they'd dressed for their grandmother's service. Under her winter coat, Heather wore the same navy blue wool pinafore dress with big white polka dots, and her best navy blue flats with real, grown-up stockings, and a white bow tying back her blond hair. She even carried a little navy purse. Clutched it, actually. Ian had on his too-short suit, and his best shoes and socks; the only thing awry about his appearance was that his mother hadn't been around to comb his hair, which stuck out in cowlicks front and back. They walked close together, their eyes downcast, looking appropriately mournful for a funeral.

"Good little actors," I murmured.

"Little shits," Geof repeated, and I snorted with laughter, and prayed they wouldn't hear me and look over our way. They were distracted, however, by a funeral home employee who bent over to say something to them. They must have replied in some sort of acceptable manner, because he smiled in a sad, pleasant way, and allowed them to pass on by him. We watched, amused and fascinated, as the children scuttled over to a far wall and then stood there, huddled together, as if waiting for their parents to arrive. They watched everybody else file through. We watched them.

"Are they going to *do* anything?" I whispered.

Geof shrugged. I pressed myself against his back, enjoying the excuse to get physical. He pressed backward against me, also appearing to enjoy it.

And we waited.

And across the hall, Heather and Ian waited.

And the last of the visitors filed in through the front door, and the funeral home employee walked toward the first chapel and quietly closed its double doors so that the service could begin. Then he walked to the doors of the second chapel, and closed those. And then he disappeared into another door marked, "Employees Only."

Heather and Ian glanced at each other and then they broke and ran. Ian to the first chapel! Heather to the second chapel! Ian grabbed the guest book off the first pedestal! Heather swept the guest book off the second pedestal! Ian raced back for the front door! Heather ran after him, catching up to him, blond hair flying out behind her! They were neck and neck as they drew abreast of the ficus plant, when Geof stepped out in front of it, and said quietly:

"Stop in the name of the law!"

"Uncle Geof!" cried Heather, and stopped in her tracks.

"Oh shit!" said little Ian, and broke for the front door.

Geof caught up with Ian at the bottom of the front walk, and hauled him back to where Heather and I stood shivering on the porch of the funeral home. I took the guest books out of their cold hands and quickly returned them to their pedestals before anybody noticed they were missing. And then I rejoined the cop and the culprits outside on the porch.

Now it was Heather who looked defiant, and Ian who looked terrified at the possible implications (five years of being grounded?) of what they had done.

"We were only trying to help," Heather protested. Her lips were blue, and she stomped her feet up and down to keep warm. "We were only going to look at them, and then we were going to return them!"

"I'm sorry, Uncle Geof," Ian said, in a pitifully small voice. He stuffed his hands in his pockets and danced up and down beside his sister. "I'm sorry, Aunt Jenny. I'm really sorry. Aren't you really sorry, Heather? We're really sorry. We didn't do it. I mean, we didn't mean to do it. It was an accident. Can we go now? It's really cold!"

Geof and I looked at each other and laughed.

The children saw it, glanced at each other, and then looked hopefully back up at us. Maybe we wouldn't kill them, they were thinking. Maybe Uncle Geof wouldn't toss them in jail and throw away the key. Maybe Aunt Jenny wouldn't tell their mother and father and maybe they wouldn't really be confined to their rooms until they were dead. Maybe they were going to live!

"Were you going to . . . examine . . . the signatures?" I asked them.

Heather stopped stamping her feet long enough to nod her head. "We were gonna see if anybody signed anything weird like they did at Grandma's funeral."

Geof said, "Have you done this before?"

"No!" they cried in unison.

"Honest," Ian added, and crossed his heart as he danced around us, creating little drafts of even colder air.

"How'd you get here?" I asked. They were far too young to drive and it was several miles from their home. "Hold still for a minute!"

"Taxi," Heather admitted. "We used our allowances and we walked to a friend of Ian's house and called a taxi from there. It was easy."

Ian broke into a grin. "It was fun!"

Geof shook his head, trying to hold on to a grave expression. "Listen up, junior detectives. It's nice of you to want to help, but I think the grown-ups can handle it from here on out. Are we agreed on that?"

They looked solemn, and even stood still for a moment as they nodded their heads.

"Promise?" I said. "Swear it on a stack of Bibles?"

They nodded again, but I wasn't convinced.

"Swear it on a stack of Star Trek comic books?"

They giggled, but they nodded vigorously that time.

I bit my lip, to maintain the seriousness of their pledge, and it was then that I became aware that Heather wasn't quite holding my gaze. Geof's, yes, but not mine. She'd look at me, and then her blue eyes would seem to cloud over and her glance would shift away from me. And suddenly I realized what was going on. If she'd been younger, littler, I'd have crouched down on my haunches and taken hold of her arms and looked up into her blue eyes. As tall as she was now, I could only put my right hand behind her head and turn her face to me.

"Heather?" I said. "Did you hear what happened to me?"

Her gaze slid away again, and Ian grew positively frozen with silence. I asked her, gently, "What did you hear, honey?"

She drew a shaky breath. "Mom said you got sick. But—" Her voice grew shakier, and she still wouldn't look at me. "But some kids at school said—"

"I'll bet they said that your aunt tried to kill herself. Right? Well, listen to me, both of you. It isn't true. I am fine. I am one hundred percent, positively, absolutely fine. I am a walking advertisement for mental health." (Lord, I hoped it was true.) "I will tell you both exactly what happened so that you won't have to wonder about it. Very few people know all of the details, but I want you to know everything that I know." (Almost.) "You know how you've always heard that drugs and alcohol don't mix? That they can be deadly?" (I couldn't resist the aunty urge to sermonize.) "Well, I went to the doctor's the other day and he gave me some vitamins and his nurse gave some pills to help me relax. And later on I went to The Buoy and I had some beer, and I took one of those relaxing pills by mistake, thinking I was taking a vitamin. And the combination of the drug and the alcohol made me fall asleep in the car after I got into our garage. And the garage door came down and shut me into the garage, asleep, with the engine still running. And that's how it happened. It *was* dangerous, and it *was* a close call, but your uncle got there in time to save me." I smiled up at him. "My hero." (Why was he frowning, and looking down in such a puzzled fashion at me?) "And I'm really glad he did. I love life. I love both of you! Do you really think I'd kill myself? I would never *ever* do that to you! Never! And besides, I can't die yet. I haven't put it in my will that I want Ian Guthrie to have my lifetime supply of sugarless bubble gum and that I want Heather Guthrie to have my earrings." I tugged at the lock of her hair that hung below her navy bow. "Do you want my earrings?"

"Yes!" she said, and smiled up at me, and then she added, shyly, sweetly, "But not real soon."

I bent down and kissed her forehead. "I promise."

"Aunt Jenny?" said Ian. "Do you really have a lifetime supply of bubble gum?"

"Yes!" I reached behind Heather to punch her brother's arm. *"Used* bubble gum! On the floor of my car! I'm sorry I missed soccer practice yesterday, kid."

"That's okay," he said, and grinned.

"Come on, junior detectives." Geof placed his hands on their shoulders, but he was still looking at me with that curious expression on his face. He opened his mouth as if he were going to say something, but then he glanced down at the children and seemed to change his mind. "Let's go get a soda, and I'll tell you some gory stories from the cop shop."

Their faces lit up—partly from anticipation of their uncle's always-exciting police stories, partly from the knowledge that they could probably hit him up for hamburgers and a banana split to share, and partly from an awareness that they were getting off easy, at least until they got home and faced their parents—but I smiled away the offer.

"You go on," I said, and then I added, in answer to Geof's inquisitive stare, "There's something I need to do while I'm here, so I'm going back in. Why don't you come back and pick me up after you take them home?"

"You have to do something *here,* Jenny?"

I nodded, and gave him a look over the children's heads.

"Francie may be here," I explained to him. "She works in the office part-time."

Geof nodded in understanding, and said, only half joking, "My advice is to grab a wreath out of one of the chapels. Take the flowers with you as a peace offering."

I knew from previous experience that behind that door marked "Employees Only"—the door through which the funeral greeter had disappeared—lay a warren of administrative offices. Though I was acquainted with the owners and some of the employees, I hoped to be able to avoid everybody but Francie, as I just wasn't up to having any more confrontations that day, even if they were sympathetic and friendly. I wondered, with no little nervousness, how Francie would greet me this time.

I needn't have worried on either score.

In the first place, when I popped into the women's restroom first, I found Francie Daniel there by herself. And in the second place, it had not occurred to me that by this time her sense of guilt would so far exceed my own as to eclipse it altogether.

"Francie?" I said, tentatively, upon seeing her by the sink.

Even as she met my gaze in the mirror, tears began to roll down her cheeks. "Oh, Jenny." She ran to me, and pulled me into a fierce embrace. "Oh, Jenny, I can't tell you how sorry I am. I'm just so very sorry."

It took me a moment to grasp her meaning. During that moment, she mistook my silence for anger. "Oh, honey, Duke and I feel so guilty. You came to us asking for help. And we turned you away. Oh, Jenny, I think it's the most unforgivable thing I've ever done." My face was getting wet just from being pressed so close to hers. "If we'd only known how lonely you must have felt, and how desperate . . . to go home the very next night and to . . ."

Oh shit, I thought. Now I got it. Francie and Duke had heard that I'd tried to kill myself and now they were wallowing in guilt because they hadn't "saved" me. For a vengeful, petty moment, I was tempted to let her wallow. Then my conscience kicked in. Or maybe it was my mother's voice again: Here was this poor woman who'd never been anything but kind and compassionate to my family, who stood by my mother when nearly everybody else fled, and who always was the soul of goodwill to me. And she let me down once, just once, just one measly time in

157

all of those years, and I couldn't find it in my rock of a heart to forgive her? *Nice, Jenny,* I thought as I reached up with my free hand to touch her soft, wet cheek. My other hand was still trapped in her embrace. *How wonderful that you've never made a mistake, yourself, or ever let a friend down. God, what a self-righteous little prig you are. How about thinking about somebody else for a change?*

I forced both of my arms around her and hugged her back.

"It's not your fault, Francie—"

But she pushed me away from her, to hold me at arm's length and to continue without letting me get another word in. "If we'd only seen how desperate you were, we could have made you stay with us that night. We could have gotten help for you. Oh, and we would have, Jenny, we would! I realize now that if I'd told you the truth, maybe you would have been satisfied, maybe you would have found some of the peace you were looking for and you wouldn't have felt so desperate, but I didn't know! I thought it would be worse for you to know—"

"The truth?" I said. "What do you mean?"

I felt my body go rigid under her hands, and I thought: *If this is what it takes to get you to talk to me, Francie, then maybe you will have to wallow a while longer. I'm sorry, but you've got to talk to me, goddammit!* I pulled her over to a metal and leather couch under a window, between the sinks and the stalls, and I made her sit down beside me. I pulled tissues from my purse and dabbed at her face until she smiled a little at me. "Shh, shh," I murmured, "it's okay, it's going to be okay. Now. Tell me the truth about what, Francie?"

I hoped she wouldn't notice that my fingers were shaking.

She sniffed, gulped, blew her nose on the tissue I handed her.

And then she told me a story, never quite looking at me for more than a split second at a time while she told it, mostly looking at her lap, or into a tissue, or at the walls or the door, but hardly ever looking me straight in the eyes.

"It's about your mother," she said.

"Yes? It's okay, you can tell me, Francie."

"Maybe I should check with your doctor first—"

"Francie, please."

"All right. You know that she got so sick after she had her hysterectomy. Mentally, she just deteriorated. Well. Well, Jenny, that wasn't the first time your mother was ever hospitalized for mental illness." I stared at her, willing her to keep talking, and yet dreading every word that dropped from her mouth. "Or for emotional illness, or whatever you want to call it, I never know which, it's so confusing, it seems like one year they call it one thing, and then it's something else—"

"Francie," I said softly. I hid my shaking fingers under my purse, and caught my lower lip between my teeth to keep its quivering from being obvious to her. *If she doesn't tell me what she was going to tell me, if she doesn't get this over with soon,* I thought, *I'm going to hit her, I swear I'm going to hit her.*

She let out a breath, which seemed to relax her a little. "The first time was right after you were born." She shot a glance at me. Under my purse, my hands found each other and held on hard. "Of course, you wouldn't have known, you were just a tiny baby. But your mother got so . . . depressed, I guess. And she, well, she stopped caring for you, Jenny. She couldn't nurse, and she . . . well, she just got really sick and your father had to put her into the hospital. Hampshire. She was gone about a year, Jenny."

"A year?" I said in a whisper.

My first year of life? Without my mother? Even all those years later, I felt bereft and abandoned, knowing it to be ridiculous, but feeling it anyway. *Mother!* my child's heart cried out within me.

"And the next time," Francie continued, unaware of the awful turmoil she'd set off within me. "There were a few episodes after that, but the next really bad time didn't come until after your sister was born. Your mother wasn't gone so long this time. Only a few weeks, I think, maybe not even that."

I would have been two years old when Sherry was born. Did I remember anything about my mother being gone that time? I searched my memory, my feelings, but nothing came, no buried longing.

"Was it depression again?" I asked.

Francie let out another breath, and then looked down at her hands, which were tearing a tissue apart. Clearly, there was something more she had to tell me, something she really, really did not want to say to me. How to get her to release it?

I touched her hands, gently.

"Francie, you loved her through everything. And I'll always love her, too, no matter what happened, no matter what you tell me."

She took a sharp breath and then plunged into speech. "Your father said, he told me, I don't think he ever told anybody else, that she . . . oh God, Jenny . . . she may have tried . . . she was depressed, she was . . . well, Jenny, the thing is, he said your mother tried to hurt herself. And Sherry." Francie started talking very fast. "Sherry was a colicky baby, you see. Well, if you ever have children, you'll know that's the worst, I mean, that's just the worst you can endure, the baby cries all the time, just all the time, and oh, you feel so helpless and so annoyed and angry, and that makes you feel so guilty, and oh, gosh, you've just had the baby, and you're tired, so very tired, and you can't cope, even the strongest of people can't cope very well with a colicky baby, and your mother wasn't strong, she was . . . oh, Jenny, she was desperate, I think—"

Francie was crying again, and by then I was, too.

"Like you," she said, and clasped my hands in hers. "She was desperate like you. And I couldn't save her. And I didn't even try to save you, because I couldn't stand to see you become like her, I couldn't go through it again. And I didn't want you to know about her. I thought I owed that much to her. I wanted to protect you—and her memory— from that. But I was a coward. Duke and I both, we were such cowards. And now look at you, Jenny. Forgive me. Please, please forgive me."

I reached for her to embrace again.

"Yes," I whispered into her shoulder. As I grasped her I suddenly realized—with apparent irrelevance—that Francie was wearing a wool jumper over a Peter Pan blouse. The dress was tweed, rough and knobby to my touch. But there was something comforting about it, maybe it was just the sort of jumper I thought a mother should wear. And Francie's sensible shoes and her modest blouse and her comfortable, huggable, motherly body under her soft wool dress—it was all so damn motherly. So much like the way that my assistant, Faye Basil, dressed, I suddenly realized. And they even kind of looked alike, Francie and Faye. My two motherly friends and supporters. And then there was my old teacher, Miss Lucille Grant, so much older than they but also a sturdy, comfortable, steady kind of woman, who served me cookies and tea and who gave me good advice. Funny, I'd never put them all together in my mind before this. But then maybe I'd never before realized just how desperately I'd been looking—all my life?—for a mother.

Francie disentangled herself from me, gently, and got up and washed her face at the sink. As I watched her I thought of that other Francis— Father Francis Gower—and of his warning to me: Don't mess with other people's memories—they are none of your business. I had no memory of any of the events that Francie had just confided to me. But now I knew unforgettable, searing things that I had not known before, and would never have recalled on my own. Was I better off for knowing them? The priest had also said of my mother, "You might not even like the woman you find."

Well, now I knew, I'd finally filled in those blanks.

And now, how did I feel about her?

"Francie? What did you mean the other day when you said that people accused Mom and Dad of something? What was it?"

"Oh, it was so unfair, Jenny. Half the time they'd say he mismanaged the company. And then they'd turn around and say it was fraud. Some people thought that he took all the money and ran. I mean, it was so illogical, wasn't it? If he was too dumb to manage the company, how could he have been smart enough to commit fraud?"

"What about Mom? Where'd she come into it?"

"Oh, that was the part that was really so unfair, but they said, people said, that your mother could never have been kept in such a fancy private hospital otherwise."

"Yeah," I said, bitterly, "I guess she really scooped the cream off the top, didn't she?"

"There were so many rumors," Francie said, "mainly because there wasn't anything in the paper about it. Nobody really knew what was going on, so people just assumed the worst, and your parents took the brunt of it." She turned, and gave me a quick, guilty smile that was like a tic. "I don't know, Jenny, but what maybe your father deserved it." Francie turned back around to the mirror. "But I know your mother didn't."

Rumors. Which might have stopped if Sam Hayes's father, who had sat on the board of PFF, had investigated the truth, and printed it. Rumors. Which had probably helped to drive my dad out of town, and which had probably helped to put my mother away for the rest of her life. And Sam Hayes, Jr., had sat there and lectured me about how grateful I ought to be, and my own dear Jack Fenton had defended the "good business" practices that had greased our slide into disgrace. Rumors.

"I've got to go," Francie mumbled. "I've done my damage. Now I've got to get back to work."

I met her eyes in the mirror above the sink, and gave her the best smile I could manage. "Nothing's changed, Francie. Except that you've done me a wonderful favor, you've told me the truth, you've freed me from the pain of not knowing. I feel so much better."

"Oh, honey, do you, really?"

"Yes." She looked tremendously relieved, but of course I was lying. I'd never felt worse in my life. "And Francie, I didn't try to kill myself. I fell asleep in the car with the engine running, that's all. I'm sorry for the way I behaved at your house."

She seemed to believe me. She looked as if she wanted to believe me, and I realized there wasn't anything else I could do or say to make it so. Any more than I could fight the rumors that would probably dog me all of my life, just as they had my parents.

A little truth, I thought, might set us all free.

After she left the restroom, I put my head down on the seat she had vacated and drew my feet up onto the couch and rolled myself up into a ball. I immediately fell asleep. It was a form of shock, I figured out later. When the system overloads, the system shuts down. When Geof came frantically searching for me an hour later, it was Francie who found me for him, still asleep in the ladies' room.

18

IT GRADUALLY BECAME CLEAR TO ME THE NEXT MORNING, FROM the way Geof behaved, that he didn't know anything about what had transpired between Francie and me in the restroom of the Harbor Lights Funeral Home the day before. I knew I hadn't said anything about it, but I guess I assumed that Francie might have. Evidently still in the habit of keeping the secret, she had not.

"Well, hello," he greeted me, smiling from the bedroom doorway.

I turned my face to see the clock: Seven. I'd slept sixteen hours.

"I'd say you were still tired from the hospital," he observed, wryly. He asked me if I wanted breakfast and I nodded and mumbled something about "half an hour." My face was stiff, my tongue and lips didn't want to move, and my eyelids were gummed together. It was going to take me at least that long to creak my way out of bed, into the shower, into some clothes, and then downstairs.

"It's a good day to go to Boston," Geof declared, and then he disappeared from view. As I listened to the muffled tread of his steps on the stairs leading to the first floor, I thought: *Boston?*

We were driving to Boston to see Cecil Greenstreet, it turned out. It appeared that I had agreed to it the day before, and since that was entirely possible, I went along with the plan, asking only that we postpone it until after lunch, because I had a couple of other things to do first.

I didn't say much during breakfast—Kix cereal and coffee—but Geof seemed to accept that as a natural effect of so much sleep. And that much was true: My head was awakening more slowly than my limbs, and the connection between my brain and my mouth was the last one to fall into place.

While I put the dishes in the dishwasher, he answered a call on the portable phone in the kitchen. After saying, "hello," and listening to the person on the other end for a moment, he walked out of the kitchen with the phone, and I couldn't hear the rest of his end of the conversation. "Who was it?" I asked him, when he returned, and replaced the receiver in its cradle.

"It was the department."

"What did you tell them today, Geof?"

"I'm still sick with the flu."

"Do they believe it?"

"They can believe what they want. Did you find that new dish-washing powder I brought home?"

"Geof—"

"I forgot something upstairs. I'll meet you at the car."

It seemed that I wasn't the only one who had certain subjects he didn't want to discuss.

We agreed that I could probably stay safely in my sister's house without a bodyguard, particularly as Geof still felt confident of his theory that the attack on me was one of opportunity, and not of premeditation. So he drove me there, dropped me off, and arranged to pick me up before noon.

"Don't be too hard on her," he said, as I got out of his car.

I turned to him, surprised. "What do you mean?"

"You've been pissed about something all morning."

I nodded. "Maybe I'm looking for a target."

"You plan on saying things you may regret?"

I thought about that and then said, "Yes."

He didn't try to talk me out of it, which seemed to me a fine quality in a husband.

Sherry was definitely surprised to find me on her doorstep at eight-thirty in the morning. I'd timed it so the kids were already off to school and Lars was gone to work. And I just happened to know that her housekeeper didn't work on Fridays. I was taking a chance with Dad and Randy, but maybe I didn't really care if they overheard what I had to say. It turned out, however, that they were gone, too.

"Jenny?"

"Thank you, I think I will come in," I said, although she hadn't invited me, but only stood, looking dumbly agape, in her doorway. "Why yes, thanks, I'd love some coffee. Okay, we'll have it in the kitchen, that would be fine."

I strode past her into her entryway, and then kept walking, forcing her to follow my footsteps through her living room into her huge, modern, industrial-strength kitchen. I walked to her freezer, pulled out a bag of coffee beans, and then ground them and started them brewing in her fancy German coffee maker. I turned around to find Sherry seated at her own kitchen counter, looking nervous. And defensive. Well, a good defense deserves a good offense, I always say—

"The flowers were lovely," I said, talking fast, so she couldn't interrupt. "Small, but lovely. So nice of you to send them. And to identify yourselves so clearly on the card. I guess you thought I might have confused you with some other Guthries I know, my being in a befuddled mental state and all. Much too confused to entertain visitors while I was in the hospital, you must have thought, or of course you would have tried to visit me. Or phone me, other than to complain about my influence on your children, of course. Sorry about that. They only wanted to help their crazy aunt. So I guess you were only thinking of me, that's why you haven't come to see me. Or called to ask about me. Or made some fucking effort to find out how I am!"

I discovered I was shouting at her.

"Jenny—"

I just keep shouting.

"What's the matter with you, Sherry, that you could even think I might try to kill myself? How could you think that? I'm your sister! Don't you know me any better? Or didn't you care if it was true? Was it all too embarrassing, just simply, oh, my darling, just too, too mortifying for you, Sherry? How dreadful for you to have a sister whom others might accuse of trying to commit suicide. Never mind that I didn't do it, that I am constitutionally incapable of doing any such thing. Never mind me. Never mind that I was in the hospital puking my guts out, needing the love of my family—"

My voice broke on all of that self-righteous self-pity, which only infuriated me even more, so that I couldn't stop, but had to keep right on screaming at her, hoping the neighbors heard, hoping Sherry was "mortified" beyond bearing, hoping this hurt, hurt, hurt her in every way that it was possible for her to hurt—

"Do we embarrass you, Sherry? Crazy dead Mother? Loony Dad? Your cop brother-in-law? And me. What horrible crosses we are for you to bear. Poor, poor Sherry. Well, let me tell you who's dead. You are. You've got a dead heart, baby sister. And let me tell you who's crazy. You are, for giving a damn about everything that doesn't matter and for being too cowardly to place any value on the things that do matter." I walked over and leaned in her face and shouted at her. "Like your sister."

Sherry shoved me out of her face.

Literally, with both hands, physically shoved me.

I stumbled backward, caught myself, and then shoved her back. Hard, so her chair tipped and tumbled her sideways to her kitchen floor. She uttered a frightened, pained little scream as her shoulder and head struck the tile, but then she quickly scrambled to her feet and grabbed my arms and began to shake me. I broke loose from her and hauled back my right hand and hit her across the face as hard as I could. She gasped and fell again, crying, clutching her right cheek. And then she was on me, hitting my head and chest, kicking my legs, screaming wordlessly at me, and crying. And I was giving it back to her. We fought like heavy, desperate, furious, heartbroken, overage, out of shape wrestlers, until our clothes were torn and our skin bloodied and bruised, and until we were merely clinging violently to each other and sobbing.

Sherry whispered furiously, *"I hate her."*

"I do, too."

"She left us."

"Goddamn her!"

"And now we hate each other, too."

"Do we?" I breathed deeply, but it hurt.

Sherry drew away from me and stared at my face. We were panting like dogs. She actually managed a little smile. "God, this is really embarrassing."

I started to laugh. "Good old Sherry."

"Well, really." She pulled completely away and I could see that the full horror of what we'd just done was beginning to sink in on her. "Look at us, we're a mess. If anybody ever hears what we've—"

"Oh, well, they already think I'm crazy."

She gazed at me a moment. "I never did."

"Then why didn't you come to see me?"

"Because you are a disgrace and an embarrassment to me, always getting yourself into these disgusting predicaments involving violence and death. Frankly, if you weren't my sister, I wouldn't want any part of you."

"Sherry," I said, "we have to talk about Mom."

She bit her lower lip, tasted blood, grimaced. "I don't really hate her —do you?"

I shook my head, unable to speak. I felt, in fact, unspeakable.

"Just sometimes," Sherry added softly, like a little girl.

I nodded, still unable to get my voice to work. All I could think of was the baby that Sherry once had been, and what sadness had befallen her, had probably even formed her, and she didn't even know about it. And I, instead of feeling compassion for her, had hurt her, too—as if it were her fault, as if my mother would have gotten well and maybe never have gone away from me, if only Sherry had never been born.

My sister sighed and then did something that, for her, was remarkably brave. "Let's go upstairs and clean up," she said, "and then, let's talk."

We limped upstairs—both of us in pain from the blows we'd inflicted on one another—and we took showers, Sherry in her bath in the master bedroom and I in the children's bathroom. Then we both wrapped ourselves in matching white terry cloth robes that belonged to Sherry and Lars and we sat cross-legged on their king-sized bed. One of her eyes was turning black and blue and that cheek was red and swollen. Beneath the robe I wore, I felt bruises swelling and throbbing, but the bathroom mirror had shown me a face that was free of marks. In that regard, I was luckier than I deserved. Lord, why hadn't we done this when we were kids and tough enough to bear it? I ached in every tendon and surely she did, too. How would she ever explain that cheek to her bridge club? Fortunately, my sister did have a reputation for clutziness, so she just might get away with claiming that she'd banged into the edge of the dining room table. Again. It actually had happened once before. And what excuse would I devise for limping and groaning? Well, that was easy—everybody knew I was crazy, so maybe they'd just assume I had tried to beat myself to death.

Sitting there on the bed, with every appearance of sororal coziness, I

167

confided my discoveries that our mother had had a hysterectomy and that she had been institutionalized after our births. I didn't tell Sherry about Francie's claim that Mom had, evidently in a postpartum state of psychosis, tried to harm her. Maybe I was wrong, but I felt that was information nobody ever needed to know about her own mother. If Sherry ever wanted to go to a psychiatrist—and I doubted she ever would, she wasn't the type—or if she ever showed any sign of wanting to delve into her own psyche, then . . . maybe . . . if she really, truly, desperately seemed to need to know . . . everything . . . then I'd tell her. But for nothing less than that. In the meanwhile, it was plain that I'd given her enough shocks for one day.

"I didn't know anything about any of this, Jenny."

"Of course you didn't, how could you know? You were a child, and Mom wouldn't have wanted to frighten you, and it wouldn't have occurred to Dad to tell us anything. But Sherry, you must have been frightened anyway—"

She frowned. "I can't remember. And to tell you the truth, I don't think I want to remember."

"To tell you the truth, I don't blame you."

With her right forefinger, she traced the inner seam of her robe, saying, "Now that we know, what good does it do us?"

"I don't know."

She looked up. "Does it make us happier? It doesn't make me happier, Jenny. Does it finally satisfy you that you know truth, whatever that is? It doesn't satisfy me. That's something you'll never understand, will you? I don't care about the truth. It's bound to hurt. It does hurt. There isn't any satisfaction to be had for either of us, from any of this, ever. All there is is forgetting. And going on."

"You're good at that," I said, without bitterness.

"Better than you," she agreed, without malice.

"But you won't fight me if I keep trying to find, I don't know, happiness, satisfaction? I don't know what it is . . . whatever it is I'm after?"

"I don't even know what you're talking about." She smiled slightly. "But I don't care to *fight* you again, about anything. Once in a lifetime is enough, thank you."

We were silent for a few more moments.

"Did we get it all fought out?" I asked.

"No," she said, decisively. "I don't suppose we ever will. We don't even know what 'it' is."

"What's it all about—"

"Alfie?"

We smiled at each other, at the shared cultural reference to the movie from our childhood. But I was saddened to realize that it still wasn't the kind of smile that you share with your best, closest, bosom friend. There was still, even now, a distance to it, a coolness, an . . . unrelatedness, if you will . . . and that knowledge hurt me more than any of my bruises did. We would always be sisters, but for the first time I had to face up to the fact that we might never be friends. Tomorrow, I still might not like her very well, or she, me. Tomorrow, she'd be embarrassed again, mortified by the visible evidence of family discord. And between two women, at that. Hell, I was mortified, too, but only because of the implication of our lack of love.

"Where's Dad?" I inquired.

"At the club, playing golf."

I laughed. "My God, it's cold and it's March and it's the middle of the morning! It's not even 50 degrees outside!"

"He has his love to keep him warm."

"I wonder if Randy *likes* to play golf in any weather."

"You want to see them?" Sherry asked, surprising me with her perception. When I nodded, she surprised me even more. "I have some clothes you can wear. Come on, I'll help you get into them."

It struck me as a willing, friendly act on her part, although I couldn't help but protest. "Sherry, don't bother. I'll wear my own clothes, I don't need anything special."

She looked with disdain at the pile of my clothes that lay humped on her bedroom carpet—red sweater, blue jeans, socks, and Weejun loafers—and shook her head in mock exasperation. "Jenny, Jenny, Jenny, were you raised to go on a golf course looking like that? I'm ashamed of you. If you go dressed in jeans, Dad will be embarrassed in front of his friends and then he will spend the entire morning fretting about your clothes and telling you how *Randy* always knows exactly the right things to wear at all times, and how *Randy* wouldn't step up to a tee without golf shoes, the proper pants, and a pretty little golf sweater."

"There is wisdom in what you say," I admitted.

"Bet your ass." She swung her legs off the bed and limped over to her closet where she began pulling out ensembles for my appraisal and tossing them to me on the bed. "Leave it to me. I'll fix you up so even Nancy Lopez wouldn't be ashamed to putt with you."

"But Sherry, I'm not going to actually play golf. I'm only going to ride around in the cart with them."

"Right." She pulled a crimson velour jogging suit out on its hangar and threw it to me. "That's like saying you're not going to worship in church, you're only going to sit there. Makes no difference at all. You go to church on Sundays, you wear a dress and heels. You go to a golf course at the club, you wear golf shoes. You know I don't care what you wear—" (I didn't know that.) "—you can wear tennis shorts for all I care, but Dad will care, and that will make a difference as to whether or not he pays any attention to you."

"I guess I appreciate this," I said as a white jogging suit followed the crimson one in an arc to the bed. *Lordy,* I thought as I fingered the velour, *could it be possible that I was a shade melodramatic? Might I even have been wrong about my sister, and about the possibilities for us? Surely not, not I.*

"The red one," Sherry decided for me. "The white makes you look like you've been lying in a hospital bed."

I glanced up at her.

She was smiling at me. Slightly. But still.

"Oh dear," I said. "I forgot. Sherry, I don't have a car. Geof drove me here, and he won't be back for awhile."

She sighed, hugely, but I thought I detected a hint of mockery in it. "Okay, okay, I need to pay our club bill for this month anyway, I'll go to the office, and then maybe I'll sign the kids up for their spring tennis lessons while you find Dad."

19

AT THE COUNTRY CLUB GOLF SHOP, I WAITED FOR THE ASSIS-
tant golf pro to call out an electric golf cart for me. There wasn't a
whole lot of competition for them in the middle of March. In the sun,
the day felt pretty warm, but I was bundled into a lined trench coat
anyway, which took some of the snap out of Sherry's stylish suit and
her regulation cleated shoes. I'd had a few golf lessons as a girl—
enough to convince me that life wasn't long enough to spend it walking
eighteen holes—and I remembered feeling like Lyle Alzado in those
shoes. I still felt like a football player in them. (An exhibitionist football
player, considering the trench coat.) It didn't increase what little
aplomb I felt in regard to talking to my Dad and Randy.

The assistant pro said, "Mr. and Mrs. Cain ought to be at about the
fifteenth green by now." She was a tanned, big-shouldered, friendly
woman about my age. "They have the place to themselves this morning,
so they ought to be zipping through. Do you know how to find them?"

"Do you have a map?"

"Sure." She laid a little map on the counter between us and pointed
out the path winding around the course, which I hadn't been on in
probably twenty-five years. "Here we are. And here's the fifteenth hole.
They'll be in that vicinity, I expect. Your dad's wearing a plaid tam with
a big red puffball on top and Mrs. Cain is wearing a mink sweater."

I looked up at her. "To play golf?"

She remained poker-faced. "Well, it's chilly out."

"More like silly out," I said under my breath. She didn't charge me
any green fees, but I paid for the use of the cart by signing my dad's
name to the bill. "Thanks."

"You're welcome, Mrs. Bushfield."

"It's still Cain. Better yet, Jenny."

She smiled. "Thanks, but I can't do that. Club rules."

"Ah." It's the petty rules I most like to test, so I glanced at her name tag and said, "Thanks, Ms. Finney."

"Susan," she said, and grinned.

What a colossal pain in the ass I am sometimes, I reflected as I climbed into the golf cart and turned the switch to On. Or was I just practicing for what lay ahead? Maybe every astonishing thing that had happened so far this day was only groundwork for the fifteenth tee.

I shifted into gear and zipped off between two bare birch trees, down the narrow gray asphalt cart path, to Daddy.

"Yo! Pop!"

That was my first mistake. Never yell at a man as he tees off. He paused at the peak of his swing, his head jerked, his arms jerked, he swung down and topped the ball, sending it flying, about an inch off the grass, to the west. The hole was north.

"Damn it!" my father exclaimed, and threw his tam to the ground.

Randy alighted from their cart and stood waiting for me, her hands on her hips, her lips pursed in a showy display of pique. Her expression accused me of ruining his shot, which was the same as ruining his day, which wouldn't improve hers. Shame on me. I aimed my little cart in his direction, and rolled over the putting green on the 14th hole. That was my second mistake.

"Jenny, for heaven's sake!" Randy cried. "Don't drive on the putting green." Her tone implied: Don't you know *any*thing? She saved me from making a third mistake by calling, "And stay out of that sand trap!"

I managed to land my cart safely beside theirs, but I didn't get out.

My father was still at the tee, practicing the swing he'd missed.

"What in the world brings you out here, Jenny?" Randy asked. Not, Jenny, how are you? Or, Jenny, how wonderful to see you! Just, what in the world brings you—of all the unwelcome people—out here?

"It's an emergency, Randy," I told her, faking breathlessness. "I came to get Dad; I've got to get him back to the clubhouse right away. Can you bring your cart back alone?"

"What emergency? What's the matter?"

"Dad!"

172

That ruined another of his swings, but at least I got his full attention. I pressed on the pedal of my little cart and did a quick end run around Miranda. *"I'm coming, Dad!"*

Behind me, Randy came running, too, yelling, *"Wait!"*

I put the pedal to the metal and easily outraced her to the tee.

"Sorry, Dad. Get in! There's an emergency down at the clubhouse. They need you. I'll take you."

My father, who in his golf attire looked as handsome as Seve Ballesteres and as distinguished as Jack Nicklaus, said with almost pathetic hopefulness, "Really? They need me? Well, let's go then!" He called back to the running Randy over his shoulder, *"It's an emergency, dear! Follow us in!"*

In the seconds it took for her to race back to their cart, get in, switch it on, and start it moving, my father and I had vanished over the hill separating the fifteenth from the twelfth. I abducted him, wheeling into the woods off the twelfth instead of rolling back to the clubhouse.

What can I say? Dealing with them was, at the best of times, like walking onto the set of a slapstick movie. Unfortunately, it also made me feel like the comedienne dangling from the window ledge by a rope tied to her ankle. *Help. Somebody get me out of this.*

Dad didn't protest at any of this, he just went along for the ride, looking dashing as we scooted over hill and dale. As usual, he never paid any attention to where he was going until he got there, and even then you were never sure he had his bearings. Wherever he was, he was. That's about the most that could be said for him.

Where he was when I finally stopped the cart was at the furthest corner of the golf course, away from city streets and clubhouses, away from prying second wives and helpful golf pros. It was just my daddy and me, alone together under the old sycamore tree, in the brisk breeze of a cool March morning.

I switched off the cart and turned to face him.

"Dad," I began.

"I feel a bit hungry," he said. "Is it time for lunch?"

"Dad," I began again.

He came into focus. "Didn't you say there was an emergency, Jenny? Something on which they needed my help?"

"They're going to meet us here," I told him.

"Here?" His expression seemed to say: Where are we? Mars? Venus? Palm Desert? "What do they want me to do, do you suppose?"

"I don't know, but it's important, and they'll tell you all about it when they get here. Maybe something to do with greens rotting, or gophers digging new holes, or something. Dad?" I made a third try. When he continued to gaze pacifically into the trees, I plunged into my speech. "Dad, I have some questions for you and I really need specific answers. Here's the first question. Okay, Dad? Why didn't you tell us that Mom had a hysterectomy?"

He sighed and crossed his arms.

I waited. Nothing.

"Okay," I said, "then here's the second question. What happened to Mom after that operation? I mean, did she have pain, was she ill? What happened? Did that operation trigger the mental illness?"

He sighed, more heavily this time, and shook his head as if in silent negation at something in his own thoughts.

I touched his arm. "I know you're in there, Dad, just as I know you were with her when everything happened. Dad, I'm not trying to be hard on you, I'm not. I have more understanding now of what you must have endured with Mom. I've learned about the other bouts of mental illness, after I was born, and Sherry. It must have been awful for you, too." I wished I could stop talking to him as if he were a child. Short sentences. Easy words. But he was so hard to communicate with that he was like someone who spoke another language, and so I always felt I had to resort to the basics. I wished I could break that insulting habit now, but it was ingrained, and would he understand me any better, even if I did? I cringed at my own tone, which sounded to me like a kindergarten teacher talking to her slowest pupil. "I'm sorry we've been kind of hard on you sometimes. If you've been happy with Randy, well, then I'm happy for you, too. It's just that I still need to understand a little more about Mom. Can you tell me anything more, please?"

My father didn't say anything, but he reached over and took one of my hands. His own was trembling. He had his face turned away from me. When I leaned forward, trying to catch his eye, trying to turn him toward me, I was shocked to see that my father was crying.

"Dad—"

"I did everything wrong, Jennifer," he murmured, looking not at me, but at the tree to his right. "I'm awfully sorry."

I sat frozen for a little while, horrified at what I had done. *Are you happy now,* I asked myself, *now that you got your father to apologize for living?* I didn't press him to say more. I couldn't. Not ever, anymore. I would never, I swore, ask him about those days again. Gently, he withdrew his hand from mine. He pulled out his handkerchief, wiped his eyes and blew his nose.

"I'm sorry," I said.

"Mustn't be," he said, and patted my hand.

"I love you," I said.

My father folded his handkerchief back into a neat square and pushed it back down into his back pocket. "Can't imagine why," he said, and broke my heart. He cleared his throat and placed his hands on top of his knees, striking a posture of brisk resolve. "Well, I'm really getting very hungry. Do you suppose they've started serving lunch yet?"

I started the cart, and drove us back to the clubhouse.

And what excuse would I present to Randy for having kidnapped Dad?

Surprisingly, it was he who saved me.

"Miranda, dear," he said, climbing down from the cart and smiling sweetly at her, "it's all taken care of. The sprinkler system wasn't working correctly on the back nine, it was simply flooding the greens, and they had quite a nasty little swamp out there on the 18th, we would never have been able to play it anyway. I was able to give them the benefit of my experience with California golf course irrigation systems. I do think they quite appreciated it. Shall we go in to lunch, darling?" He turned to me, and, as usual, directed his question to the air over my left shoulder. "Will you join us, dear?"

"No, thank you, Dad."

Randy, who had been glaring thunderclouds at me, was all smiles now, as it appeared that I had vastly improved Jimmy's day, and thus, hers, too. I could tell that she had noticed his red-rimmed eyes, but I hoped that she'd attribute that to our wild and windy ride. The assistant golf pro had been listening, and looked baffled, but caught my warning glance, and kept her mouth shut.

When my stepmother walked toward the ladies locker room to freshen up before their lunch, I followed her.

"What was that all about, Jenny?"

"Oh, just as Dad said."

"Mmm."

"Randy?" She sat down on a pink tufted stool at a long vanity table, and I took the stool next to hers. "What did you mean the other day at

Sherry's house? When you said that Pete Falwell stole the company from Dad?"

She gave me an undecipherable look in the mirror as she applied fresh mascara, and then she took her time recapping the wand. Finally, she appeared to make up her mind about something. "Well, what do you think I meant, Jenny? Do you know where I worked before I went to work for Jimmy?" (I didn't know. It wasn't just that I was only seventeen at the time, but also that I had tried to ignore her existence in my father's life. Our lives.) "Well, I was the receptionist at PFF, that's where. Now I'm not saying I heard anything specific, I wouldn't want to accuse anybody of anything and get sued for libel—"

"Slander. Sorry. I'm sorry, please go on."

"But they wanted Cain Clams so bad they could taste it. Pete Falwell used to say Jimmy was a lousy businessman and he was going to run that company under if somebody didn't step in and save it. And lo and behold, what an amazing coincidence, doesn't it just turn out to be PFF who ends up owning everything?"

"Well, I don't know, Randy—"

"Well, I do know," she said, throwing the mascara wand into her purse. "Because when I went to work for your dad, they came to me for information—"

"What? Who did?"

"Mr. Peter Falwell and his people did, that's who. Wanted financial records and all sorts of papers I can't even remember what, wanted me to copy them or just plain steal them. And I said I wouldn't do it, you wouldn't catch me working with that greaseball Greenstreet, not for anything."

"Cecil Greenstreet? What do you mean—"

"I mean he was their man! Brought into this town by Pete Falwell, sent to apply for the job of vice president of Cain Clams, sent to sabotage your father's business, that's what I mean! And I was supposed to report to him, get paid by him—" She broke off, and shivered violently.

"But Randy, if you knew all this, and you didn't like it and didn't want to be any part of it, why didn't you tell Dad?"

She pressed her lips together and took several deep breaths through her nose, as if trying to get herself back under control. Then she turned to look directly at me, with what I could only interpret as affectionate scorn, with the emphasis on the latter. "Jenny," she said, patiently, slowly, "have you ever tried to tell your father anything he doesn't want

176

to hear? He liked Pete Falwell. He still does. Pete Falwell was his . . .
'friend.' Cecil Greenstreet was a fine, upstanding businessman, according to your father. And, frankly, I was only a receptionist, and his—"

"Lover."

She flushed. "Yes."

I took a deep breath of my own. "Randy? Knowing how my father is,
why in the world did you ever marry him?"

Her mouth curled. "You're not assuming it was the money? Well,
you're wrong, the money helped to convince me. Sure, it did, I was
young, and he was rich and gorgeous. But I'll tell you something that
you don't have to believe, neither you nor your sister. It wasn't exactly
that I loved him. It was that, God, he needed somebody to protect him!
I couldn't save him from going bankrupt, he was determined to let his
friends make a fool of him, and he never has admitted what they did to
him, but I thought maybe I could save his . . . I don't know, his peace
of mind and his . . . happiness."

She flushed again, and turned away toward the mirror, not meeting
my eyes. I crossed my arms on the top of the vanity and rested my head
on them, face down, eyes closed. In a little while, about the time I heard
Randy running a comb through her hair, I sat up again.

I got up from the little tufted pink stool.

I leaned over, and kissed her cheek.

And then I left my stepmother alone to finish making herself beautiful for her Jimmy, and I walked off to pick up Sherry at the clubhouse.

In the space of one morning, everything had changed in my family
and nothing had changed. I understood them better, I loved them more,
I even liked them a little better. But my sister wasn't suddenly going to
turn into my best friend, and my father and stepmother weren't going to
change overnight into generous, witty, articulate people who were a joy
to be around; they were all going to continue to be as aggravating as
they'd always been.

But something sure felt different.

Maybe it was me.

Sure enough, when I told Sherry what Randy had confided to me, my
sister brushed it off, saying, "Oh, come on, Jenny, that woman would
say anything to make herself look better." Of course, to be fair, Sherry
was plenty cranky by that time, having already fielded too many stares
at her bruised cheek and black eye.

* * *

Geof was waiting for us at Sherry's house. I half expected him to give me hell for leaving without him, but he seemed distracted, and didn't scold. He was so distracted, in fact, that he didn't appear to notice that Sherry kept her sunglasses on inside the house or that I ran upstairs, came back down with an armload of my own clothes, and went home dressed in Sherry's jogging suit. I had to point out to him the "evidence" of our battle; and even then he barely reacted to the latest chapter in my family's continuing soap opera.

Finally I said, "You've been to the police station, right?"

He muttered something noncommittal.

"Are you in trouble because of me, Geof?"

He looked up sharply at that and grinned. "Almost always."

"Come on, what's going on with you?"

Geof shrugged. "I'm hungry and I want to go home."

I wanted to push, to get him to tell me what was bothering him, but I'd learned long before that the man would talk when he was ready to talk. Until then I might as well change partners and dance. Short of that, I changed the subject.

"You know, with my excursion this morning, I may have proved that you were right about the fact that nobody is trying to get me. At least, not in any premeditated sort of way. Maybe life can return to normal, whatever that is, some day soon."

He was about as convinced of that as Sherry was about Randy.

But he believed me absolutely when I said, "Cecil Greenstreet isn't going anywhere. Boston can wait until tomorrow. I've had enough for one day, thank you."

It will probably come as a surprise to no one to learn that he drove me back home and that I went directly to bed and took a nice long nap.

He, however, didn't waste the day, but spent it tracking the whereabouts of several people who had reasons to resent my continued existence on earth. There was a former museum director who might have liked to hang me on a wall; there was a murderous realtor who used to be a friend of ours, but wasn't any longer; there was a funeral director who might have enjoyed burying me; but they were all safely tucked away in prisons, or at least they were on the night someone shut me in the garage. Geof also checked on the whereabouts of enemies of his, criminals who could have been waiting to see *him* that night, but who might have viewed me as their opportunity for a route to revenge. As is frequently the case with such efforts, it took a lot of time—more than usual, even, because he had to think of devious ways to get around the fact that this wasn't a police inquiry into the "incident" and he wasn't even supposed to be asking—and he didn't come up with much.

"Actually, I didn't come up with anything," he confessed over a dinner of lobster casserole in our kitchen that evening. "It's goddamn frustrating. Here we sit, glancing right and left, looking over our shoulders, checking the bushes and the shadows. Boo!" I jumped, startled, and then laughed at my own jumpiness. He viciously stabbed a chunk of lobster meat, and said, "Hell, what's the use of being paranoid if you can't find any enemies?"

"Maybe we'll find one in Boston tomorrow," I suggested.

Later, as he stroked linament into the bruises from my fight with my sister, he couldn't resist observing, "Who needs enemies when you've got a family like yours?"

"They're all right," I said defensively, surprising myself even more than him. A little embarrassed, not quite accustomed yet to this new, warmer feeling toward them, I quickly altered my tone to a joking swagger: "If you think I look bad, ya oughta see da other guy."

Because of my nap, I didn't fall asleep as easily as Geof did that night, so I got out of bed and got my little notebook out of my purse. I sat in the bay window of our bedroom for a long time, wrapped in a blanket, watching the clouds pass over the moon. Finally, I wrote in the notebook:

> *Because* she had a history of mental illness, my mother couldn't bear the heavy emotional and psychological burdens brought on by the unusual constellation of her illness, the business failure, and her husband's affair. It was all too much, all at one time. *And so,* she descended into her final mental illness, from which she never returned.

When I returned to bed, I felt as if I finally had my answer. If there wasn't any joy in it, at least there was a little peace.

20

SATURDAY WAS ANOTHER LOVELY DAY TO GO TO BOSTON, AT least by Geof's standards. We took the BMW and he drove. God knows I couldn't have managed the physical coordination it took to shift, steer, and clutch at the same time. I hurt from the fight with Sherry. And I felt as if I were emotionally hung over from . . . everything.

Geof chose the scenic route. For the first half of the drive, he put cassettes into the tape player and let the music and the beauty of back-road Massachusetts roll over and by us, as if he understood that I wasn't up to conversation. The first tape he put on was travelin' music —the soundtrack from the movie *The Electric Horseman*. It fit the weather, somehow, and it suited my sense of temporarily escaping, as the cowboy of the title had escaped from his past and from Las Vegas.

As for the weather, it was New England gray, Geof's favorite kind of driving weather. He hated to squint for miles and miles, preferring to eschew the pleasure of sun glinting off maple leaves for the bleaker beauty of a gray road blending into gray fences merging into a gray ocean melting into gray clouds. I sighed, leaned back, and let my body feel as one with the car as it snaked around the windy roads, over narrow lanes, and through seaside villages where the lights were turned on inside the houses to ward away the gloom.

It was two days later, and I still had not said a word to him about my conversation with Francie about my mother. I *wanted* to tell him. And sometime soon, I would. But I had to live with it inside of me for a while, first, sharing it only with the two other people I knew who had known her best: my dad and my sister. I had to find a place of acceptance for it in my heart, before I could lay it out in the open for somebody who hadn't known her—even if that was my husband—to probe and poke and question.

After a while, he inserted an Elton John tape and, in spite of my being lulled by our companionable silence and by the road itself, the lilting melodies pricked me into a more cheerful, wakeful consciousness.

"Let's talk," I said.

Geof reached out to turn down the volume and said, as if he'd been waiting all morning for me to finally say that, "All right, here's how I see it. It's Saturday. I've called ahead, so we know the office is open. He's the president, so he'll probably be there. If he isn't, we get his home address and go there. Wherever he is, we find him, and we get in to see him. We confront him with his statement that he doesn't know Pete Falwell, and the contradictory evidence. After he admits that well, yes, of course, he just misunderstood your question, we ask him when he first met Falwell. We'll need to verify that. We also ask him some pointed questions about his relationship with Falwell during his tenure as VP at Cain Clams, and we ask him how he happened to come to Port Frederick in the first place and how he got the job at Cain. I think you should handle that end of things, because you understand the business end of it better than I do. We want to know when he got—no, when he was *promised*—this job he has now. And we want to know what he was doing, where, and with whom on the night you were—"

"Attacked? Assaulted? What was I?"

"Nearly killed," Geof said, bluntly, and I felt a chill go through me as I gazed out at the weathered barns and houses passing by us at forty-five miles an hour. "He's going to want to know what business it is of ours to ask, and I'm also wondering whether I should identify myself as a cop or just as your husband."

"If I introduce you as my husband, could we get into trouble later if he came to trial for something, like maybe whatever we discover might not be admissible?"

"Jenny, to tell you the truth, I'm not sure about that."

"You're not on duty and you're out of your jurisdiction."

"Yeah, but I don't know, I'll have to find out. The thing is, I don't see that we have much choice, do you? We have to know. There's nobody else to do the asking. If we get anything incriminating, I figure the worst that happens is that I'll have to find other admissible evidence to back it up, that's all."

It was my turn to be wry. "That's *all?*"

He laughed a little, acknowledging the difficulty of coming up with even one solid piece of evidence in any given case, much less two or three.

"Geof," I said, "let me get this straight. You think it's possible that he did it, don't you? You think he's the one who tried to kill me. All right, I'll admit that's possible. But I'm worried about its *probability.* Am I really that much of a threat to him? Let's say it's true, that he did grease the Cain Clam slide into oblivion, and let's say it was even a true case of corporate sabotage, with Pete Falwell and PFF egging him on. Maybe they even hired him to do the job, maybe they even paid him while he was on the Cain payroll, maybe this job he has now as president of Downeast Marine is a virtual payoff for handing Cain Clams over to Pete and PFF. How would we ever prove it? And what possible harm could ever come to him? You and I both know that PFF would pay his court costs into eternity, and that's exactly how long any civil suit that my family might file would drag on, and he'd probably get off anyway! If there were damages, PFF would pay them for him. And he'd go right back to work, with an enviable reputation as a rough, tough businessman. You think anybody'd mind? Hah. Even if there were criminal charges, he'd probably get nominated to the U.S. Senate on the Oliver North and Ivan Boesky Presidential ticket. Now just where, exactly, in that scenario is a motive to kill me?"

Geof drove past a sign that said: BOSTON, 5 MILES.

He shrugged. "We don't know everything yet."

I sighed. "Truer words . . ."

"Boy, are you cynical," he added, which was clearly an imbecilic thing for a cop, of all people, to say. I did not deign to reply. After a minute, he said, "So which one would run for president, North or Boesky?"

By the time we reached the headquarters of Downeast Marine, at Boston Harbor, we had opted in favor of omission and prevarication over honesty and forthrightness. Maybe it was all that talk about Oliver North. We wouldn't come right out and say to Cecil Greenstreet that Geof was a cop, although he might already know it anyway. And I'd play innocent as long as I could, telling him that my reason for asking was that as soon as I learned that he worked for PFF, I just knew he'd misunderstood my question, and I wanted to give him a chance to clear things up. We'd start out easy and gentle, we decided, and try to avoid coming across so tough and accusing that he'd think he ought to call his lawyer.

"It's not going to work," I said, as we held our coats against the cold wind coming off the harbor. "He's going to see right through it."

"Fine," Geof said. "Maybe he'll give us some more lies to use against him. I like that, that's always good. Or maybe we'll ratchet him up enough to make him panic into giving us some indication of the extent of his guilt. I like that, too, gives us psychological leverage at a real basic, emotional, gut level. He might make a mistake, contradict himself, give himself away—you just never know what may happen. That's the pleasure of interrogations."

I held the door open for him, and said, "I do so like to see a man who enjoys his work."

Instead of the perky receptionist who had been on duty at the front desk the day I visited Greenstreet, there was a weekend security guard in a uniform. He picked his teeth with his thumbnail as he observed our approach.

"Hello. We have an appointment with Mr. Greenstreet," Geof announced. Our first lie. We could blame it on confusion, say I thought I'd made the appointment, but maybe I hadn't, but could we please see Mr. Greenstreet anyway, for just a few minutes, as long as we had come all this way, and we were already in the build—

"You do?" The guard sucked on his thumbnail, looking skeptical, which was only natural, given that he wouldn't have had us written down on his calendar.

"Yes," I interjected, and then added for verisimilitude, "we're a little early."

"I'll say." He grinned at us. "Like maybe several weeks early. Mr. Greenstreet's in Japan. At an international maritime convention. He left a couple of days ago, won't be back until—" He checked a desk calendar under his elbows. "Well, I don't even know when he'll be back, 'cause they didn't write down no date here."

"Japan?" I said.

Geof, who was quicker to adjust than I was, slapped the side of his head with the palm of his left hand, and groaned. "Oh, damn, that's right! I forgot he said he might be gone. When did he leave?"

The guard glanced at the calendar again. "Says here, two days ago."

That would have been my first whole day in the hospital, the day after the night before . . .

I turned to Geof. "He didn't say anything to me about going to Japan—"

"Thank you," he said, nodding at the guard, and pulling me away from him. But then he turned back, as if he had suddenly recalled something. "Say, I wonder if you could help us with something else. We need to send some flowers to some friends here in Boston, and we don't have any idea who the good florists are. Do you know who this company uses?"

The guard grinned again, obviously enjoying our yuppie predicament. *Golly, they got to send flowers, and they just don't know who to call. Ain't life a bitch?* "You askin' me?" But then he turned helpful, by picking up the telephone. "Hey, Grace," he said into it, after a moment, "who'd I want to call if I was to send flowers to somebody and I was to want to bill it to this company? No, babe, I don't mean what accountant, I mean what, whatdoyoucallem, florist?" He wrote down a couple of names in a large, scrawling longhand, and then he laughed. "Yeah, babe, it's three dozen roses for you!"

"Bouquets of Boston," he said, handling us the names on the paper. He seemed to find the name funny. "Or Faneuil Flowers."

We thanked him, and he said, "Have a nice day."

Outside, I said, shivering partly from the cold and partly from an internal chill, "What do you want to bet that Pete Falwell suddenly had to attend an international maritime convention, too? You're the cop, tell me: Is this incriminating, or what?"

"Could be coincidental. Come on, let's find a café with a phone."

We found a working-class bar near the harbor where it looked as if we could get good hot bowls of catch-of-the-day chowder and big mugs of cold beer. We picked well. The chowder—a tomato-based stew, really, with corn and green peppers and onions and thumb-sized chunks of white fish bobbing in it—was scalding, filling, comforting, and the draft beer, a local brew, did arrive at our table in icy mugs. While I picked at my half of our shared dessert of apple pie, Geof made his way through the lunchtime crowd to the pay phone.

He shook his head as he returned, sliding back into his side of the booth. He picked up his fork and stabbed the point of the pie—(I prefer the fat end with the crust on it)—and said, "I told them that Mr.

Greenstreet wanted to duplicate his order of the other day. And they said, which one was that, the Bird of Paradise centerpieces for one hundred and fifty tables or the dozen roses? And I said, no, you know, the carnation. Carnation? they said, are you sure? Maybe it was Faneuil Flowers, said the woman at Bouquets of Boston. Must have been Bouquets of Boston, said the man at Faneuil, but we have some lovely carnations just in today, so why don't we just go ahead and take your order—"

"A dozen roses?" I interrupted. "Did I tell you he's a randy dandy? Bet you they weren't for Mrs. Greenstreet."

"On the other hand," Geof pointed out, as he swallowed the last piece of apple. "They weren't sent anonymously to you, either."

"Jenny," Geof said, on the way back to Port Frederick. We usually shared the driving duties, but I let him pamper me this time. I did, however, take over the responsibility for the tape deck, and now Tracy Chapman belted her poignant songs about wronged women, strong women, and welfare lives. She put my own troubles into perspective. (As in: Things could be worse. Unless of course, he'd killed me. That was worse. Hard to find the silver lining in that one.) "What was that story you told Heather the day before yesterday? About you taking some sort of drug, thinking it was a vitamin?"

"I did," I said, and explained about the confusion between Marjorie Earnshaw's Valium "prescription" and Doc Farrell's vitamins. "The other night, when you were already so mad at me about driving home drunk? It didn't seem like the best time to tell you I was also stoned. You weren't in the best mood."

"Well, Jesus, Jenny, no wonder you passed out in the car."

"Exactly." I felt uncomfortable with the subject, not wanting to recall his anger, not wishing to reminisce about my stupidity at a bad time, on a terrible night. "Geof, there's something else I've been thinking about. Let's go to St. Michael's when we get back. I have a feeling there's something I ought to talk to Father Francis Gower about." I paused, then added, "On second thought, I think maybe we both ought to talk to him about it."

"What?"

I spent most of the rest of the ride telling him.

By the time I finished, he agreed that I'd want a cop along when I visited the retired priest in his little home.

21

SINCE WE HAD TO DRIVE NEAR THE NEW EAST GALLERY TO reach Father Gower's home, I asked Geof if he'd like to stop in and see the art show, while we were in the neighborhood.

We had a more difficult time finding a place to park than we might have had only a few days before, probably thanks to publicity over the MOAC protests. There was a good Saturday crowd inside the three-room gallery. Every wall was painted white, the floors were refinished oak planks varnished to a high sheen, and minicams in the ceiling spot-lighted the works of satirical art. The rooms seemed even more packed than they really were because everybody had on winter coats, except the staff, and even they wore bulky sweaters. Small Chinese bowls filled with red potpourri sat atop the heating vents in the floor, emitting wafts of a cinnamon scent. But it wasn't hot inside. For one thing, the gallery kept their furnace on "low," as much to economize on heating bills as to protect the art. For another, everytime somebody opened the front door to enter or exit, they let in a blast of chilly air with a smell of snow in it.

Geof's uncontrollable fit of laughing started mildly enough with a mere chuckle as we stood in front of a parody of Peter Paul Rubens's masterpiece in oils, *The Rape of Hippodameia.*

Do you recall ever having seen poor Hippodameia?

In the original painting, her chubby breast is bared and her fleshy arms are flung back helplessly as she reclines like a board in the arms of a centaur while her male defenders struggle to wrest her from the monster's grip. A small photograph of that painting hung in a frame beside the newer version so we could compare the two.

What had Geof chuckling was that the artist/parodist had substituted a seminaked likeness of a handsome young man in place of Hippodameia. Now, both the centaur and the defenders had women's heads and bodies.

"Makes you wonder," I murmured, "if Rubens painted mythology or just his own sexual fantasies."

"Are you kidding?" Geof laughed, causing one or two heads to turn our way. Bursts of hilarity, and little gasps, were popping up all over the gallery, however, as visitors discovered old masters interpreted a brand new way. "Think of those huge naked women he always painted, that ought to give you a clue. Anyway, maybe that's all mythology is, just some horny old guy's sexual . . . Oh, now this is interesting, Jenny, look at this." We had moved on to the next painting, which was a wickedly clever lampoon of Edouard Manet's famous painting, *The Execution of Emperor Maximilian.* In the new version it was women soldiers, instead of men, who loaded their guns and fired them into the Emperor and his two aides.

"Impossible," Geof declared, with a snort of derisive laughter. "I can't even imagine women doing that, which I suppose is the point. And if women wouldn't, why do men?" He dug his elbow into my side. "Is that it, Jenny? Have I got it?"

"You're asking me?" I felt chagrined as I gazed at the painting. After all, I'd let down the side—the one that wasn't supposed to be as violent as men. "The woman who beat up her sister?"

He smiled as if I'd said something that amused him almost as much as the painting did. "Yeah, but it took you more than thirty years to get there."

It was the parody of Manet's *Luncheon on the Grass* that ultimately did Geof in, collapsing him in such a fit of mirth that he infected nearly everybody else in the gallery—including me—so that soon we were nearly all chuckling, as much at his reaction as at the painting itself.

Picture the original: those dark-suited men reclining in the grass, that lone nude female among them, so clearly the object of their real appetite, and the artist's. But what Geof saw was this: Paul Newman, painted from the rear, in the nude, his glorious face turned half-smilingly, seductively toward the viewer; while around him, the business-suited women, looking smug, reclined amid the dappled grass, the shading trees.

"That's outrageous!" Geof chortled.

"A travesty," I agreed, also laughing.

"And the goddamned funniest thing I think I've ever seen!"

Out of the corner of my eye I had noticed the gallery director, looking in our direction. She, too, smiled at Geof's reaction to the painting. I excused myself, leaving him to enjoy the show alone for a few minutes, while I walked over to talk to her.

"How's it going?"

"Great crowds," she said. "But we keep getting those damn letters, Jenny. And now they're starting to get them in Minneapolis."

"Is that where the show goes next?"

"Yeah. I hope it doesn't scare them off."

"Any other trouble?"

"No, not really." But she frowned, and suddenly looked near tears. "Except, I'm tired of having to be alert all the time, you know?" (Boy, did I ever.) "I'm tired of being brave, Jenny." (I knew what she meant there, too.) "I don't like coming in to work, wondering if we're going to get bombed, or something—"

"I don't think—"

"I know, I know," she said, impatiently. "Nobody's gotten violent yet, but I'll tell you I feel pretty violated by the things they say about us. I really *hate* these people, Jenny, whoever they are. Now I think I know what it feels like to work in an abortion clinic. Can't *he*—" She jerked her head angrily in Geof's direction, "—*do* anything about it?"

"They're trying," I said, defensively. I hoped it was true. Since Geof wasn't going in to work—and bringing home the latest cop gossip—I couldn't be sure. But I knew that it was tough, often impossible, to trace anonymous letters, particularly ones, like these, that were handprinted —so you couldn't even trace a typewriter—on a generic kind of stationery that could have been sold anywhere to anybody at any time, and always posted from a different mailbox. The letters weren't likely to betray their source; something else, some stroke of luck or coincidence, would have to do that.

On the way out of the gallery, Geof read aloud to me from the curator's introduction to the show's brochure. " 'The object of this exhibit is, first, to lure the eye, and then to spark an emotion—whether that be humor, anger, desire, joy, or sadness—and, finally, to fire the brain into questioning the most basic tenets of civilization as they are portrayed, reflected, predicted, and established by those artists traditionally considered to be our greatest.' I suppose you understand that?"

I shrugged. "Beats me. But I sure do like them pictures, Pa."

"Me, too, Ma," he said, and tossed the brochure away. "Let's save 'em."

"Here it is," I said.

"Father Gower's house? Which one?"

"His house is the little brick one next to the rectory, but that's not what I meant. What I meant was, here it is, the last big snow-storm of the year."

The flakes that were falling were big and thick enough to remind me of the blizzard of doilies in Father Gower's living room. The snow started when Geof and I left the New East Gallery and in only the short time it took us to walk to the car, and then drive to St. Michael's and park, the streets and sidewalks got slick, and the trees, pedestrians, cars, and rooftops got heavily dusted with white. A winter wonderland was in the making, all right, promising just the sort of romantic atmosphere that usually made us want to curl up together in front of a big fire back at our cottage.

"We're going to wish we'd worn boots." Geof looked morosely down at the snow that dampened the soles of his good leather loafers.

"Boots, nothing, we're going to wish we had dogs and a sled." I grasped his arm. "Come on, let's mush before we freeze into snow-covered statues."

"Like Pompeii," he suggested, and I laughed at the accidental appropriateness of his jest.

"Yes, and wait 'til you meet the volcano inside."

We quickened our pace—cautiously—on the front walk, which was already so slick that walking on it was like treading on wet plastic with bare feet. An evening newspaper, camouflaged by the snow, lay in the yard. I picked it up—so it wouldn't get buried—and stuck it down into the outside pocket of my purse. When we reached the porch, Geof rang the doorbell. I heard Mrs. Kennedy's approach before she reached the door.

"I'll get it, Father!" her voice sang out. "Don't you be botherin' yourself now, that's what I'm here for!"

Darn right, I thought, smiling a little to myself, *you bother him, Mrs. K.*

She flung open the door and pantomimed great astonishment and pleasure upon seeing two large snow bunnies on the porch. Mrs. Kennedy wore a baggy, faded yellow sweat suit with tennis shoes; this time she held a bottle of furniture polish and a dust rag with which to punctuate her conversation. She must have recently had her hair done, because she'd gone to the trouble of protecting it with a scarf which she'd tied at the nape of her neck. Her expressive face projected nothing but joy at the sight of us.

"Well, and if it isn't Margaret Mary's oldest girl and a handsome young gentleman with her! Father!" She turned with her whole body, and bellowed in a hospitable sort of way into the interior. "Yoo hoo! You've visitors!"

Having made her announcement, she turned back to us and smiled happily, clasping the polish and rag to her bosom.

"Is this your husband, dear?"

I made the introductions with a flourish I thought she'd like, knowing it might be the only part of our visit she *would* enjoy. "Yes, Mrs. Kennedy. May I present my husband, Geoffrey Bushfield? Geof, this is Mrs. Kennedy, who has been a devoted housekeeper for many years to Father Gower and to St. Michael's." He inclined slightly at his waist in a mock but charming little bow. She flushed and dimpled, liking it very much. I could hardly blame her; he had a similar effect on me. "Geof," I continued, "is a lieutenant in the Port Frederick Police Department."

She turned quickly and yelled again into the interior: *"Father Gower! Company!"*

A male voice bellowed back at her. "It's not a 48-room mansion! I can hear the damn doorbell myself, Mrs. Kennedy!" The old priest, dressed in the same frayed black pants and red plaid shirt again, but this time with brown suspenders, appeared in the doorway that led to the living room. His face was screwed up and red as a monkey's. "I'm not senile, for God's sake. I am even capable of deducing that when a doorbell rings it means somebody's at the door." He shuffled closer, in old brown house slippers. "And unlike you, Mrs. Kennedy, I wouldn't leave them standing out there, freezing! Step out of their way, Mrs. Kennedy," he exclaimed, swinging his short arms as if they were brooms for sweeping her out of the hall. "For the love of Mike!"

"He loves visitors," Mrs. K said behind her hand to Geof and to me, as she moved aside and then closed the door and shut off the snowy world outside. "Does him such a world of good to see people, him bein' retired and all."

"I'm right here, Mrs. Kennedy," he snapped. "I'll thank you not to talk about me as if I weren't here. We'll take coffee in the living room, thank you, Mrs. Kennedy."

"Now that's a lovely idea, Father," she said, approvingly, although she didn't make any move to follow his directions. "And you'll be interested to know that Jennifer's young man is a police officer. Now isn't that thrilling?"

It was pathetic, the way she tried to make him out to be a lovable old Bing Crosby sort of priest. Around him, she had that kind of forced vivaciousness that you find in some wives who have surly husbands. He threw her a look of pure disgust, and then shuffled into his living room, as if he expected us to follow him.

"We'll just hang up our coats," I said.

Father Gower turned back around quickly, but Mrs. Kennedy was closer and beat him to it. Reaching out to take the coat I slipped off, she said, "It's wet, isn't it? I'll just hang it over the newel post to dry. Lieutenant, I'll take—"

But Geof was already opening the hall closet door, his black ski jacket in his hand. Mrs. Kennedy froze with my coat, the furniture polish, and the rag in her arms. The priest glared at her from the entrance to the living room, as if it were her fault that she hadn't jumped quickly enough to assist Geof.

He pushed aside coats, apparently searching for a hanger. His black jacket slipped from his grasp. Geof bent down to pick it up, bringing himself to eye level with the assorted contents on the floor of the closet. He paused, looking for what I had told him he would find, and in the process, creating a moment in which nobody else seemed to breathe. He reached into the crowded closet and pulled out several large rectangles of white cardboard, and displayed them to us.

"This your art supply closet, Father?" he asked.

I slipped past the priest into his living room. There, I found what I wanted and brought it back into the hall and held it out for the inspection of all three of them. It was the penholder containing felt-tip pens of many colors.

"Where are the stencils, Father?" I inquired.

The old man raised his shoulders and lowered them in a heavy, surrendering, disgusted breath.

"In the kitchen," Mrs. Kennedy said quickly. She pointed with the can of furniture polish. Her vaudeville Irish accent disappeared entirely. "That's where I do it. That's where I made the signs. I wrote the letters.

I'm sorry, Father, forgive me, I shouldn't have done it, but you said yourself those women artists are an offense against God with their blasphemous paintings!"

"Mrs. Kennedy," Geof said, "what about that coffee?"

"But—"

"Black will be fine," he said.

"But don't you want to interrogate me?" She pressed my coat to her chest. "I'll go downtown with you right now—" she said, pointing to the door, with the furniture polish. "I'll sign a confession—" She made scribbling motions with the dust rag. "—whatever you need—"

"Mrs. Kennedy, you've been watching too much television," the priest snapped. "Get the damned coffee!"

With a last desperate glance at me, she obeyed.

"The living room," Geof said, so the remaining three of us trooped in there and sat down. Geof crossed one of his long legs over the other, folded his hands over his abdomen and said, calmly, "Okay, Father Gower, let's hear it."

"She had nothing to do with it," the priest said immediately. He looked so red in the face, so angry and defensive, that I worried that he'd suffer a stroke right then and there. "Of course, you can see that. She's lying, because she has a misguided notion about trying to protect me. Stupid woman. I don't need protecting. I am under the wing and the divine protection of God in this endeavor. As an agent of His will, I am responsible."

At first, I had thought he was trying to protect her, as she was him, and I started to like him a little better for it. But then I grasped a less flattering, more unpleasant truth: He wasn't trying to absolve Mrs. Kennedy of any blame; rather, he wanted all of the "credit" for committing acts that he considered to be justifiable and even divinely ordered.

"Oh, I'll accept that it was your idea, all right," Geof agreed. "I'll bet you wrote the letters and you dictated the messages you wanted on the posters. But she made those posters, and it was she who took the masking tape and put them up on the gallery windows. She addressed and stamped the letters for you, and she delivered them to the various mailboxes that she used. She was pretty smart about that, Father—"

"Only because I told her to do it."

Mrs. Kennedy had crept back into the hall, where I could see her from where we sat. Father Gower had his back to her.

"Well, then tell her this." Geof stood up, and I suspected that he knew very well that his height and size created a towering presence—all official and all male—in that small room with its little priest and its feminine doilies and the lavender smell of sachet. "Tell her to get the advice of a good lawyer in your parish, because if you keep this up, she's going to need one."

"My parish is full of lawyers who will help me."

"Well, good for you." Geof was suddenly deeply sarcastic, causing even my stomach to clench. "But what about her? You think they'll leap to do pro bono work for a housekeeper? She'll be lucky to keep her job. You'll get farmed out to some old priest's retirement home, a little sooner than you'd planned, and she'll be turned out. No more salary, no retirement pay. And that's the good news for her. That's what will happen to her if she doesn't go to court, or to jail."

"I'll tell them she wasn't responsible."

"Yes, she is. Morally, legally, any way you want to look at it. She's a grown woman and she's responsible for her actions, just as you are for yours. Nobody forced her to lick those envelopes, Father, and I seriously doubt that you kicked her out the door and made her walk to the mailbox. She is responsible for her part in this, and she'll pay for it, only the price will be higher than the one you pay, because I seriously doubt that the Church will go to the same lengths to protect a housekeeper that it will to protect one of its priests.

"You have three choices, as I see it, Father Gower. You can continue as you're doing, and take the inevitable consequences, and maybe that's what you want, a little public martyrdom to enliven your retirement. I doubt that's what she wants. Or you can cut it out. Or you can continue your protests, but do it openly and within the law, which is your constitutional right."

Father Gower avoided our eyes, refusing to respond.

I had been covertly watching Mrs. Kennedy during Geof's entire speech, and I thought—hoped—that she looked terrified.

"This is a warning, Father," Geof said.

Still, the old priest said nothing.

"Consider it a sign from God, if you like," Geof added, in that same profoundly sarcastic tone. "And the sign says, *lay off.*"

He held out a hand to me, and pulled me up out of my chair. We started for the door.

Suddenly the priest spoke. "Your mother could not have been buried in the Catholic section."

I turned, slowly. "Why not?"

"I would not have allowed it."

I waited, hating him.

"Because women who have abortions," he said, "are damned to unconsecrated burial."

Behind me, Mrs. Kennedy moaned, then murmured, "Father!"

"My mother had an abortion? She confessed this to you, and you're breaking the sacred trust of the confession to tell me?"

He smiled, a slow, smug, cunning smile that said he would have his little revenge for this afternoon. "I have broken no trust. She never confessed it to me. But I know it's the truth."

"If she didn't tell you, then how do you know it?"

He closed his lips on his awful secrets.

"I don't believe you," I said.

We left his house in silence, and walked out into another kind of silence—the muffled kind produced by several inches of new snow.

22

"I'VE GOT TO FIND THE WIPER TO SCRAPE THE WINDOWS BEFORE we can go anywhere," Geof said.

"Don't bother." I jerked open the door on my side. "I'm so furious I could melt the snow off the car all by myself. He made all that up because he hates us for revealing his nasty little game. He said himself that she never confessed it to him, so there isn't any way he could know a thing like that. Damn him! You didn't even scare him with your warning, and he sure as hell doesn't give a shit about Mrs. K. I wish you'd pulled him in and locked him up in a cell full of exhibitionists and porno queens." I punched open the door to the glove compartment, nearly pulling it off its hinges as I rummaged inside it. "Here, I'll help you look."

"No, get in the car, Jenny. Leave that alone before you break it. I'll take care of it."

I got in and slammed the door, knocking most of the snow off the window on my side. Geof found a scraper on the floor of the back seat. I watched him clear the other windows, although everyplace he scraped was quickly coated with more snow. I pulled out my keys, started the car and the defroster, and turned on the windshield wipers and the rear-window de-icer for him. All the while, I muttered imprecations against the priest. *Damn him, damn him, damn him!*

"Jenny." Geof got in, after knocking snow off his shoes and brushing it off his clothes. He took my keys out of the ignition, traded them for his own, and tossed mine back to me. His voice still held some of the impatient tone he'd used with the priest. "Listen to me. You're pissed off, so you're not thinking. He could know."

"Oh, bullshit. He said himself that she never con—"

"She wouldn't have to confess an abortion for him to know she had one. She could have confessed a *pregnancy* to him, and told him she wanted to terminate it. And then when the pregnancy didn't continue and no baby ever appeared, he'd know, wouldn't he?"

I leaned my head back against the seat.

"Well, wouldn't he?"

"Oh, shit," I said.

Geof relented, coming down off his tough tone. "I'm sorry, honey, but I think maybe that's the way it was."

"My God. She was pregnant. At forty-six. With an unfaithful husband. And a business going bust. And worst of all, a history of postpartum psychosis."

"Psychosis? What are you talking about?"

I looked over at him. "Francine Daniel told me that Mom was hospitalized after I was born and after Sherry was born. She may have tried to kill herself the second time, and Francie thinks that Mom hurt, or tried to harm Sherry." I spoke pedantically, to hide the pain. "Today, they call that postpartum psychosis. It's probably behind a lot of cases of infanticide. Women can be treated for it now. But back in those days, they would have just called her crazy, and treated her for God knows what, and made her think she was a horrible mother and a terrible person."

Geof reached over to touch my shoulder, but he didn't interrupt. I suddenly realized that I was lecturing to a cop about a phenomenon that he'd probably seen in other women, other cases.

"I need to see Doc Farrell," I said. "I'll bet you that's why he gave her the hysterectomy—because he performed the abortion and botched it, and then he had to cover it up, the bastard."

"And you think he's just going to confess that to you, as if *you* were a priest?"

"Geof, I don't give a damn what he says. It's too late to do anything about it, and we'd never prove it anyway. I just want him to know that I know."

But when Geof tried to pull out into the street, the wheels slid and wouldn't go forward. Cursing, he got out to retrieve a shovel from the trunk and then to hack away at the snow and ice that blocked the tires. There was only one shovel, so I stayed in the car. When I reached for my purse to put my keys away, I discovered the newspaper that was still stuck down into the outside pocket. I pulled it out, and then out of its cellophane wrapper, and spread it over my lap, just for something to do with my hands. I didn't intend to read it; I was too worked up, too distracted to read the news. I leafed through it without looking at it, seeing instead my mother's face when I was a child, and her face in the hospital, and Dr. Calvin Farrell's face as he told me about the hysterectomy—some of the truth, just enough of the truth so he didn't have to lie. And I saw the tears on my father's face and I wondered, did he know? I thought of my mother and of how she'd been that Christmas, and I realized that what I had seen then, without knowing it, was utter depression and hopeless desperation. She was Catholic, raised to believe abortion was a mortal sin. But she couldn't have that baby, no way, not a woman who'd already been hospitalized for psychosis related to childbirth. What if she had the baby, and hurt it, as she had tried to hurt Sherry? What if she had it, and then tried to kill herself? Those must have been the horrible worries afflicting her and paralyzing her. And where could she turn for help and counsel—to male priests and a male god and male doctors and her philandering husband, to an entire universe of powerful, controlling men who couldn't possibly understand the anguish growing within her. My mother, I decided, had been a woman torn by her love and fear of her God and by her fear of the horror this pregnancy could inflict on the baby, on her husband and daughters, and on herself.

I understood perfectly why she had the abortion.

She saw no other way out.

And now, finally, it all made sense. Now, finally, I could also understand why she withdrew into madness. Maybe it was a repeat of the postpartum psychosis. Or maybe there wasn't any other escape from the guilt.

My eye was caught by the words *Port Frederick Civic Foundation* in the newspaper.

I focused on where it appeared in a Sam Hayes editorial that was headlined: FOUNDATION SEEKS STABLE, SANE NEW DIRECTION UNDER STRONG NEW LEADERSHIP.

> Thanks to the resignation this week of longtime director Jennifer L. Cain, the Port Frederick Civic Foundation is now poised to reestablish itself as a powerful force to maintain and enrich the important institutions of this community: family, church, and government. *The Port Fred-*

erick Times welcomes and applauds this signal of positive, conservative change. Under the controversial leadership of Miss Cain, the foundation too often embroiled itself in costly and morally bankrupt endeavors, like the current pornographic exhibit at the New East Gallery, the local AIDS hospice, and support of Planned Parenthood. Now, with her fortuitous departure, the foundation is free once more to invest its funds where they will work to the best interests of the businesses and families of Port Frederick. Though it is unkindly hinted by others—although not by this paper—that Miss Cain now joins her father James D. Cain III in well-deserved exile—we wish her well, particularly in light of the death last week of her mother, who was a victim of mental illness, and also in light of Miss Cain's own recent near-asphyxiation, which has been attributed, by the police department, where her husband is a lieutenant, to accident. We wish her good health and every success. There is no need to express such wishes for the foundation, because Miss Cain's departure assures that the Port Frederick Civic Foundation will thrive, right along with the community it is pledged to serve.

I handed the editorial to Geof when he got back into the car.

"He said he would do it," I said, "and he did."

Geof read it, then handed it back to me. "I think," he said, "that I'm going to go have a little talk with Sam Hayes."

"Drop me off at the doctor's office first, will you?"

"Don't you want to go with me? Aren't you upset?"

"About this?" I gestured toward the editorial. Seeing it in print wasn't nearly as painful as I would have thought it might be, or maybe the pain was only relative to my obsession about my mother. The article would embarrass my sister, but I wouldn't lose any friends over it. If I did, then they were not, by definition, friends. I shrugged. "What can I do? It isn't the sort of thing I can defend myself against. I can't demand a retraction. I can't write a letter protesting that I'm really a wonderful person. I've got to let it go. Sam doesn't need me to tell him how I feel about this. He knows."

"Well, he doesn't know how I feel about it," Geof retorted, "and I'm going to make sure that he does."

"You and Harry Truman."

"What?"

"Defending your women."

He snorted, as he pulled the gearshift back into first gear and tried it again. "Hell, no. My woman can defend herself. I'm only thinking of myself and the poor, defenseless Port Frederick Police Department."

He let me out in front of the medical center, as close as he could get to the building without getting stuck in the snow. I was determined to see Doc Farrell; Geof was determined to give Sam Hayes a piece of his mind. As hot under the collar as we both were, it's a wonder any snow stuck to either of us.

Unlike any other doctor I ever heard of, Doc Farrell kept regular Saturday hours. But then, he wasn't married, had no children, and had never been seen on a golf course.

When I reached Marjorie Earnshaw's reception desk, I said, "I have to see him, Marj."

"You can't, Jenny, even with this snow and cancellations, he's backed up something awful because of deliveries this morning."

"I'm having a miscarriage. I'm hemorrhaging, Marj."

"Well, my God." She got up from her chair. "Why didn't you say so? For heaven's sake, stay where you are, I'll get you a wheelchair."

By the time Doc Farrell arrived, a nurse had already examined me and said, kindly, "I expect it was only a little spotting, honey. You'll be fine."

The doctor was not so friendly.

"What's this all about, Jennifer?" He looked harried and tired. "You're not pregnant. Weren't you just in here a few days ago, had a urinalysis? Didn't I examine you then? I'd know if you were pregnant. You're not. So what's this about having a miscarriage? And hemorrhaging?"

"My mother had an abortion, didn't she?"

He snapped his mouth shut, and folded his white-clad arms over his chest.

"Only, you called it a hysterectomy," I continued. "Either that, or she had an abortion that went wrong, maybe it was septic, maybe she got seriously infected, and so you had to do a hysterectomy to take care of the problem. Really took care of it, too. Boy, she didn't have a problem in the world after that, just blissfully comatose, no more worries."

"She had—" Doc Farrell leaned forward and said it slowly and distinctly. "—a hysterectomy. Period. I do not perform abortions. I never

199

have. I never will. Not on any woman. And certainly not on your mother. I will show you the records to prove it."

And he whipped out of the room. I heard him yell at Marj to get my mother's medical charts. And then he returned, and dumped the thick folder on my lap.

"Read that," he said. "And then apologize."

I clasped the folder and, feeling a weird sense of glee that I'd finally managed to get my hands on it, slipped out of the doctor's office. Then I took the elevator down to the canteen in the basement. From the vending machines, I bought an egg salad sandwich on white bread and a can of Mountain Dew.

I sat down at one of the small metal tables to eat and to read, losing track of all time as I perused my mother's medical history. It wasn't easy to read, what with Doc Farrell's indecipherable scrawls, all the Latin medical terms, and the various hieroglyphic lab reports. Her first visit to the gynecologist was right before her marriage. *Were you a virgin when you got married, Mom?* I wondered. None of your business, Jenny, I decided. I looked through many years of lab tests, finding a miscarriage . . . no, two of them, that I'd never known about . . . one in the eighth week, the other in the fourth month. Ah, here was her pregnancy with me, along with complaints of morning sickness and swollen ankles. After my delivery (7 lbs 4 oz), the doctor had scribbled a note after a postpartum visit: "Excessive crying, lacks energy, reports feeling inadequate." There were similar notations made after Sherry's birth (7 lbs 6 oz), including a terse notation that, "patient says feels angry a lot." *Homicidal was more like it,* I thought, as I read that phrase so many years later. Only she wouldn't have been able to say that, probably couldn't have brought herself to admit, *Doctor, sometimes I think I want to kill my baby.*

I read all the way through, front to back in that file, including the full report of the hysterectomy. I found nothing untoward. Nothing to indicate an abortion. Nothing even to indicate a suspected or confirmed pregnancy. Nothing unusual reported about the operation itself.

"Fool," I said to myself. "What did you think you'd find, incriminating statements with red arrows pointing to them? If any such things ever happened, he'd have destroyed any record of them. Of course, he can hand you this file and say, 'Read it.' There's nothing in it to incriminate him."

* * *

About that same time, Geof was standing out in a blizzard, waiting for a tow truck to come and help get the BMW out of the parking lot at *The Times*. It wasn't that his car needed to be towed. That wasn't the problem. The problem was the other cars around him that were stalled or stuck, and that blocked his exit and prevented him from driving away.

He stood in the snow, stamping his feet, which were cold and wet in his loafers. But he was too hyped up to get back in his car and wait for the truck. He thrust his ungloved hands in his pockets, and hoped I wouldn't worry about him, that I wouldn't think he'd been in an accident. He had tried to reach me at Doc Farrell's office, but Marj Earnshaw had told him that I'd already left. So now he pictured me standing at the front door of the medical center, staring out at the snow, searching for his headlights, looking woebegone.

He was eager to erase that pitiful expression from my imagined face, and he had just the story to do it. After letting me off, he had burst into Sam Hayes's office—all macho posturing and bluff, as he knew I would describe it—ready to haul the publisher out of his chair and slam him into a wall.

And then Geof discovered the publisher had already been beat to a bloody pulp. Not literally, just figuratively. The "perpetrators" were my trustees, my employees, and my friends, as well as the directors of practically every charitable organization in town, their employees, and dozens of other people whom the foundation had helped in some way through the years. They'd been calling and haranguing him ever since his editorial hit their front porches. By the time Geof reached him, Sam Hayes was already typing up a "softened editorial stance" in order to appease subscribers who threatened to cancel, and to stave off angry advertisers, like my friends who owned restaurants and my friend who managed the health spa and the friends who owned a bookstore and my friends who ran a gas station, and a respectable number of Geof's friends who advertised, as well.

Geof left Sam's office, satisfied and smiling.

The feeling lasted until he got to the parking lot.

With nothing else to do, he started thinking about how to break the *bad* news: The day before, while I was at the golf course, he had been suspended without pay for dereliction of duty, disobeying orders, falsifying sick leave, and failing to report to work.

* * *

I was still lost in thought about my mother when I looked up and saw, not only that it was six o'clock at night, but that Marjorie Earnshaw had entered the canteen.

She nodded at me, and approached my table.

"Mind if I join you, Jenny?"

"Sit down, Marj."

She touched a hand to the black and white striped band around her hair, and pulled out the other chair.

"Don't you ever go home, Marj?"

"Three nights a week I volunteer over at the hospital." She inclined her huge head of hair to the left, in the direction of the hospital just across the street, the one where I'd been a patient only a few days previously. "I usually pick up a sandwich down here."

"I'll bet you can tell those interns a thing or two."

She smiled sardonically. "A few doctors I could name, too."

"Yeah." I tapped the medical file in front of me. "He's a real winner, isn't he?"

She looked where I was pointing, then up at me, her face registering surprise and insult. "Well, I didn't mean *Doctor—*"

"He killed her, Marj."

"What in heaven's name—"

"My mother. It's not in here, is it? Did he have you expunge it? Or did he just never write it up, so you didn't have to take out anything at all. Her last pregnancy. The abortion."

I stared at her bitterly. She had to have known all about it; nothing ever occurred in that office that she didn't know all about.

I thought she'd rail at me, but she became surprisingly quiet and gentle. "Jenny, I don't know where you get these ideas, but they just aren't true. He's a fine doctor, and he never did any such thing. Look, I'll be glad to talk to you about it, but I've got to have something to eat."

I nodded, nonplussed by her unexpected kindness.

"You know what, Marj? If you'd been a doctor, you would have had a better bedside manner than he does."

She smiled, with a touch of her old, familiar arrogance, and went off to the vending machines. I focused my gaze on my mother's file, but looked up as I heard the sound of the coins rattling down the machine. A sandwich popped out of its slot and Marj opened a little plastic door to take it out. She put coins, twice, in the coffee machine, and I watched as the plastic cups plopped down and the liquid filled them. She walked over to the condiment table, where, although her back was turned to me, I could tell that she was mixing cream and sugar into the drinks. She returned to the table, setting a cup of coffee in front of me and then settling down to drink her own coffee and eat her own sandwich. It appeared to be tuna fish.

"Why, thank you, Marj."

I gazed at the whitish, sickening looking instant brew in the brown plastic cup with a white rim. I preferred black, but I didn't say so. I looked up, to find her gazing encouragingly at me.

"You'll feel better if you drink it, Jenny."

"Thanks—" I smiled. "—Dr. Earnshaw."

I picked up the cup and it finally registered. *Brown plastic with a white rim.* Just like the one Geof had found in our driveway. Dumbly, I held it in my hand halfway between the table and my mouth, staring at it, frantically attempting to understand the implication of it.

"Something wrong with the coffee, Jenny?"

"What?" I didn't dare to look at her for fear that she'd see the awareness in my eyes. "No."

This was it! This was the proof that Doc Farrell had something to hide, including my own attempted murder! Here was a brown and white plastic cup from the vending machine in his own office building. He'd picked up a cup of this crap before he drove out to my house, and it had fallen out of his car when he'd gotten out of it in order to shut me into the garage. This was it! Wait until Geof saw this! I hid the exultation on my face as I gulped a swallow of the vile brew.

"Ugh." I set it down.

"Better drink it all," Marj advised.

She was right. I couldn't carry a full cup of coffee out to Geof when he arrived to pick me up. Grimacing, I downed the rest of it.

While Marj ate, she chatted about her years with "Doctor," although most of the stories revolved around her and about how she'd always managed to save the day, in one way or another. She told me about patients she'd diagnosed quicker than he had, about lab tests she just *knew* had to be wrong and sure enough when they were redone she was right, about bandages she'd applied and pills she'd prescribed that had helped the patients "so much." I felt lulled and comforted by her droning voice, and her boring, egotistical stories. *Tell me more, Marj,* I thought, sleepily, as my head came to rest on my hand, *put me right to sleep.*

"Do you need a ride home, Jenny?"

"Hm?" I couldn't seem to get my mouth to work.

"I think you need a ride home. Your husband called a long time ago, but I thought you'd already left, so that's what I told him. There's a blizzard outside, you know. You'd better come on back to the office with me, while I get my keys."

"Umkay."

I allowed her to take the file, which she put under her arm, and to help me to my feet. *Must look like a patient,* I thought, *with Marj propping me up like this.* She guided me to the elevator, and then inside of it, and punched the button for the right floor. I watched her do it all, but it seemed like a dream to me. When the elevator opened again, Marj pulled me out, letting me fall heavily against her as we walked—she walked, I dragged my feet after her—to Doc Farrell's door.

Marjorie was talking again.

"I've been a great help to many patients, Jenny. I helped your mother once, when she was pregnant and desperate. I saw the lab tests, and I heard her crying in Doctor's office. I knew she couldn't have that baby, and I knew I could help her even if none of the fancy doctors would. We did it at my house. It was April 10, 1971. Even in my own kitchen I'm a better doctor than most of them will ever hope to be. I did everything right. It wasn't my fault that she got infected. She just didn't take care of herself, the way I instructed her. Well, we won't blame her. It was an accident."

Marj pushed me through the door, and turned to lock it.

My knees buckled, and I collapsed onto the floor.

"That's what I tried to tell you at the funeral." Marj bent down to grasp my wrists and she began to pull me across the floor. "I saw in the paper that your mother died and, I don't know, something in me felt so bad. I wanted you to know it was an accident. I even sent flowers, special flowers, baby's breath and rosebuds for the baby, and a white carnation for your mother. Because she was dead. That's what you wear on Mother's Day, you know, a white carnation if your mother's dead. I wanted you to know! Not that I was sorry; there wasn't anything for me to be sorry about. But that it was an accident."

She pulled me through a swinging door and down a corridor in the direction of the examination rooms. I was limp, so very limp in her grasp, and she was struggling, grunting, against my weight.

"But you weren't satisfied with that. You had to know more, to ask questions, and pry. And Doctor was worried, because he had performed the hysterectomy to cover up my—the accident. Didn't want his practice compromised, he said, by a malpracticing nurse! Afterward, I told him I'd never do that again, and I kept my promise. I went to your home, Jennifer. I was going to tell you that you shouldn't ask those questions. I was going to let you know it was an accident, so you'd leave us alone. But there you were, already asleep in the garage, waiting for me. I knew you were tired and so upset, and I wanted to help you. But it didn't work out, and I was so scared that people would find out, and they wouldn't know that it had all been an accident. So now I'm going to help you at last."

Marjorie dragged me into one of the little cubicles.

She began undressing me, starting with my left shoe.

"I'm going to exchange lab tests, Jennifer, so now yours will say you are pregnant, just as you claimed in front of so many people in the office today. Like your poor mother, you can't have this baby. Too much mental illness running in the family, you know, can't take that risk. And so you tried to abort yourself, and well, it just went wrong, that's all, just like your poor mother. And you managed to get up here, to cry for help, and I was here to help you."

She had my shoes off, and had pulled off my mother's black trousers and was tugging at my stockings now. *Help me,* I cried inside myself, *oh, please, somebody help me.*

"But there was a blizzard, and the telephone wouldn't work, so I couldn't call for help. So I had to leave you here, bleeding profusely from the hemorrhaging of your womb, while I ran through the blizzard, across the street to the hospital, to get help."

I felt her pull at my panties.

"But they didn't get here in time, and you died."

Inside my head my mother's voice screamed: *No!*

I rose up from the floor—desperately fighting the effects of the drugs with which she had doctored my coffee, and I hurled myself against her, knocking her against the examining table. I hit her, once, twice, again and again, causing her head to bounce against the hard tile floor. It all felt like slow motion to me, like an underwater battle fought by a furious, clumsy, lumbering creature. Finally, she sprawled, bleeding from her nose and mouth, unconscious.

I dragged myself to her desk, pulled the telephone down onto the floor, dialed 911, cried help, and then fell asleep on the floor with the phone off the hook.

Epilogue

Memorial Day

I WAS NEVER ONE TO VISIT CEMETERIES ON MEMORIAL DAY, and neither was Geof, but this time we both went to the Harbor Lights Memorial Park.

We ignored the rules against fresh flowers. Removing the plastic tulips from my mother's grave (installed "compliments" of the management), we replaced them with our vase of Shasta daisies. The vase, which was clear, heavy glass, tilted when Geof set it on the ground. He straightened it, and then we stood back, admiring the effect of the big pink daisies against the green, green grass. Geof put his arm around my waist, and I leaned into him.

"I'm going to go sit on a bench," he said. "Don't hurry, Jenny, I'll wait as long as you want." He kissed my hair. I turned my face up to his and caught him full on the lips. He squeezed my waist, and then I watched him stroll away to a cement bench about a hundred yards from my mother's grave.

I climbed from there up a little incline past the graves of assorted relatives and friends. A few steps beyond was a flat marker which, on the day of my mother's funeral, had been concealed by the green mat that had covered the gravesite. On that day, an edge of the mat had rolled up, revealing to me only a small corner of this little brass marker. My mother's friend, Francie Daniel, had prevented me from seeing it that day, but it was also she who had finally told me of its existence.

Now it lay openly revealed to this sunny Memorial Day.

There was no name on it, only an engraving of a child's hands clasped in prayer. This was where my mother had buried an empty coffin. I had a feeling it was here that my mother had symbolically buried her heart.

I felt no grief, no sentimental tug toward this grave. The embryo that was killed was only a potential person, not a real one. But there had been a real person who had lived in my mother's full grown, vital, beautiful body. Somebody I loved. Somebody I needed then and now. I turned away from the empty symbol, and returned to my mother's grave and sank to the ground beside it.

Finally, I could fill in the blanks.

Because . . . and so.

Because my father was a fool—something he couldn't help, it seemed to me—and because the businessmen of Port Frederick stuck together in a collusion of old-boy power, I was pretty sure that Cecil Greenstreet had been able to conspire with Pete Falwell to bankrupt Cain Clams. And so they got away with it. Whether or not my family cared to spend the money it would take to fully investigate and maybe even to file lawsuits, none of us knew yet. Given my father's unwillingness to face the truth, and the lateness of the date, I rather doubted we would, or could.

Because I had been ignorant of all of that, I came back to my hometown after college loaded with guilt for the damage I thought my family had wreaked on the people who worked for us. Because the old men felt a bit of communal guilt, they hired me to run the foundation. And so I had devoted the last decade of my life trying to compensate for sins I had not committed and that, in fact, my father hadn't committed, either. And so, I discovered that even the sins that parents don't commit, but are only perceived to have committed, are visited upon their children.

Because an old-boy network of another sort ruled my mother's life, she died. And so, she turned to the only person who offered to help, a woman, but one who was warped by the sacrifice of her own ambitions and desires. And so they were both, my mother and Marjorie Earnshaw, female strangers in a strange male land.

The only question remaining about Marjorie Earnshaw had been why she removed the PFF annual report from my lap as I sat sleeping in my car. And that, it turned out, was simply explained: because it was sliding off my lap, she picked it up and then didn't know what else to do with it but to take it with her. And so Marj inadvertently caused us to

I.O.U.

follow false trails that led away from her, although they helped to uncover the sabotage of our business.

I touched Mom's gravestone.

Good-bye, womanly Margaret.

Good-bye, lovely, female, blessed, cursed Margaret. You had no place to turn but inward, and so there you retreated, cocooned within yourself, for yourself, by yourself, defeated but victorious. Having found all of the other doors closed against you, you opened the one remaining door to the only home where you felt entirely welcome, the home of yourself.

With my hand on her headstone, I made a vow to her.

"If I ever have a child, Margaret, I'll have it for you, too. If it's a girl, I'll name her after you, but I won't raise her to be you. If it's a boy, I'll teach him to love the kind of woman you wanted to be, but never could be."

And then I realized: *I was that woman.*

All of my debts were paid.

I looked over toward Geof, wanting to wave at him or to shout out the news of this marvelous epiphany. *I was free.* And so, in a way, was he. We were free to return to our jobs or to leave them for good. I was free to start a foundation of my own, if I wanted to put my newly formed philosophies into action, or free to sail my life into other directions entirely. We were free to remain in Port Frederick, or to leave it.

I picked a daisy from the vase and started plucking petals to predict my future.